Praise for the novels of Janet Chapman

"Janet Chapman is a keeper."
—Linda Howard, *New York Times* bestselling author

"Full of intrigue and passion . . . red-hot romance."
—*Publishers Weekly*

"A story filled with wit and tenderness." —*Booklist*

"[Chapman] is unmatched and unforgettable."
—RT Book Reviews

"The combination of wit, clever dialogue, charismatic characters, magic, and love makes this story absolutely enchanting." —Romance Junkies

"A Perfect 10 is a fitting rating for . . . a novel which is both tender and joyful." —Romance Reviews Today

Call It Magic

Janet Chapman

JOVE
New York

A JOVE BOOK
Published by Berkley
An imprint of Penguin Random House LLC
penguinrandomhouse.com

Copyright © 2020 by The Estate of Janet B. Chapman
Excerpt from *From Kiss to Queen* copyright © 2016 by Janet Chapman
Penguin Random House supports copyright. Copyright fuels creativity, encourages
diverse voices, promotes free speech, and creates a vibrant culture. Thank you for buying
an authorized edition of this book and for complying with copyright laws by not
reproducing, scanning, or distributing any part of it in any form without permission.
You are supporting writers and allowing Penguin Random House to continue to
publish books for every reader.

A JOVE BOOK, BERKLEY, and the BERKLEY & B colophon
are registered trademarks of Penguin Random House LLC.

ISBN: 9780515155204

First Edition: May 2020

Printed in the United States of America
1 3 5 7 9 10 8 6 4 2

Cover art by Jim Griffin

A heartfelt thank-you to all the brave men and women who hit the ground running every time those alarms go off, and in particular, thank you to Orono Fire & Rescue.

Prologue

Gunnar Wolfe lifted the landing gear the moment he cleared the small Colorado runway, directed one last scowl at the mountains he'd wasted three days searching, and turned the small private jet east. Already having called once to say he'd be a day late to his new job in Spellbound Falls, Maine, he was damned close to blowing a second 7:00 a.m. roll call. The last thing he wanted was to waste the favors he'd had to cash in to snag the last firefighter position on one of the top fire and rescue squads in the country.

Engaging the autopilot once he reached cruising altitude, Gunnar signed off with the tower, switched the radio to cabin speakers, and pulled off his headphones. He leaned back in his seat with a heavy sigh and wondered, for the hundredth time since setting out on this crazy odyssey nearly a week ago, what in hell he was doing chasing halfway around the world after a woman he'd never even met.

A woman, he'd finally concluded, who didn't want to be found.

What had begun as a potential distraction provided by a good friend's matchmaking wife had, as of three days ago, turned into a personal mission to track down Katy MacBain, who'd mysteriously gone missing after finishing a four-week wilderness rescue course in Colorado. About the only thing Gunnar could say with any level of confidence was that Miss MacBain was still alive. Or she had been four days ago, when she'd driven off alone in the rental pickup delivered to the motel she'd spent two days holed up in—also alone, the desk clerk had assured him.

There, the paper trail Gunnar had been following just flat-out vanished. Hell, his computer hacker couldn't even get a ping on her cell phone signal. And here he was—a man who made his living hunting down and severing the heads of criminal organizations, independent terrorist cells, and petty regimes, stymied by a twenty-eight-year-old part-time real estate broker and volunteer paramedic who still lived at home with Mommy and Daddy. Or she had, until somehow managing to wrangle herself a position on one of the more premier fire and rescue squads in the country.

Christ, he hoped Katy had pointed that rental truck east and was driving to Maine, as he didn't want to think he might be abandoning a woman in trouble. In his experience, women only went into hiding for one of two reasons: to nurse a broken heart or to escape some no-good bastard trying to break them.

This should teach him to mind his own business the

next time he stumbled upon a kidnapped queen. Why hadn't he just called his royal buddy, Markov Lakeland—king of the young country of Shelkova, just across the Bering Sea from Alaska—and simply told the man where he could find his missing wife and aunt? Getting mixed up in their reunion had led Gunnar straight from the frying pan into the fire.

He sighed, remembering the look on his friend's face when Markov strode into the village carrying the weight of six desperate days of not knowing if he'd ever see his wife again. Gunnar could swear he'd felt the ground shift when Markov had pulled Jane into his arms. For the first time in his life, Gunnar had found himself wondering what it would feel like to love someone that much.

And so had begun a three-month-long fantasy, fueled by a persistent queen who sent email after email with outrageous stories about her very tall, very beautiful, very best childhood friend who, having missed the royal wedding, had given her promise to be in Shelkova in time for the royal birth.

Only Katy MacBain had once again been a no-show, and Jane had gone into labor two weeks early smack in the middle of a palace overrun by well-groomed, ill-mannered nomads on a collective mission to find wives. And now it was Gunnar's mission, once again, to locate a missing woman and restore order in at least one small corner of the world.

Chapter One

Two weeks later

Katy MacBain's heart sank when she saw that one of the late arrivals they'd been holding the plane for was a kid.

Please stop. Please stop walking, she silently pleaded to the young boy striding down the aisle of the crowded commuter jet. Katy sighed in relief when the decidedly winded, harried-looking woman following him grabbed the loop on his backpack and pulled him to a halt five rows away.

It wasn't that she didn't like kids, but this one looked more excited than an astronaut boarding a spaceship to Mars. And in her experience, excited little boys liked to fidget. And talk. Considering she'd just spent the last ten hours zigzagging across the country, trying to get from Idaho to Maine, Katy feared her head would explode if she had to spend the final leg of this hellacious journey being nice. It would be too much for her, when she was barely keeping it together.

She groaned inwardly when, after eyeing the man next to the vacant seat, the woman nudged the boy forward once more. Katy looked back in hopes there were more empty seats behind her, but the duo stopped at her row.

"I wasn't able to get us seats together." The desperation in her eyes contradicted her congenial smile as she apologized to Katy. "But don't worry," she rushed on, her gaze dropping to the book in Katy's hands. "Shiloh brought plenty of things to keep him busy."

Two deep dimples punctuated the six- or seven-year-old's bright grin. "I brought a book to read, too. Mine's on raising chickens."

How . . . weird. "Why don't I just go take your other seat," Katy said, bending to grab her own backpack from the floor in front of her.

"I already asked the flight attendant, and he said it's too late to change seats because the passenger list has already been filed."

Katy grabbed her backpack and straightened. "I'm sure they won't mind if he at least takes the window seat."

"I prefer Shiloh be on the aisle where I can see him," the woman said, jostling her carry-on and large purse in order to slip off the boy's backpack.

"Could you ladies swap recipes after we're airborne?" came a male voice from a couple of rows back. "We've been stuck at this gate over twenty minutes waiting for you."

The woman aimed her congenial smile in his direction. "And I greatly appreciate your patience."

Only the kid ducked past her to face the man. "Our other plane was late, and we had to run across the whole terminal. But I needed to stop and use the bathroom, 'cause I don't like the toilets on the planes, and I knew I couldn't hold it all the way to Maine."

Several chuckles and a loud feminine gasp drowned out whatever the man muttered. "People don't want to hear about that," the woman said, settling the boy down beside Katy, tucking an array of games, books, snacks, and other items into the pocket in front of him and then popping his backpack into the overhead compartment.

As she dug around for his seat belt, he said, "But I had to explain it to him, Mom, 'cause he thinks it's your fault we're late." Shiloh leaned into the aisle, twisting to look back at the man. "Mom picked me up and ran like a cheetah so we wouldn't miss the plane. And if you don't know, cheetahs are the fastest land animal on the planet."

That well-aimed salvo effectively put the grump in his place, and Katy found her first smile of the day. Because really, who wouldn't want to sit next to a little boy willing to defend his mother at his own expense? In fact, Katy was afraid she was already halfway in love with the little warrior herself. More than that, she was relieved to have a distraction from the dark thoughts that threatened to consume her.

"You don't gotta worry I'll make you sick or anything," the boy said as he twisted toward her to help his mother hunt for the other half of his seat belt. "Even though Mom told me to hurry when I used the bathroom, I made sure to wash my hands real good so's to kill all those nasty public germs."

"Thank you for that." Katy fished the buckle out of

the crack and handed the belt to Shiloh. Smiling at his mother, she said, "Go spend the next couple of hours relaxing. We're all good here."

Ignoring the heavy male sigh from several rows back, the woman leaned down and gave her son a quick kiss on the cheek. "Don't go talking the lady's ears off," she reminded the boy over the soft whoosh of the jet's front door closing.

"Let me help you stow your bag and get seated," the flight attendant offered, taking the woman's carry-on and walking up the aisle as the plane gave a slight lurch backward.

"I'll be good, Mom," Shiloh said as he pulled a book from the seat pocket. "I'm gonna study which breeds are the best layers and see what dates I can get the chicks delivered."

Ah. The kid was going to raise chickens. Katy leaned her head back and closed her eyes to the drone of the idling engines as they taxied to the runway.

"You're supposed to watch while he tells us what to do in an emergency," he whispered.

"This is my fourth flight today. I could probably give the demo myself. In fact," she added, opening only one eye at him, "I happen to know you're supposed to put on your own oxygen mask before you help put on mine."

The kid gaped at her for a full three seconds, but Katy saw his tiny shoulders go back and his chest puff out as he returned his attention to the attendant. The captain came on the speaker, thanked everyone for flying with them, and said they were next in line for takeoff. The weather in Bangor, Maine, was seventy-three degrees with clear blue skies, and thanks to a good tailwind, he expected to be landing in one hour and forty-seven minutes.

Katy figured she could subtract several degrees off that temperature for her eventual destination up in the northwestern mountains. In fact, by the time she got there around nine or ten tonight, it would probably be closer to fifty.

She'd hadn't given herself much time before starting her new job in Spellbound Falls—and that was by choice. She didn't want to spend even one day at home in Pine Creek answering questions about the two months she'd been in Colorado—mostly because she'd actually spent the last two weeks in Idaho trying to forget what had happened in Colorado.

She'd agreed to only a quick dinner in Bangor with her folks before heading up the mountain. She hoped she could make it through that much. Because even though she'd gotten really good at lying over the phone, Katy wasn't sure how long she could hold up under her father's scrutiny. And if by some miracle she made it through dinner, there was still the chance her mother would know all was not well—physically or emotionally—with her youngest daughter.

Which brought Katy back to her ongoing litany of the last few days. Please, please let me be healed—at least enough to fool Mom. Deep down, Katy knew she'd been getting by on adrenaline and denial, but she had to. This was no time to fall apart. She needed to make the most of this job, needed to become the person it would demand her to be. By rescuing others, she'd rescue herself. That was her new, and only, mantra.

As of three weeks ago, when she'd finally decided she

could no longer deny inheriting her mother's little . . .
gift, Katy had obsessed over whether or not it was possible to actually hide an injury or illness from a former
trauma surgeon who also happened to be a medical in-
tuitive. If not, then a motherly hug might be all it was
going to take for everything to go to hell in a handbasket
right there in the middle of Bangor International Airport.

Please, please don't let Robbie be with them. Because
hiding anything from her magical big brother was nearly
impossible, considering he was Guardian of the Mac-
Keage and MacBain and Gregor clans and could friggin'
travel through time at will.

Was there a reason she couldn't have been born into a
normal family with plain old everyday talents instead of
being a first-generation Highlander whose father hailed
from twelfth-century Scotland? Not to mention her two
male MacKeage cousins who could manipulate the energy of mountains and Winter MacKeage Gregor was an
actual drùidh.

Funny how the MacKeage and MacBain males were
strongly encouraged to do at least one tour of duty in the
military—in essence putting themselves in harm's way
on purpose—but a MacBain female who was strong and
capable and a damn good equestrian couldn't do something even remotely dangerous if it served no intrinsic
purpose to humanity in general or the clans in particular.

So Katy had rebelled by not going to college. Instead,
she'd taken a night course at the regional high school and
gotten her real estate license. The problem was she'd
been damn good at that, too, which was why everyone
had been surprised when instead of buying the business
when her boss retired five years ago, Katy had run off to

Bangor and enrolled in a two-year course to become a paramedic.

She'd felt crazy and brave and filled with more purpose than she'd found in her life to that point. And if her family didn't quite understand, that had to be okay. Just like they might not understand how monumental it felt to finally be on the verge of something most people her age managed years before, having a place of her own, however small and humble. In a family the size and intensity of the MacKeages, solitude always seemed both impossible and undesirable. But these days, for so many reasons, a new wind was blowing in Katy's life. It was time to find her own spot in the world.

And then came the news story four months ago about a rescue squad being formed in a small mountain town a hundred crooked miles to the north. Once again, she'd quietly left home, then called her parents from Colorado to tell them she was taking a wilderness rescue course for her new job on Spellbound Falls Fire & Rescue. It was also why she'd waited until there had been two thousand miles between them before mentioning she'd even applied for the position, much less gotten it.

But good grief, this was the twenty-first century, not the twelfth. If she'd been born in her father's original time, she'd be considered a hopeless spinster at twenty-eight—assuming she hadn't been married off at fifteen and already anticipating the arrival of her first grandchild.

No, she definitely would have been a spinster, likely shunned for her . . . gift.

How in heck had her mother not gone insane?

The major reason Katy had decided to become a

paramedic was to help her understand what she was seeing whenever she inexplicably found herself rooting around inside someone else's body in her mind's eye. Unfortunately, every anatomy class in the world wouldn't help her make sense of the pulsing colors and conflicting emotions that assaulted her every time she went hurtling through bone and cartilage and various organs.

Well, except for three weeks ago, when she sure as hell hadn't had any trouble recognizing Brandon Fontanne's loathing.

Darkness threatened to overtake her, and Katy shuddered. She pushed it back as best she could but didn't feel confident she could keep it at bay.

"You don't gotta be afraid," a soft voice whispered. A small hand touched her arm, and Katy's eyes snapped open. The young boy, Shiloh, sat looking up at her with shining, alert eyes. "That loud thump was just the landing gear going up inside the belly of the plane, so the wheels won't drag in the wind and slow us down."

Oh, good Lord, she'd forgotten where she was. "How old are you, Shiloh?" Katy asked. Talking had to be better than remembering.

His small shoulders went back. "I'm almost nine, and in September, I'll be in the third grade."

Nine? The kid barely looked seven. But then what did she know, having been born into a family of giants? Well, except for her mother, who topped out at five-foot-three.

"Mom named me after my grandfather, 'cause she said that, even though he was born too early just like I was, he still managed to grow up big and strong and live to be ninety-four." Shiloh leaned over to glance up the aisle then looked back at her with a heavy sigh. "But I'm still waiting for the growing big part to kick in, 'cause even though I was the oldest kid in my class, people kept thinking I was too young to even be in school."

Poor little guy.

"Well, you've definitely started the strong part of growing up," she said, giving his forearm a quick squeeze. "And I predict you're going to be six feet tall by the time you're done growing. So, Shiloh . . ." She nodded at his catalog. "How many chickens are you planning to get?"

He stared at her for several heartbeats, his big brown eyes both hopeful and skeptical as he apparently tried to decide if he believed her about being six feet tall. Finally, he said, "I might only be able to get six pullets. But I'm really hoping to get four dozen so I can sell their eggs to the resort where we're gonna live. Mom said she's gotta ask the top boss lady if I can have any chickens, 'cause I don't want to keep them penned up if I don't have to." He gave another glance up the aisle then shot her a grin. "And if Mom lets me go with her when she asks, I can tell the boss lady that she wouldn't have to spray chemicals around the resort, 'cause free-range chickens would eat all the bugs and worms and even small frogs and baby snakes."

"Hens might be a good alternative to pesticides," Katy drawled, "but they do like to leave little . . . packages all over the place. So don't be surprised if the boss is reluctant to have resort guests dodging chicken droppings. Also, four dozen are a lot of birds to take care of," she added at his frown. "I know because, from the time I was five, it was my job to take care of my family's eighteen laying hens."

"It was?" Shiloh gasped, looking like he'd just won a

prize. "So you must know a lot about chickens. Did you order them as chicks through the mail? What breeds did you get? Did you have a rooster? I'm thinking I should get some roosters so I won't have to keep ordering chicks every year. And that way I won't have to set up a brooder, either, 'cause the hens will raise them for me."

Katy bit back a chuckle at the kid's enthusiasm over going into the chicken business. "Well," she said, "I don't know where we got our hens originally, since there have been chickens at home for as long as I can remember. And we always have at least one rooster, and every year we end up giving half our chicks away to neighbors."

She wanted to tell him the fancy boss lady at the resort might not want her guests waking up to crowing roosters, but she didn't have the heart to dampen his excitement.

"You say your mom has a job at a resort, and you're going to be living there? Is it in Maine?"

He nodded.

"Do you know the name of the town it's in?"

"The resort's called Inglenook, and it's far, far up in the mountains almost all the way to Canada in a town called Spellbound Falls."

"No," Katy said on a gasp of her own, imagining she also looked like she'd just won a prize. "I'm going to be living and working in Spellbound Falls, too."

"At Inglenook?" he asked.

"No, I'm going to be a paramedic at the new fire station right in town. Which," she rushed on at his crestfallen look, "is only about eight or nine miles from Inglenook. And not only do I happen to know your mother's boss personally, I also know that Olivia keeps a large flock of laying hens up at her other resort on the top of Whisper Mountain called Nova Mare." Katy shrugged. "I'm not sure what she's doing at Inglenook, but I bet she'd be open to your proposal about supplying the dining hall with eggs."

"When Mom got back from her interview to be the director of family activities," Shiloh said, back to being excited, "she told me Inglenook's got a huge barn full of horses and that the workers and their children are allowed to ride them." His chest puffed out again. "I've never ridden a horse before, but I bet I could learn real quick."

"I bet you could, too," Katy agreed, giving him a wink. "In fact, I might even be able to teach you, seeing how I'm going to be boarding my own horse at Inglenook."

"You are?" he asked, his face exploding into dimples again. "You have your own horse?"

Katy nodded. "Her name is Quantum Leap, and I've had her since I was twelve."

"And you'll teach me to ride her?" he whispered, back to looking hopeful and skeptical.

Katy chuckled and shook her head. "Very few people can ride her, I'm afraid. Even though she's twenty-three years old, Quantum can still be quite a handful. But if it's okay with your mom, we can borrow one of the resort horses and go on trail rides together."

"Oh," he said, dropping his gaze to his forgotten hatchery catalog. "I don't think Mom will let me ride outside the fenced area, 'cause she'd be worried my pony would run away like what happened to her when she was a little girl. She told me she held on a really long time before she fell off and broke her arm." He went quiet for several heartbeats then suddenly grinned up at her. "But if my pony had a lead line and you held it, Mom might let me go on a trail, since you must know a lot about controlling horses if you got your own."

"That would work," Katy said with a nod. "But just so you know, Inglenook doesn't have ponies, only full-sized horses."

He blinked up at her, then shook his head. "Mom's definitely not going to let me go riding, then. If she broke her arm just falling off a pony, she'd be afraid I'd break my neck falling off a tall horse. Even if it was just walking, it's a long way down."

Katy was pretty sure Shiloh was the one who was worried about that possibility. "I'm going to teach you how not to fall off. And I'll explain to your Mom that horses are generally safer than ponies for kids to ride and that the ones at Inglenook are especially gentle."

"And we wouldn't go out on the trail until I'm really good at it?"

"Nope. You'll be trotting and even cantering like a pro before we leave the paddock. And we'll use a lead line if it will make you—your mom—feel better."

"Okay, then," he said, his dimples back in full force. "I guess I'm gonna like living at Inglenook after all." Just as suddenly, he looked down at his catalog. "I wasn't sure before, 'cause I really didn't want to move almost all the way to Canada. I mean," he said with a shrug, looking up again, "Mom gave me the resort brochure to read, and it looks real nice and everything, but we don't know anybody there. I won't have any friends."

"Sorry, buddy; wrong on both counts."

"Huh?"

Katy shot him another wink. Where she'd first bristled at the idea of sitting next to this little chatterbox, she now felt grateful—both for the distraction and for the honor of meeting this champ of a kid. "You know me. And I'd feel honored to be your very first friend in Spellbound Falls."

"You want to be my friend? But I'm just a kid."

"But you're such a smart, strong—" Katy halted in midsentence when a shadow fell over them. She looked up to see the boy's clearly stricken mother.

"Shiloh," the woman whispered, darting an apologetic smile at Katy then scowling down at her son. "You're supposed to be reading, not talking the lady's ear off."

"But Mom, she's going to Spellbound Falls, too," Shiloh said before Katy could speak up. "And she's been raising chickens since she was five, and she knows your boss lady personally. She owns a horse that she's gonna keep at Inglenook, and she wants to teach me to ride and even take me out on the trails. But on a lead line," he rushed on between breaths, "so's you don't have to worry about my horse running away." He grasped his mother's sleeve. "I don't mind moving to Maine no more," he added, gruffly, "'cause Katy wants to be my friend."

Katy stuck out her hand when Mom lifted her misty-eyed gaze to her. "Katy MacBain. I'm a paramedic on Spellbound Falls Fire & Rescue."

The woman grabbed her hand in a nearly bruising grip. "I can't believe this is happening," she said, her voice also thick with emotion. "What are the chances of our meeting someone going to the same town, and . . .

and . . ." Her eyes started to tear as she looked down at
her son. "And Shiloh sitting beside you." She gave Katy's
hand a squeeze. "Thank you, Miss MacBain, for showing Shiloh he's going to find warm, welcoming people in
Spellbound Falls."

Katy's cheeks warmed, and she gently pulled her
hand free. "Trust me, Mrs. . . ."

"Oh. Oh! I'm sorry." The woman swiped at the moisture in her eyes. "Marjorie Fox. And it's Ms.," she added,
softly, darting a worried glance at Shiloh. "But if you
would consider being my friend, too," she rushed on
with a tentative smile, "I would like if you called me
Margo."

"Then Margo it is. Shiloh told me you're Inglenook's
new director of family activities."

"Yes," Margo said, though she dismissed the title with
a little wave. "Mrs. Oceanus seemed to feel my being a
counselor at a large, multicultural school in Phoenix for
twelve years more than made up for my lack of experience in the hospitality industry."

Katy nodded. "Once you get to know the various di-
rectors at both Inglenook and Nova Mare, I believe you'll
find that Olivia not only prefers hiring people from outside the industry but that she has an uncanny knack for
choosing exactly the right person for her positions.
You're going to love working for her."

Margo relaxed on a soft sigh. "I've never looked forward to anything more." She smoothed a hand over her
son's neatly cut straight black hair. "And Shiloh's going
to love living in the cute little house that comes with my
job. Spending time outdoors hiking and fishing and

swimming with children from all over the world instead of being holed up in his room all day, reading."

"Only when I'm not taking care of my chickens," Shiloh said. "They need lots of attention while they're little, so I'll be too busy to do all that nature stuff. Especially with kids I don't even know and who'll only be there for a week." He looked over at Katy. "But I'm sure my chicks will be okay for a couple of hours while you teach me to ride."

What Katy could see was that young Mr. Fox was a hermit in training. And that his fears lay close to the surface, poor kid. It wasn't easy making a big life change. She knew all about that.

"I'm afraid I'll only be able to get to Inglenook two or three times a week," she told him, stifling a smile at his frown. "As a paramedic, I have to live at the fire station twenty-four hours at a time every third day, and if I end up running ambulance calls at night, I'll probably spend a good part of the next day catching up on my sleep."

"What's Quantum supposed to do on the days you don't come see her? Isn't she gonna get lonely?" The boy brightened. "I could visit her and even bring her carrots."

"That's why I'm keeping her at Inglenook, Shiloh. Just like people need to get outdoors and do stuff with other people, Quantum's going to make friends with the other horses and play with them in the pasture on the days I'm not there."

She shot Margo a wink when Shiloh scowled down at his catalog, then touched the boy's arm to get him to look at her. "And trust me; hanging out with a bunch of chickens all day isn't nearly as exciting as kayaking on an actual inland sea full of playful dolphins that'll come so close you can almost touch them."

"Do you kayak?"

Katy nodded. "I do. I've been kayaking since . . . well, for as long as I can remember," she added with a laugh. "Only Pine Creek doesn't have interesting ocean creatures like Bottomless does." She leaned closer and lowered her voice. "I have ten-year-old twin cousins who live right on the fjord just a few miles from Inglenook, and they told me they have a pet whale named Leviathan that only a handful of people have ever seen."

Fear replaced the curious expression on Shiloh's face. "Whales are big. And a kayak isn't—" The plane gave a sudden shudder, and a chime sounded. Katy looked up to see the "Fasten Seat Belt" sign illuminate just as a distinct crackle of a mike being keyed came over the speakers.

"The captain has asked that everyone please stay in your seats and keep your seat belts fastened," a male voice said over the speaker. "Nothing to be alarmed about, folks, we're just heading into a small bit of—"

The plane gave a rather violent shudder, forcing Margo to grab Shiloh's seatback. "Okay," the voice drawled as the female flight attendant made her way toward them, "let's nix the small and go with nuisance turbulence."

"Shiloh?" Margo whispered just as the attendant reached her.

The boy leaned into the aisle to look up and down the length of the plane, then looked at his mother again and shrugged. "They're all smiling."

They? Katy wondered as she stretched to her full

sitting height and also looked up and down the plane—not seeing one smile on one passenger but plenty of concern.

"Let's get you back to your seat," the attendant told Margo, stepping to the side to let her pass just as the plane gave another violent shake. "Hold on to the seatbacks as you make your way forward."

"There's nothing to worry about, Katy," Shiloh said, and opened his catalog with a resigned sigh.

They fell into a companionable silence broken only by the drone of the laboring engines and startled gasps of passengers as the plane pitched and yawed with soft shivers and a few violent jerks.

It took Katy a moment to realize Shiloh kept looking in her direction and grinning. Or rather, he kept looking past her left shoulder. When she looked at him, he dropped his attention back to his catalog.

She went back to reading only to catch him staring past her and grinning again—finally turning that grin on her when he realized she was onto him.

"Your angel is very shimmery," he whispered, his eyes large and shining with wonder.

"Excuse me?" Katy said, leaning toward him. "Did you say my angel?"

He nodded, first at her and then at the wall beside her. "She's one of the brightest I've ever seen."

"She?" Katy repeated, involuntarily glancing over her shoulder.

"Well, except for mine," Shiloh said, his grin broadening. "He's so bright sometimes I have to put on sunglasses." He darted a glance up the aisle then leaned closer. "Mom said I shouldn't tell anyone I see angels, but mine said it's okay to tell you." He shrugged. "Most people don't believe they're real 'cause they can't see them."

"But you— Wait. Earlier when the turbulence started and you told your mom they were all smiling . . . you were seeing smiling angels?"

He nodded again. "I saw everyone's."

Excitement pulsed within her. Katy closed her book, looked around to see if they had any eavesdroppers, and pivoted to face him. "You called my angel she but yours he. Do girls have female angels and boys have males?"

He shook his head. "They're not really male or female. They . . . they're . . ." His brows puckered in thought. "They're all. You know, like everything. They don't even have bodies, 'cause they're really just energy." He grinned. "Angels can be whatever we need them to be when we ask for their help. But you gotta ask. Well, most of the time. Sometimes they know what's gonna happen before we do and they'll give us warnings to make us ask for their help." A pained expression crossed his face. "But people don't always get the message, even if their angel smacks them upside the head, trying to get their attention."

Katy stilled, her mind racing back three weeks. "Do they ever not warn us?" she asked, searching her memory for anything happening that night that she should have taken as a sign. "Like, do they ever decide to just let us deal with . . . things on our own?"

Shiloh stared at her with a look of deep concern. He could read her pain, she thought. Or the angels were cluing him into it. Too much, she thought. For him, and for me.

She shot him a crooked smile and touched his arm.

"Do they talk to you?" she asked, wanting to lift the dark mood she'd created.

He brightened again and nodded. "I don't hear them with my ears, though. I used to talk back to them out loud but only when I was alone in my room." His eyes took on a troubled quality again. "But I stopped after my dad came in one night and asked who I was talking to. He got a funny look on his face when I told him, and then just walked out without saying anything." Shiloh glanced down the aisle then lowered his voice. "Later on, I heard Mom and Dad in their room, fighting. But in that whispery way, 'cause they didn't want me to hear, you know? I think it was about what might happen if people found out I see angels. So I started talking to them inside my head after that. Even when I'm not visiting Dad, so I won't forget and do it when I am." He shrugged. "Mom says I'll probably outgrow it."

"Only if you stop believing. I'm a grown-up, and I believe you see angels."

"Then how come you can't see them?"

"I see . . . other things." Amazing how good it felt to say that to another person.

"Like what? Spirit guides? I see them, too. One of yours is letting me see it right now. It's a—" His eyes widened as he continued to stare past her shoulder. "It's a snake wrapped around a stick."

Katy laughed. "You just described the symbol for medicine," she explained. "Which fits, I suppose, since I'm a paramedic. But no, I don't see angels or spirit guides. Sometimes, though, I can see inside a person, see what's hurting them. I get pictures in my mind of what's wrong with them so I can help fix it."

Dark, nagging thoughts threatened to sweep into her mind, but she pushed them away and focused on this miracle of a boy, smiling at him.

He smiled back. "Um, can I ask you a question? About the Bottomless Sea?"

"What do you want to know?"

He hesitated, his eyes turning guarded. "The reason Mom wanted the job at Inglenook so bad was because she heard the Bottomless Sea was formed by . . . magic," he whispered. "And that's why she thought it would be a good place for us to live," he rushed on nervously. "Mom said that up until five years ago, Bottomless was just an ordinary lake. But then a big storm and earthquake happened all at the same time, and the mountains moved, and all the fresh water rushed out, and an underground river rushed in from the ocean and filled the lake up again with saltwater." His eyes narrowed on hers. "Is that true?"

"It is," Katy said with a nod. "It was big news five years ago. Oceanographers and geologists descended on Spellbound Falls the very next day. They even built a permanent facility to study the area. But because they couldn't figure out how or why it happened, a lot of people started saying it must be magic."

"Do you think it was magic?" he asked, back to looking guarded.

"I do. And you know why?"

"Why?"

"Because even though I can't see angels, I can feel the energy you say they're made of all around Bottomless. And when you get there, I bet you'll feel it, too."

His brow puckered as he shook his head. "I'm not gonna tell anyone if I feel it, though. Except you and

Mom," he added, quickly. "Because I don't want people thinking I'm weird." He scowled. "Mrs. Akins, my first-grade teacher, made Mom and Dad come to school after I said I didn't want to get on the bus because my angel told me there was gonna be an accident."

"Did Mrs. Akins make you get on the bus anyway?"

Shiloh's chin went up. "I cut out of line and hid in the bushes, and I didn't come out until I saw Mom running up the sidewalk when they called and told her they couldn't find me." His eyes turned sad. "My dad left us a couple of weeks after that. Mom said they fell out of love with each other, but I think he left because he couldn't handle my seeing angels."

Poor guy. "I'm sure that's not true, Shiloh." Though she wasn't sure at all. "And was the bus in an accident?"

Shiloh dropped his gaze to the catalog in his lap. "My friend Andrew got a bloody nose when the bus hit a garbage truck. And other kids got hurt, too." He looked up. "You won't tell anyone in Spellbound Falls that I see angels, will you? It'll be our secret?"

She nodded. "Of course."

"Some of the kids at my new school might tease me if they knew, and my teachers will tell me I shouldn't make up stuff like that."

"I promise not to tell. But remember, Shiloh, Bottomless is a very magical place." She canted her head. "Do you see them all the time? Everyone's angels?" she asked, wondering if it wouldn't drive a person crazy.

"No. They only show themselves when mine says it's okay, like he did to yours." He grinned. "He can tell if someone believes, and I think he wanted to let me know there's gonna be nice people in my new town."

"Oh, Shiloh, you're going to feel right at home in Spellbound Falls," Katy said with a laugh and finally gave in to her urge to hug him. "Because your very wise mama is taking you to a very magical town filled with some of the nicest people on the planet."

She felt every part of him relax and his energy grow lighter. And, she realized, the same was true for her.

Chapter Two

The rich, delectable scent of seafood wrapped Katy in the feeling of home when she and her parents stepped through the restaurant door. Instantly, she knew she'd be ordering the lobster, and he'd better be a big one. Of course, this was Maine, so the odds of that were great.

She followed her mother to their booth in the back, then scooted across the bench and basked in the glow of her parents' smiles. No matter how nervous she was about this conversation, she'd really missed having them this close. She would so hate to bring her unhappiness into this moment.

"It's good to see ye looking so strong and fit," her father said.

Her mother nodded enthusiastically. "You look wonderful, Katy."

Katy's shoulders relaxed, just a bit. So far, so good.

She'd passed the appearance test. No red flags so far. "Thanks. It's really great to see you guys, too. It was hard to be away." Her voice wobbled, but she cleared her throat and widened her smile.

Her mother's brow twitched slightly, but the server appeared at exactly the right moment and swept them into ordering. While she listened to her parents make their choices, she tried to line up some safe topics in her mind. But suddenly everything seemed like something she'd rather sidestep. Even talking about Jane and her baby was fraught, since her plans hadn't exactly unfolded as expected.

They caught up for awhile, and it did Katy's heart good to hear about her brother and cousins, about the goings on in Pine Creek and just a bit beyond. That's as far as Katy wanted her mind to travel.

"I left something in your truck," her mother said, smile as big as ever.

"Ooh, did you bake me cookies?"

"Ye won't stay fit for long if ye start indulging in your mother's sweets," her father said with a grin of his own.

"I'll keep that in mind, Papa," she said and glanced back to her mother. "Seriously, do I get cookies?"

Libby shook her head. "Not this time. Just a copy of the Pine Lake Weekly Gazette. It's not every day that one of our town daughters becomes a real, live queen, and I thought you'd like to see the story."

Katy bit her lip, then thought better of it. Her mother missed nothing. "Oh, thanks. And yes, our Jane is a queen with her very own princess to love."

"Is she beautiful?" Libby breathed.

Fortunately, Katy only had time for one smiling, duplicitous nod before the server—clearly an angel with impeccable timing—appeared at the table with their food. Her stomach practically snarled in anticipation of dinner. Not sure if she was dizzy because all she'd eaten in the last twenty-four hours was airline snacks or from relief that she just might survive this reunion, Katy attacked the two-pound hard-shell lobster with ravenous gusto. Exactly as delicious as she remembered.

She'd finished both claws before she recalled she was also supposed to be carrying on a conversation with her parents. She glanced up to find them both watching her with bemused grins.

"I guess it's good?" her mother said.

"Amazing."

Her father cleared his throat. "On a completely different note, since ye failed to say where you'll be living in Spellbound Falls, I took the liberty of speaking with Duncan, and he insisted ye stay with him and Peg." His eyes lit with amusement. "MacKeage also agreed to let ye bring that delicate mare of yours. Ye can give him a call on your way through Turtleback Station, and he'll be at the dock by the time you arrive in Spellbound tonight. And in return for his generosity, I told him you'll be glad to help Peg with the children and whatever farm chores need doing."

Katy had seen that one coming from a mile away. No, from two thousand miles away, actually, knowing that within minutes of her call from Colorado telling her parents about her new job in Spellbound Falls, this overprotective tower of granite would be on the phone with Duncan. This was her moment, her fork in the road.

"That was sweet of him. And you," Katy added with a bright smile, knowing he didn't much care for being referred to as sweet. "But a nine-mile water commute, especially in the winter, isn't very practical if my pager goes off in the middle of the night. That's why I already booked a site at a campground twenty miles south of Spellbound. They have these great platform tents, like the cabins I used to stay in at summer camp." She shrugged to keep from squirming when his eyes narrowed. "Once I'm settled into my job, I plan to look for a small house to rent closer to town."

"A house ye intend to live in alone?"

Katy kept her eyes locked on his. "Considering the crazy shifts I'll be working, I'd rather not deal with a roommate." Dammit, she was twenty-eight, not eighteen. "And these last couple of months, I discovered I like living alone."

Michael MacBain set down his fork, leaned back in his chair, and folded his arms over his chest. "You've changed."

"One of us had to," Katy returned just as softly. "And since it's my life we're talking about, I decided it would be me."

The din of the restaurant receded into a silence that stretched one heartbeat . . . two . . . only to be broken by a feminine sigh. "Welcome to adulthood, Katy," Libby said with a smile.

Okay, she must still be asleep on the plane and this was some weird, impossible dream. Katy darted glances between them before finally settling on her now beaming mother. "Contrary to popular opinion, I've been an adult for quite awhile now."

A soft male snort drew her attention. Her father shook his head, amusement lighting his—no, not amusement this time. Good Lord, could that possibly be moisture making his eyes shine? "Ye have our blessing to live in Spellbound Falls," he added, thickly. "Alone in your own home, if ye prefer."

Oh yeah, definitely dreaming. "Let me get this straight," she said. "I take a job in a town a hundred miles away without telling you, then run off to Colorado without telling you, and you all of a sudden decide you don't have a problem with any of that?"

"Nay, you finally decided that what I think no longer matters."

"That's the real test for any child," her mother said. "It doesn't work unless you figure it out for yourself, Katy. Like when it came to you riding that horse, though it was ultimately your father who convinced me."

"Really?"

Libby gave a small laugh. "If he hadn't, you'd still be writing to Santa asking for that Olympic-caliber horse."

Katy reared back in her chair. "You . . . you were against my getting Quantum?"

Her mother instantly sobered. "Do you have any idea how many riding accident victims I patched back together when I was a full-time surgeon in California? Or how many people I had to tell that their child or loved one probably wouldn't ever walk again?"

Katy slid her gaze to her father, then back to her mother, at a complete loss as to what to say. Or think. Or feel. She propped her elbows on the table and dropped her head into her hands. "What about Brody getting his motorcycle?"

"I managed to postpone that until his senior year in high school, when Michael finally asked if I wanted our son learning to handle a bike in Boston traffic instead of on our open roads, since we both knew he intended to buy one the moment he got to college."

Katy felt her mother's touch on her arm and lifted her head. "Robbie was almost nine when I realized I was only hurting myself by insisting Michael make the boy wear a helmet when he rode his pony." She gestured at her husband. "To which he not-so-eloquently informed me that he had no intention of raising 'a weak modern who was too afraid of dying to truly live.'"

Katy had grown up knowing "modern" referred to anyone born in this or the last century and that all the original time-traveling MacKeages and MacBains and Gregors thought most modern men were soft—which was why the displaced Highlanders insisted on raising their sons to be warriors and their daughters to be . . . well, eventually rebellious, apparently.

Michael slid an arm around his wife and drew her to him with an affectionate squeeze. "Your mother may be stronger than me in many ways," he said, smiling down into Libby's big brown eyes. "But she just couldn't see the value of buying a twelve-year-old lass a young, spirited horse." He turned his smile on Katy. "Looking at you now, I do believe I made the right call on that one."

Katy dropped her head back into her hands. Okay, he might have killed her dream of being in the Olympics, but she couldn't deny the many pleasurable years he'd given her racing the wind on Quantum. She lifted her gaze and shook her head at her parents. "You two are something else."

Michael stood and pulled back his wife's chair, then shot Katy a wink. "Why don't you ladies head to the parking lot so your mother can see for herself that ye didn't spend the last two months falling off mountains in Colorado."

Katy's body went cold. Wonderful. Just when it looked like she might actually pull this off, her father offers her up for examination. Well, at least the explosion would be in a deserted parking lot instead of the middle of the airport.

"A hint wouldn't have killed you," Katy said as she slipped her arm through her mother's, deciding to go on the offensive the moment they exited the restaurant. "It would have been nice to know that disagreeing with you two was even an option."

Libby pulled her to a stop. "And just how would telling you that have made you an adult?" She reached up and took Katy's face in her delicate surgeon's hands. "When I was your age, I was still being a dutiful daughter to a father who had been dead for two years." She twined their arms together again and proceeded across the parking lot. "I hid my passion for making jewelry from my parents all through medical school and climbing the ladder at one of the most prestigious hospitals in the country, always doing what everyone expected of me until I finally imploded at the age of thirty-one." Her smile turned crooked. "And I ran clear across the country and straight into your father's arms."

"After he fished you out of his farm pond," Katy added, recalling the story of Libby Hart's rental car murdering several prize Christmas trees on its flight into the pond, as well as the ensuing discussion between Michael and then nine-year-old Robbie as to whether or not they should throw their new tenant back in hopes she might finish growing.

"The point I'm trying to make," Libby said, "is that

everyone matures on their own schedule." She stopped and squeezed the arm she was holding. "You didn't only grow up these last two months," she said, turning to face Katy and grasping her other bicep. "You also grew out. Those are some pretty impressive guns."

Katy stepped away with a laugh. "Compliments of Colorado." She pulled out her key fob and unlocked her truck.

"So as one adult to another, you're saying there's no need for me to give you a quick little mental examination?" Her mother's eyes searched hers, and Katy did all she could to return a calm, steady gaze.

"I've never felt stronger or healthier, Mum." Katy tossed her backpack across the console, relieved to break contact, even for just a few seconds, then turned back to Libby. She clenched her fists, telling herself the lie was for her mother's sake as much as her own. "Or happier," she whispered before stepping back when she spotted her father coming toward them. "Especially now that I have Papa's blessing to get my own place," she added loud enough for him to hear.

"So long as you're living there alone," he said gruffly, pulling her into a fierce embrace. "Ye be mindful of yourself around those firemen, daughter. And if any of the cocky bastards give you any grief, you're to tell Niall or Duncan or Alec."

"What?" Katy gasped in mock surprise as she leaned as far back as his embrace would allow. "Are you saying you didn't ask the three of them to go to the fire station and flex their collective muscles at the cocky bastards before I arrived?"

He answered with a grunt and pulled her back against

him, Katy presumed to hide his guilt. "Ye may be a grown woman, but you will always be my baby girl."

"Well, it's time your baby hit the road," her mother said dryly, playfully tugging Katy away from him. "Or she's going to end up sleeping through her first day on the job."

"That wouldn't be a problem if she hadn't cut it so close," her father grumbled as Katy gave her mom a quick hug and climbed in the truck. "Ye keep a sharp watch for moose," he added as she fastened her seat belt. "And if ye feel your eyelids getting heavy, find a well-lit public place to park and sleep in the truck. They won't give your precious job away if ye're not there at seven sharp in the morning."

Katy took pity on him, knowing his brogue only deepened the closer his emotions got to the surface. "I'll drive careful, Papa." She arched a brow—partly to lighten the mood but mostly to keep her own emotions in check. Lord, she loved him, as maddeningly overprotective as he was. "Just remember to bring sleeping bags when you and Mum pop by for a visit in"—she cocked her head—"less than two weeks, I figure."

"We'll do that," Libby said with a laugh as she poked her head through the open window for one last peck on Katy's cheek. "Along with a cooler filled with healthy food. Enjoy your new job, ba—Katy."

"I intend to," Katy drawled past the growing lump in her throat. "And thanks for . . . Thanks for everything. I love you," she added as she closed the door, then started the truck and drove off with a wave.

She would have been fine, too, if she hadn't glanced in the rearview mirror when she reached the parking lot exit and saw her mother's petite body engulfed in a bear of a hug as her father stared after his youngest child officially leaving the nest.

Katy blinked against the sting in her eyes as she drove away, only to concede defeat less than a mile later. She pulled to the side of the road instead of turning north onto Interstate 95, put the truck in park, and covered her face with her hands.

Well, crap. What was so all-fired great about being an adult, anyway, if it meant she could no longer run home crying to her parents when the world knocked her flat on her ass?

Gunnar slipped into the corner booth of the lively Bottoms Up Bar & Grill, tossed the fire chief's badge on the table, and took a long guzzle of the beer he'd gotten at the bar because he'd been too impatient to flag down a waitress. He pulled out his phone and took it off silent with his free hand even as he continued to drink, then lowered the glass and read the text he'd gotten a little over an hour into the council meeting.

He took another guzzle of beer to hide his grin, figuring Miss MacBain should be arriving at the campground anytime now, and that in less than nine hours, he would finally be standing face-to-face with the mysterious missing woman. And while it was on his mind, he decided to head off what he knew would be queen-sized trouble if he didn't report in soon. Fingers flying, he dashed off a text of his own, telling Jane that her BFF was back home and safe, apparently none the worse for wear. Hopefully she'd be all caught up in baby management and simply read the message without firing back a wave of questions. Fat chance, bonehead.

He slid his gaze to the badge and gave a snort. Instead of being a mere coworker like he'd planned, tomorrow morning he would be introducing himself to Katy as her new boss. All thanks to Chief Gilmore's sudden resignation, which had forced the town councilmen to spend the last four days pouring over their roster of firemen, then most of tonight's meeting arguing over which one of the two best candidates should fill the temporary position while they searched for a replacement.

That should teach him to be more careful what he put in his resume.

Duncan MacKeage had been the only councilman who'd remained calm throughout the three-hour meeting, and Gunnar didn't know if he was flattered or concerned that the apparently influential man had gotten him named interim chief. Which should also teach him to pay better attention when three burly Scots—one of whom had been Duncan—made a point of coming to the station en masse to introduce themselves to the mostly male squad before their sweet, pretty, favorite cousin started her new job.

The reason for their visit couldn't have been clearer, even though one of the Scots giving the unspoken warning had been Niall MacKeage, chief of the Bottomless Sea Police Force. And although Scot number three, Alec MacKeage, had affably introduced himself as a trail groomer at his family's ski resort over in Pine Creek who lived in Spellbound Falls during the off-season, even the cockier firefighters had seen the deadly potential in those sharp green eyes and had all politely smiled and nodded when they'd shaken his hand.

Gunnar had known who the three men were, having researched Katy's extended family at the onset of this little odyssey. He'd also crossed paths with Chief MacKeage at a couple of accident scenes, as well as having seen both Duncan and Alec in town, though he'd gone out of his way to avoid speaking to them. Katy's resident watchdogs had, however, inadvertently been responsible for keeping him sane these last two weeks by their very lack of concern about where she was. Though he did wonder how the seemingly astute men were unaware their sweet, pretty, favorite cousin was lying through her teeth to her entire family.

Gunnar concealed his surprise by taking another sip of beer when he realized the police officer sliding into the booth across the table from him was familiar.

The uniform most definitely was not.

"Is there something about to go down here I should know about?" his uninvited—and sure as hell unexpected—visitor asked, eyeing Gunnar's own uniform. "Or is business slow?"

"Apparently I'm not the only one affected by global economies tanking, Officer . . ."

The man extended a hand across the table. "Sheppard. Officer Jake Sheppard, Chief . . ."

"Gunnar Wolfe," Gunnar said, fighting back a grin as he shook his hand. He picked up his beer again. "And about the only thing I'm aware of going down in this backcountry tourist mecca is my blood pressure."

The man he knew as Jayme Sheppard—or rather, Shep—stopped his coffee mug halfway to his mouth, amusement creasing the corners of his intelligent brown eyes. "You obviously haven't had any dealings with the Grange ladies yet. And maybe if you charged reasonable fees, several of those global economies would stabilize."

"I'll start charging less when they stop trying to hang me out to dry right along with the bad guys so they can skip the payment part entirely." Gunnar also stilled in the act of lifting his beer. "Wait. Is there something going down here I should know about?"

That got him a chuckle. "Not unless an uptick in jaywalking constitutes the beginnings of a conspiracy. Hell, I've seen rowdier tombs." Shep's expression turned hopeful. No, more like desperate. "Come on, Wolfe, you can tell me if you're after a particular . . . tourist you heard is planning to visit this ninth natural wonder of the world. I promise not to buy a full-page ad in the *Bottomless Press Herald* announcing you're here."

"Sorry, my friend, I'm merely on sabbatical." Good word, he told himself; could mean lots of different things—change of scenery, romantic interlude, career transition. If even he didn't know why this mission mattered so much, it sure didn't make sense to give Shep any accidental clues.

"Last I knew you liked hanging out with a bunch of nomads in northern Russia whenever you got tired of acting like a civilized human being. You get the tribal leader's daughter pregnant?"

Gunnar merely snorted and took another sip of beer.

Shep gestured at the badge on the table. "I thought I was finally going to get to draw my weapon when the council voted to make you interim chief instead of the other guy."

Christ, Shep had been at the meeting? "Is there a reason our paths haven't crossed in the last two weeks?" Gunnar drawled to hide his consternation. How in hell had he missed the only black guy in the room tonight—especially one wearing enough law enforcement paraphernalia to stop a full-blown riot?

"Because I always made sure I saw you first," Shep drawled back.

Gunnar cut himself some slack, recalling the bastard had once spent two weeks searching an English manor right under the noses of the entire family and staff.

"Those were some pretty impressive credentials I heard Duncan listing off," Shep continued. "Refresh my memory. Instead of getting a master's degree in fire science, weren't you rotting in prison in some obscure little country on the Bering Sea three years ago?"

"The country was Shelkova, and I was recovering from a gunshot wound under house arrest. And since timber is their major resource, the only non-dry reading in the palace library was on fighting forest fires." He shrugged. "If the woods around here ever go up in flames, I'm the man you want to call."

"Your house arrest was in a palace?"

Gunnar shot him a grin. "Once I was healed and I promised my buddy, who was Prince Markov at the time, that I'd stop using Shelkova's remote coastline for some of my sting operations, he kindly commuted my sentence."

Of course, that hadn't stopped Gunnar from getting a little revenge four months ago by forcing the recently crowned king to spend three days tracking down Anatol's tribe in order to retrieve his wife. In his defense, how was he supposed to know Markov had been that much in love with the little termagant? "So, if you're not here on patriotic duty," Gunnar continued, "what's up with the uniform and shiny badge? Hell, Shep, aren't you afraid to trip over all that equipment while you're chasing down jaywalkers?"

Officer Sheppard leaned back while adjusting the radio mike on his shoulder, then smoothed down the front of his crisp blue shirt. "It's a proven fact women are attracted to men in uniform," he said deadpan. "And it's Jake. Our K-9 officer's name is Shep. And," Jake ground out when Gunnar choked on the sip of beer he'd just taken, "Cole and I decided to trade in our cloaks and daggers for jobs with a longer life expectancy."

Gunnar stilled, forcing himself not to look around. "Wyatt's here, too?" he asked, hoping to God he sounded casual. Shep sure as hell better be telling the truth about their motivation. Since this case was personal—Jane would hunt him down and finish him off personally if he didn't find her friend and figure out what was going on—he had zero intention of letting anyone else muddy the waters.

Jake's eyes lit with amusement. "Cole's down protecting the good citizens of Turtleback Station. I haven't told him you're here yet because I wanted it to be a surprise for both of you."

Great. He couldn't freaking wait. Even though he'd more often than not been on the same side as the two . . . civil servants, Gunnar had usually found himself having to race them to the finish, because, hell, he didn't get paid unless he delivered. And they'd separately been closing in on a particularly nasty target about a year ago when everything had suddenly gone to hell in a handbasket . . .

Oh yeah, he really needed to stop being an ass to the small handful of men in the world he actually respected. And even though he'd made sure Wyatt's hospital room had smelled like a thousand-dollar brothel, he wasn't in any hurry to meet the bastard anytime soon.

Gunnar's cell phone started vibrating, the accompanying chime indicating dispatch was toning out Spellbound Falls Fire & Rescue. He snatched up the phone before it vibrated off the table and tapped the link to hear the seventy-second message.

A good ten seconds of tones went off, followed by static, then: "Attention Spellbound Falls Fire & Rescue. Units Nine-eighty-seven and Spellbound Ambulance Two are asked to respond to the north side of Fraser Mountain—they believe near the High Bridge campsite—for a sixteen-year-old male, breathing and conscious, with a possible broken leg. Patient is with a party of nine hikers also requesting transportation off the mountain. Be advised, caller mentioned hearing approaching thunder. Confirmed with Caribou NOAA; squall line expected to reach that area around . . ." The line crackled, followed by a soft chuckle. "Ah, now. Copy units Nine-eighty-seven and Spellbound Ambulance Two: Fraser Mountain, near High Bridge campsite, for sixteen-year-old male with possible broken leg. Piscataquis out, twenty-two-twelve."

Gunnar grabbed his badge off the table and stood, then headed for the door.

"Wolfe."

He stopped and looked back to see Jake also standing. His hands hovered casually—but no less menacingly—near his gun holster. "I find out you're not here on sabbatical, you won't be recuperating in a palace."

Gunnar eyed him briefly, then merely nodded and strode out of the bar. Time to do his job.

Chapter Three

Katy had been quite proud of herself for getting to work a full forty-five minutes before the 7:00 a.m. shift change, even if a leaky roof had spurred her on more than a desire to impress her new boss. Only she'd arrived to find one of the five station bays empty and no one around to impress. Her nerves jangled in the silence, sending her thoughts directly to her lifelong anxiety fix: Jane. What a relief it would be to fill the emptiness with her best friend's laughter, with a steadying round of "atta girls" and "you can do its."

But one devastating detail kept her phone in her pocket. Jane would know. She'd hear everything—stated or not—in Katy's tone, her words, even her breathing. They'd spent decades perfecting the shorthand, and Katy knew that gift would sell her out in the end. So now she sat on a bench in front of the newly completed state-of-the-art safety building, trying to decide how she felt about what she'd been told by the teenage intern she'd discovered washing mud off the impressively large rescue truck out back.

"Chief Gillman's gone," the kid told her. "Quit."

Katy felt a hard pulse in her throat at the news. What on earth had made the jovial, grandfatherly chief who'd hired her three months ago suddenly up and quit what had to have been his dream job?

"Family reasons," was all the kid offered.

"And where are the others?"

"Taking showers," he said. "They came back dirtier than their vehicles after spending all night rescuing a bunch of backcountry hikers. One of them busted an ankle and had to be transported to a hospital about fifty miles from here."

Now Katy sat and tried to tamp down her uneasy feelings. Because even with her parents' blessing, maybe moving to this magical little town wouldn't prove to be the best decision she'd ever made. Maybe it would represent another pothole on the crooked road of her life. The empowerment that came from getting a position on such an elite squad had helped pull her through the last three weeks, but apparently Spellbound Falls Fire & Rescue was experiencing its own personal—and personnel—crisis.

Katy spent ten minutes roaming the large station before she found the kitchen. She hunted down a mug, filled it with the questionable remains of the coffeepot, and went outside in hopes the bright morning sun would help banish the chill of the morning's news.

Damn, she'd really liked Chief Gilmore. Katy smiled sadly, remembering the man's hazel eyes shining with patient humor as she'd spent her entire interview in a nervous sweat, trying to persuade him to take a chance on her. She wanted the job. She thought she would be good at it. But this squad was such a big deal, it really took a lot of guts on her part to apply.

Heck, all the national news channels had run stories on Chief Gilmore's search for the bravest and best firefighters and paramedics for the elite squad he was pulling together. He drew applicants from all over the country. Deeply qualified ones.

Katy figured she must have been temporarily insane to even go for it.

Or maybe Chief Gilmore had been for hiring her.

He'd told her he had faith in her and would be there to guide her. And now he was gone.

All of which had her worrying about how the new chief would feel, inheriting a medic who possessed a sum total of three years of volunteer experience. Oh, and a certificate from the highly respected wilderness school Gilmore had pulled a few strings to get her into, which claimed she was now competent in technical climbing, whitewater kayaking, and remote search and rescue. But would that be enough to satisfy the new chief, or would she be let go without even being given the chance to prove—

"Must be nice."

Katy lifted a hand to her forehead and squinted into the sun at the elderly gentleman stopped on the sidewalk at the end of the station's driveway. "Excuse me?"

"I was just saying how nice it must be," he repeated, gesturing in her direction, "to have our hard-earned tax dollars paying you probably double what anyone around here makes, just so you can sit and drink coffee in front of a ridiculously overpriced fire station."

Katy's mouth dropped open, but before she could reply, a deep male voice cut in behind her.

"Be glad she's sitting here instead of out on some road trying to keep your wife and granddaughter from bleeding to death while we cut them out of what's left of their car."

Katy spun on the bench to gape at the tall, broadshouldered man standing in the open bay doorway, his ice-blue gaze locked on the complainer. Despite the absence of a badge, she recognized he was a firefighter rather than a medic. Although he wore a dark blue T-shirt identical to hers, his matching station pants didn't have cargo pockets to get in the way of slipping into bunker gear.

"Well, that was aggressive," Katy said, even as she fought the urge to jump up and flee along with the duly chastised gentleman scurrying down the sidewalk.

He shrugged and turned those piercing blue eyes on her. "When people stop making stupid comments, I'll stop correcting them. And speaking of stupid, lose the badge," he added, nodding at the one clipped to her jacket.

"Excuse me? Why?"

"Our jobs are dangerous enough without pinning a target on our chests. Pissed-off people will often start shooting at anyone who looks like law enforcement."

Katy swallowed her anxiety and watched the old man disappear into a local restaurant down the road.

Welcome to Spellbound Falls, she thought, with grim humor.

She turned back to the man and willed her heart to stop racing. Holy hell, were all the firefighters on the squad so imposing? Even though she'd grown up around tall, athletic men—there wasn't a male in her family under six-foot-three—Katy doubted that even a solid wall of overprotective brothers and cousins would rattle this guy, who stood as solid and grounded as a thousand-year-old oak.

"Thanks for the advice," she said in what she hoped was an even voice, "but I think I'll wait for the new chief to tell me to lose the badge."

"He just did." His eyes flared briefly before they crinkled with his grin. "Gunnar Wolfe—with an E," he said, tapping the name Wolfe printed on his shirt.

He reached in his pocket, pulled out a flat leather case, studied it a moment, and then turned it to face her. "Yup, the badge they gave me at the council meeting last night definitely says I'm chief—at least for the next three months. And although my expertise runs more toward fire and rescue, you might as well know I intend to be hands-on in all departments."

Crap, a bossy boss. "What do you mean by 'hands-on'?"

"I mean that instead of spending all my time doing paperwork and trying to placate three crews of cocky firefighters and medics, I intend to fight fires and rescue idiots off mountains in the pouring rain like I originally signed up for."

"If you didn't want to be chief, then why didn't you just say no?"

"Because I definitely didn't sign up to take orders from the next guy in line."

Katy refrained from asking who that was—partly because she didn't want to get involved in workplace politics her first day on the job, but mostly because she preferred to form her own opinion of any coworker she might have to trust with her life. "So, does that mean you plan to tag along on ambulance runs?"

His grin widened. "Don't worry, MacBain; you stay out of burning buildings and I'll stay out of your bus." He held out his hand. "Welcome to the team."

Double crap. Not only was this guy about as grandfatherly as she was, he appeared to be persistent. Katy grabbed his hand for a quick firm shake, only to find herself trapped when he didn't let go.

"You're one of five females, Katy," he said, his tone matching the sudden seriousness in his eyes, "on a squad mostly made up of arrogant, overconfident men who don't have the words *back off* in either their professional or personal vocabularies. Anyone gives you any grief, I expect to be the first and only person to hear about it." His amusement just as suddenly returned. "And by anyone, I'm including your female teammates. Although," he added dryly, his gaze traveling down the length of her, then back to her eyes, "I'm guessing you can handle anything the women might send your way."

"I can also handle the men," she said, giving a small tug on her hand.

His grip remained firm, and his grin vanished again. "But you're not going to let it reach the point of having to handle anything, are you? Your first hint of trouble brewing, I want you running straight to me instead of those three burly cousins who kindly introduced themselves to all us firefighters last week."

Ugh. Did she know her family or what? "Did you give this same warning to the other four women?"

He spun on his heel with a rumbling chuckle and

strode away, a full two seconds passing before Katy realized her hand was being held by nothing but air. "Go feather your little home away from home with whatever lucky charms and inspirational posters you brought, then meet me at your bus in half an hour." He stopped inside the open bay door and gestured toward the far end of the station. "That would be the bright yellow and black truck with *ambulance* written backward on the hood."

Several more seconds went by with her staring at empty air before Katy took a few slow, deliberate breaths. Although Gunnar Wolfe could probably give bravado lessons to the men temporarily under his command, she really couldn't take offense at his trying to head off something she now knew could become a major problem.

And just like that, without really understanding why, Katy decided she could trust Chief Wolfe. At least professionally, like when it came to his holding the other end of a rope she might be dangling from halfway down a cliff or trusting his judgment that it was okay to crawl inside a wrecked vehicle to reach a patient.

But outside of work, such as going to the Bottoms Up with the crew for beers after a particularly bad day? Katy unpinned her badge with a snort, stuffed it in her pocket, and headed inside. No, if she ever did find herself in a bar again, she wasn't even ordering water.

But then she smiled at the realization that came over her: apparently she still had a job.

Gunnar wiped off the water he'd splashed on his face and glared into the mirror over the sink in the private quarters behind his new office. Well, that hadn't gone anywhere near like he'd imagined. "Because you obviously forgot your number one rule of not letting a woman distract you—on or off a mission," he told the idiot glaring back at him. "Even if she is the mission."

Only years of surviving by the skin of his teeth had saved him from openly reacting when Katy had jumped up and turned to face him. He'd known she was beautiful; hell, the pictures he'd found of her online had been partly responsible for drawing him here. But no photograph, nothing he'd read about her, nor any of the childhood stories Jane Lakeland had unapologetically used to pique his interest could have prepared him for the flesh and blood woman. Even knowing Katy was six-foot-one, he'd still been stunned to find himself barely having to look down to see the vibrancy in her startled gray eyes.

No, not gray. Those long-lashed, fathomless eyes were the exact color of an Icelandic fogbank backlit by the morning sun. And when she'd spun to him in surprise, the whip of that long single braid of mahogany hair as thick as his wrist had sent him even further back in his youth, to when he would sit on a bluff overlooking the wind-whipped northern Atlantic and dream of escaping his island home on an ancient longship in a bid to conquer the world.

She hadn't wanted to shake his hand, even though he had enough notches on his bedpost to know women didn't exactly find him repulsive. And having met her three cousins, Gunnar figured Katy should be comfortable around large men. Hell, her chosen profession practically guaranteed she'd be surrounded by firefighters dwarfed only by their egos.

No, he figured her reluctance, and the skittish energy

she emitted, had to do with the last two weeks of her life that he couldn't account for—or at least hadn't been able to, so far. Having tracked down the school she'd trained at in Colorado, he'd learned from one of the staff that Katy had surprised everyone by getting falling-down drunk when they'd all gone to a local bar on the last night to celebrate. Before that, no one had seen her have more than an occasional evening glass of wine. The head instructor had personally helped her into the van, taking several of the students to a motel near the small local airport, making sure one of the women promised to see Katy safely to her room.

Only instead of going to the airport the following morning and transferring the rest of her round-trip ticket for one to Shelkova like she'd promised, Katy had stayed at the motel for three days and then simply vanished.

Not that that had stopped Jane from naming her little bundle of joy after her BFF. Gunnar grinned at his reflection, figuring Princess Katherine Maine Lakeland—the first female born to a Lakeland male in twelve generations—was already ruling the palace. Hell, when he'd called two weeks ago to remind Jane how crucial it was, should she hear from Katy, that she not tell her that the guy she'd wanted her to meet was going to Maine to find her instead, Markov had said his lovestruck countrymen were still partying in the streets.

After assuring Jane he'd let her know what had sent her friend into hiding just as soon as he found out why, and after coming up several hundred palm-greasing dollars poorer from digging up more questions than answers in Colorado, Gunnar had reluctantly continued on to Maine to establish himself as one of the firefighters before Katy finally—hopefully—showed up to work. He'd swear it had been the longest two weeks of his life, with him not taking a decent breath until the computer hacker keeping watch texted him night before last, saying Miss MacBain's cell phone had suddenly started pinging loud and clear in Boise, Idaho.

Gunnar couldn't for the life of him figure out why the woman had headed north instead of pointing that rental truck east. But he hadn't been all that surprised when a subsequent text said Miss MacBain placed two calls shortly after turning on her phone—the first one to the country of Shelkova that had lasted thirty-eight minutes, and a second call to Pine Creek, Maine, lasting exactly seven. Not surprising, given what Jane had shared about Katy's rather creative rebellions against her overprotective family.

More texts came in throughout yesterday, saying the phone signal kept going off only to start up again in another city. His tech guru finally discovered that Miss MacBain was making her way to Maine by finally using her credit card to buy flights on standby.

Gunnar had known down to the minute when Katy had landed in Bangor, but he hadn't let himself relax until learning her card had been used at the campground twenty miles south of town—at about the same time the skies opened up and he'd found himself going after an injured hiker, several muddy, treacherous miles away on Fraser Mountain.

With a deep breath, Gunnar decided to cut the poor bastard in the mirror some slack. He had not only run a full gauntlet of emotions these last two weeks—from anger to frustration and finally relief—he would swear he'd felt the ground shift this morning when Katy spun toward him, looking beautiful and vibrant and seemingly fully recovered from whatever in hell sent her running to freaking Idaho.

So okay, then; it appeared he was finally going to find out if the Maine wilderness really produced angels or if he would spend the rest of his life rotting in a palace dungeon for throttling a vengeful, busybody queen. No sooner had that unsettling thought landed than another, more sobering one appeared: with consequences like those on his horizon, his mercenary days might have officially come to an end.

Gunnar let that possibility settle over him, waited for it to stir up his usual "hell no" response. But nothing happened. Well, nothing but another mini mind-earthquake as he once again pictured the magnificent Katy MacBain. Hell YES, his molecules screamed instead, and he realized that locating her had only seemed like the mission.

Chapter Four

Not really into lucky charms or inspirational posters, Katy dumped her overnight bag in the first vacant cubicle she came to in the women's quarters, then rushed back downstairs to the gorgeous yellow and black, four-wheel drive ambulance.

An angry voice pulled her from her exploration of the equipment in the vehicle—brand-new and cutting edge. She poked her head out of the ambulance and discovered their new chief putting one of the firefighters on notice.

"It's not your job to educate or reprimand the people we rescue," Chief Wolfe said.

"Hell with that," offered the other man. "You don't take a bunch of inner-city kids into the wilderness without knowing what you're doing. That guy's dumbass decision put our squad in danger, sending them out in the middle of a raging storm."

"I'm aware of the weather conditions," Chief Wolfe shot back in a tone that seemed more terrifying for its mildness. "That doesn't change the fact that our job is to help people. Not lecture them for their choices in the middle of a life-and-death situation. You made a tough moment worse. Your job is to make things better. Got it?"

The firefighter gaped for a moment, then seemed to realize he'd have better luck arguing with a rock. "Got it," he said and walked to his car, muttering to himself.

Rather familiar with men whose level of quietness was a good measure of their anger, Katy decided she would run for cover if Chief Wolfe ever started whispering.

Eventually she emerged from the vehicle, having spent the last half hour getting familiar with the vast array of equipment—some of which she'd only seen in trade magazines. The chief gave her a challenging look, filled with leftover frustration from the argument he'd just had.

Deciding the only way out was through, Katy plunged into the topic that had been nagging at her since her arrival. "Is it a big secret, or can you tell me why Chief Gilmore resigned?" she asked. "When I checked in with him a few weeks ago, he never even alluded to the fact that he was leaving."

"The official story is he called from Nevada last Thursday," Chief Wolfe said as he looked in at her through the open back doors, "and told the town manager that he wouldn't be returning because his wife had been diagnosed with an aggressive form of cancer."

"Why do you sound like you don't believe that's true?"

"I believe his wife really is sick," he said, gently. He hesitated, as if trying to decide how much to tell her.

"But I think the biggest reason Gilmore chose a treatment center clear across the country was because he wanted plenty of real estate between himself and the monster he realized he'd created."

"Excuse me?"

He grinned, gesturing at all the bays filled with vehicles except for the remote access ambulance, which was out back being washed. "Why do you think every truck in here, from the aerial to the four-wheel drive ambulances, appears to be on steroids?"

"Maybe because they're working in the mountains, where snow is measured in feet instead of inches?"

"The trucks have to be so large to fit all the oversized egos of the crews." His expression sobered, and he ran two hands through his hair, stalling again, though Katy couldn't figure out why. "I wasn't posturing earlier when I told you to watch your back. These folks have the right to be arrogant, considering everyone's skill levels, but there are also several adrenaline junkies who consider themselves God's gift to humanity. And I'm including the women."

"Which again begs the question of why you agreed to be chief."

His amusement returned. "Because I'm the worst of the lot."

Katy had no trouble believing that particular boast, despite having met the man just this morning. If his handling of the citizen complainer hadn't told her Gunnar Wolfe didn't suffer fools lightly, what she'd witnessed a few minutes ago had certainly been . . . educating.

"So, how was your course in Colorado?" he asked.

"It was four weeks of adrenaline overload punctuated by moments of sheer terror."

Her honesty earned her a rumbling chuckle that shot all the way down to her toes. Anxiety washed over her. God help her, for all the years she'd been hoping and praying to meet a man who made every cell in her body shiver, why this one? But even more maddening, what ugly twist of fate had her meeting him now? What kind of cruel God answered a prayer after tearing its owner to shreds, body and soul?

"Just wait until this winter," he said with lingering amusement, "and the tones go off for an ice climber stuck on—"

He stopped midsentence and went perfectly still, his head canted slightly as he appeared to be listening. "Bring the jump bag," he said and bolted toward the front of the station.

Crap. Katy ducked back into the ambulance, grabbed the triage bag, and found herself running down the driveway behind two other firefighters also sprinting toward the frantic screams in the distance.

Once they reached the road, she broke into a flat-out run, which had her entering the small park at the base of the sixty-foot waterfall two strides behind the chief— who followed closely behind a large brown dog wearing a ballistic vest and racing toward the panicked little boy standing next to the pool of frothing water.

When they reached him, Katy realized the kid was screaming in a foreign language. He pointed at where the fast-moving stream rushed under the train-trestle-turned-footbridge before spilling into the Bottomless Sea.

Chief Wolfe spoke calmly to the kid in what sounded like the same language just as the dog bolted toward the trestle and plunged into the stream.

"Higgins! Welles!" Chief Wolfe shouted over the roar of the falls as he also ran along the edge of the pool, his gaze locked on the two children clinging to a boulder beyond the car bridge that ran alongside the trestle. "Get below the bridges and be ready to catch them if they're swept downstream."

He started emptying his pockets as Katy ran beside him. "Head over with them," he instructed, handing her his cell phone and wallet. "And bring the boy with you. Dammit, that dog's going to make the older kid lose his grip."

Katy slid to a stop when Chief Wolfe muttered something in yet another unfamiliar language and plunged into the water without breaking stride. Turning to find the five- or six-year-old boy right behind her, she shoved the cell phone and wallet in a side pocket on the jump bag before sliding it on her shoulder, then took hold of the boy's hand and headed directly up the steep bank.

"Katy," she said, thumping her chest. "My name is Katy. And don't you worry," she went on brightly, hoping her tone would reassure him if he didn't speak English. "They'll get your friends."

Forced to halt after crossing the trestle footpath in order to avoid being trampled by the small stampede of people rushing onto the car bridge to see what was happening, Katy simply scooped up the boy, tucked him under her arm like a football, and sprinted across the road.

"Shep, hold in place!" Niall MacKeage shouted to the dog in what Katy did recognize as Gaelic as he ran up the side lane while also emptying his pockets. He dropped everything on the grassy bank and waded into the water, angling cross-current until he was waist-deep in the stream several yards below the boulder.

Katy gasped, knowing that waist-deep for Niall meant treacherous depth for an average-sized person and that there was likely a drop-off near the rocky falls. She stood her young charge on the ground and crouched down beside him, slipping a protective arm around his waist as she studied the two children on the boulder. In a few seconds, Chief Wolfe reached them. The boy—who looked to be twelve or thirteen—held a younger, unconscious girl against the rock while struggling to keep her head out of the water.

"Nay, Wolfe!" Niall shouted when the chief braced his feet on either side of the children and shoved Shep away. "Have the boy grab Shep's vest and let the dog tow him to us." Niall gestured at the two firefighters Wolfe had called Higgins and Welles—one of whom Katy realized was the truck-scrubbing intern—now standing at intervals in the stream between him and shore. "We'll catch him if he loses his grip."

Katy saw Chief Wolfe say something to the boy, and her heart raced as the kid let Wolfe take the girl. The boy lunged toward Shep when the dog swam past again.

Immediately, they both sank out of sight, and Katy's heart stopped.

A second later, dog and boy popped up several yards downstream, the boy firmly gripping Shep's vest. The dog power-stroked straight toward Niall.

She let out a thick sigh of relief as Niall plucked the kid free and swung him up onto his shoulder with a whoop of triumph. The three made their way to shore just as the other two firefighters intercepted their chief, who swam cross-current on his back while holding the listless girl.

Katy rushed to them, grabbing the chief's arm and guiding him to a grassy spot. "Set her down here," she instructed, shrugging off the jump bag and dropping to her knees. "No, move away!" she snapped when a woman, dressed in paramedic blues, knelt beside her and reached for the girl.

"Go check the boy," the woman snapped back as she crowded Katy out of the way and clasped the girl's neck to check for a pulse. "Welles!" the interloper shouted without looking up. "Go get the damn bus. Somebody find this kid's parents! We're leaving in five minutes with or without them!"

The petite, middle-aged woman glanced up and spotted Katy glaring at her. "You waiting for hell to freeze over?" she drawled as she turned back to the girl.

Reminding herself they were part of the same team, Katy tamped down her impulse to shove the woman out of the way. There'd be time for her to explain her behavior later. "I don't know if the girl speaks English," she said as she stood and backed in the direction of the older boy. "But I think Chief—"

A loud feminine scream came from the onlookers lining the side lane. People hurried out of the way as a woman and man rushed forward, only to be intercepted by Niall and Chief Wolfe. The little boy Katy had carried across the road bolted toward them and threw himself at the man with a loud sob. Chief Wolfe moved over to the frantic woman, and whatever he said seemed to take the wind out of her hysteria.

"Good to see some people are doing their job," the aggressive medic muttered as she glowered at Katy.

A sharp response—consisting of many four-letter

words—swept into Katy's mind, but she took a breath and headed for the boy who sat on the ground cuddled inside a police officer's jacket and hugging Shep as the dog licked his face. Shivering and looking exhausted, but definitely not in distress, the boy darted worried glances between the girl and the two people Katy assumed were his parents. She knelt in front of him and caught Shep's snout to make the dog stop licking. "A little early in the day for a swim, don't you think?" she said, warmly. "It's barely above sixty degrees."

"He's Danish," a man said as he crouched down beside her.

Not about to have another patient stolen, Katy moved to block him, then stopped when she saw he was the police officer who likely belonged to the jacket.

He held up his hands in surrender. He had broad, attractive features, and a hint of a smirk that Katy figured was part of his daily attire. "I swear I didn't push them in." He grinned and extended one of his hands. "Jake Sheppard."

"Katy MacBain."

Jake's grin slackened, and his eyes widened. "You're Niall's paramedic cousin?"

"Guilty."

"Yes. Well, if you need to ask Evan anything, I speak passable Danish. That's his name—Evan. He's twelve and a strong swimmer, and he hasn't been coughing, so I don't think he swallowed any water. He got banged up a bit, though," Jake went on, slipping the jacket off one of Evan's shoulders to reveal a long red welt beneath a torn sleeve. "The girl is his little sister, and they're here on vacation, staying at the inn."

Katy stared at him, knowing she needed to tend to the boy, but curiosity held her in place. "So, you just happen to know Danish?"

Jake shrugged. "It pays to study abroad."

She nodded, interest fading as duty called. She reached out but didn't touch the boy until she asked permission by arching a brow with her smile. He nodded, and she cupped his arm gently. After probing the boy's shoulder around the welt, she turned to the police officer. "Jake, could you please tell Evan that I wish I had better news for him, but it doesn't look like he'll even have a scar to show his buddies when he tells them how he jumped in the stream to save his sister."

Jake chuckled and relayed the message. Evan scowled down at his shoulder, then leaned sideways to see past Katy before clasping Shep to his chest again. He looked up at her and spoke, and his tone suggested he was asking her a question.

"Evan wants to know if his sister is going to be okay," Jake said.

Katy pulled the jacket over his shoulder and glanced back to see the now conscious and sobbing girl being strapped onto the gurney as the mother held an oxygen mask over her daughter's face. Likely, she'd been pressed into service to keep her from renewed hysteria. Not that Katy could blame her.

Evan looked toward the bridge crowded with people, and Katy touched his shoulder again. Smiling at him, she said, "You definitely earned your hero's medal today, big man. She's going to be just fine."

Jake translated. She guessed he added praise of his

own as he spoke at some length because Evan's chin rose proudly.

"MacBain! Bring the boy. He's going with us," the other medic called.

Katy look over to see the medic set the jump bag on the gurney, then watched Niall, Chief Wolfe, and a couple of other firefighters muscle it up the sloping bank toward the ambulance parked at the top of the lane. Jake said something to Evan while tugging Shep out of the way, and Katy helped the boy stand. She placed a steadying hand on his uninjured arm for support and walked him toward his mom and sister.

"I'll drive the father and other boy to the hospital," Jake told Niall when they reached the ambulance. "I speak enough Danish to translate what the doctor has to say, and I'll see if I can't get Evan to tell me how they ended up in the water."

"We don't need two medics." Madam Sunshine helped Evan into the ambulance then moved to block Katy from getting in. The woman smiled tightly. "Maybe if you're lucky, the tones will go off for a stranded climber before I'm back, and you'll get to use all your fancy new wilderness training. Meanwhile, do something useful and shut the doors," she added as she turned to buckle Evan into the jump seat.

Chief Wolfe closed the first door, but Katy stopped in the act of closing the second one. "You in the habit of taking over another medic's patient in the middle of treatment?" she asked, gesturing at the girl on the gurney.

"I've been saving lives longer than you've been alive.

And when I'm in station, I deal with the critical ones. Welles, drive!"

Chief Wolfe finished closing the door and gave it two heavy thumps with his fist, signaling to Welles that he was clear to go.

"What is her problem?" Katy muttered over the sudden blare of the siren as the ambulance pulled onto the road. She turned to the chief. "She stole my patient."

He stilled, clearly confused. "There were enough patients to go around."

"But the girl was mine. I was first on scene and had first contact. And Madam Sunshine over there just waltzed in after the fact and—"

"Gretchen," he interjected. "Her name is Gretchen Conroy."

Katy narrowed her eyes, annoyed at his casual tone. "Not even a doctor who shows up on scene will touch a patient unless the attending medic asks for help. It's an unwritten code of respect."

Chief Wolfe swiped at some water dripping off his hair, scanned the people still hanging around, then pulled the hem of his T-shirt out of his pants. He started walking up the road toward the station as he lifted the wet material—making her gasp a little at the sight of an amazingly ripped abdomen—and wiped his face, his boots squishing in rhythm with his brisk pace as Katy walked beside him. "Maybe they didn't have that particular code where Gretchen's from." He dropped his shirt and studied her. "You should talk to her about it."

She felt a flush building, one that probably had more to do with his abs than the situation, and the heat only increased her annoyance. "It's not my place, especially considering it's only my first day here. You're the chief. It's more appropriate for you to tell her." She knew bossing her new boss wasn't going to win her any brownie points, but she didn't care.

"And, as chief, I'm concerned that stepping in too early might do more harm than good and keep the two of you from developing a good relationship."

Katy stopped when they reached the sidewalk in front of the station, not thrilled to go inside just yet. "What happened to being the first and only person to hear about it if anyone gives me grief?"

He stopped and turned to her. "In the two weeks I've been here, I haven't seen Gretchen have a problem with anyone else. For now, I'm just asking you to try again. If it doesn't work, I'll step in. Fair?"

She shrugged, not quite thrilled but surprisingly soothed. Maybe he was right; a territorial problem with Gretchen was nothing like dealing with an arrogant, aggressive man. She knew that better than anyone.

Watching as he turned back toward the station, she gasped a little when he abruptly walked back and held out his hand. "My phone and wallet?" he said when she frowned in obvious confusion.

Oh, crap. Oh, damn. Oh . . . She'd left them in the ambulance.

Katy turned to face the road in the direction the vehicle had gone. "Um, is your phone password protected?" she asked without looking at him. "It's not that your stuff is lost or anything . . ."

He said nothing, though she felt the razor-sharp sting of his impatience.

Damn. Silence was worse.

"It's . . . They're in the jump bag in the ambulance." Still, she couldn't bring herself to look up him. It was quite possible those icy blue eyes of his would freeze her to the spot.

The silence stretched on. Not sure what else to say, Katy watched the onlookers disperse as the three late-arriving firefighters started back with their wet teammate, making her realize poor Welles had been pressed into service driving the ambulance in wet pants.

Hearing a sigh some distance behind her, Katy finally turned in time to see Chief Wolfe walk into the station while pulling his T-shirt off over his head and exposing an equally gorgeous set of muscled shoulders.

Wow. Did she know how to impress a new boss, or what?

Chapter Five

Barely two hours on the job and she'd already complained about a fellow medic stealing her patient and sent the chief's wallet and cell phone to the hospital. All she'd needed for an encore was to sideswipe their rescue boat on her way out of the parking lot.

She considered going to chase down his personal property. Anything to see those warm crinkles at the corner of his eyes rather than cold blue derision. His quirky, amused grin flashed through her mind, and then those rock-hard abs and rippling bronze shoulders. She bit her lip, more than shocked at her fascination. He was a lot to take in, that was for sure. And that energetic confidence he exuded threatened to overwhelm her.

Settle down, Katy, she told herself. She couldn't let something as useless as attraction make her act like an idiot. Or like more of an idiot. It had become quite clear that her new job would bring conflict on way too many fronts. She had to stay sharp and strong to prove herself, and more than ever, she wanted to do just that.

Her phone rang out, the bluesy ringer turning the small space around her into an echo chamber. Pulse racing, she pulled it from her pocket, more concerned about quieting the device than who happened to be calling. Until she saw the caller's name, that is.

Jane. Again.

With a huge gulp, Katy swallowed a hard lump of emotion—guilt, shame, disappointment, panic. This had to be the twentieth time her best friend had called in recent weeks, and her heart ached to think about the effect her silence must be having on Jane, but she just couldn't answer. Not yet.

Stuffing her phone out of sight, she closed a supply drawer in the truly badass remote access ambulance and straightened enough to peek out the side window as Madam Sunshine backed their other ambulance into the next bay. Even though the tiny control freak—all five-foot-nothing of her, Katy estimated—could barely see over the steering wheel, she clearly wasn't about to let a mere intern drive back from the hospital. Whatever, Katy told herself. What mattered was that the jump bag was finally back at the station.

"Come on, lady, go get a cup of coffee already," Katy muttered when they didn't immediately exit the vehicle. She needed that wallet and cell phone as a peace offering, since she had a favor to ask. She went back to exploring the various compartments, keeping an eye out for an opportunity to retrieve the chief's possessions.

Finally, two vehicle doors opened and closed, followed

by one set of footsteps walking away and the other set—likely poor Welles—running. Not trusting that Gretchen would head straight upstairs, Katy went back to wondering why she couldn't seem to stay focused around Chief Wolfe. The man was strong and capable and good-looking—so what? Ripped bodies and quick reflexes could be found in every fire station on the planet.

On the other hand, insanely blue eyes shining with silent laughter would make any woman with a pulse forget to breathe. Even her. Even, she was amazed to discover, given what she'd been through.

At least she had confirmation that her hormones hadn't been permanently traumatized three weeks ago—the downside being they very well might be making her act like a starstruck schoolgirl in front of the first man she'd ever actually wanted to impress.

Which again begged the question of why this man in particular? It's not like she hadn't kissed her share of guys. Heck, she'd even slept with a few. Though she had to admit those encounters might have been more exploratory—she wanted to know what was so all-fired exciting about sex—than borne of real passion.

That's probably why she'd been so disappointed.

Katy stopped fiddling with the defibrillator. Well, heck, maybe that was the problem. Maybe she kept messing up because she felt like a schoolgirl for imagining what it would be like to make love to a drop-dead gorgeous, fully mature man who, she didn't doubt, probably had bucketloads of experience in the bedroom.

Except that didn't explain why she'd never so much as skipped a heartbeat over any of the firefighters back in Pine Creek. Or any of the guys at Pete's Bar & Grill who'd asked her to dance—after, that is, they'd made sure none of her brothers or MacKeage cousins had been lurking in the shadows.

Seriously; she needed to get a grip before she truly embarrassed herself. And anyway, being her boss put him strictly off-limits. Workplace romances ended careers, and she happened to love this particular career. Even fantasizing about— No, wait. He was only interim chief, and in three months, Gunnar Wolfe would be just another coworker. And by then, she should have this healing people thing figured out, and what had happened in Colorado would be ancient history. Intuition poked her then, quick and sharp as a finger prick, but she shook off the sting. She would put Colorado behind her.

It had to mean something, the way her body snapped awake at the mere sound of his voice this morning. And when she'd found herself facing a guy who could have stepped out of any of the firefighter-hero romance novels she and her fellow female medics in Pine Creek used to consume like candy, she'd been so awestruck that she hadn't even been able to shake his hand. Heck, she actually might have fainted if he'd been wearing his dress uniform.

Yes, the guy definitely wasn't like any—

Then it hit her. His looks were one thing, but he had this other quality, a shimmer of something ancient and powerful.

"Ohmigod, that's it," she breathed. "You've never met a man like him before because he's one of them."

Well, to be more accurate, she'd never met one she wasn't somehow related to, with the exception of Olivia's husband, Mac Oceanus, and his father, Titus. And of course, Nicholas, another imposing giant who also happened to have gorgeous blue eyes.

Katy sighed in relief for finally figuring out why her hormones were so stirred up. Gunnar Wolfe was from Atlantis. That explained his being able to talk to the children and their parents this morning and his muttering something in another language when he dove in the stream. Atlanteans spoke all languages of the world. It also explained the nasty scar she'd seen on his beautiful back as he'd disappeared into the station, since she knew Nicholas had brought a handful of the island's legendary warriors with him when he'd decided to settle in this century as Olivia's director of security for Nova Mare and Inglenook.

Pine Creek might be harboring a small population of time-traveling Highlanders, several modern-day magic-makers, and a couple of powerful drùidhs, but when Maximilian Oceanus had turned Bottomless Lake into an inland sea five years ago, the mighty wizard made Spellbound Falls the new reigning seat of magic.

In fact, rumor had it that Titus—who had built Atlantis—planned to expose the mythical island any day now, since it was no longer needed. That's why the few dozen Atlantean holdouts who hadn't felt prepared to venture into the real world had been invited to form a new colony on a small island just three miles offshore of Spellbound Falls.

Katy didn't think Gunnar was one of them, though, as he seemed more than comfortable with modern society and technology. No, he had to be one of the warriors Nicholas brought with him. As such, he would be able to adapt quickly to any new environment, since the small

elite army was known to travel to any and all civiliza-
tions throughout time, upholding the Oceanuses' vow to
keep the troublesome mythical gods from interfering in
man's free will.

Katy sighed, feeling a little better. Considering who
and what he was, she really shouldn't be surprised by her
sudden and powerful attraction to Chief Wolfe. Having
grown up surrounded by magical men, plain old ordinary mortals had always seemed so . . . ordinary. And
because Atlantean warriors were the strongest, bravest,
most loyal and noble men ever to walk the Earth, those
very traits also made them the safest. Innately protective,
not only would they never brutalize a woman, they
would go after any man who did.

Just like the men in her family.

"Okay, that settles that problem," she said as she
opened the side door, looked around to make sure the
coast was clear, then shot over to the other ambulance
and climbed inside. "Now that I know who you are, Mr.
Wolfe with an E, there's no reason why we shouldn't
make this attraction mutual."

Katy stilled as that liberating notion settled around
her like a warm, gentle hug. She'd done her suffering.
Now things—her life, her purpose, her security and
peace of mind—could fall into place as intended.

She grabbed the jump bag, unzipped the side pocket
and dug out the wallet and cell phone, then stared down
at them with a crooked smile. Catching Gunnar's interest
should actually be relatively easy, considering the
breadth of her knowledge. From the time she'd first
started looking for The One in her early teens, she had
also started studying all the males in her extended

family—paying especially close attention to their love lives.

So, knowing which female traits men found attractive and which ones sent them running in the opposite direction, all she had to do was stop acting like a silly schoolgirl and start being her strong confident self again. And since the Highlander genes she'd inherited from her daddy didn't know the definition of defeat, by the time a new permanent chief was installed three months from now, Gunnar Wolfe should be hers for the taking.

Gunnar glanced up from his paperwork at the sound of a soft knock, then stood up and silently held out his hand, palm up.

His visitor forked over his wallet and cell phone. "Gretchen wouldn't have needed anything in the jump bag once she was in the ambulance, so all your deepest, darkest secrets are safe."

"Is that your way of saying I'll only have to write you a check every month?" Gunnar said dryly, slipping the wallet in his hind pocket without bothering to open it.

Those long-lashed, fog-gray eyes took on a gleam. "Yep, but I'll do you a solid and only take half your pay."

Gunnar used the excuse of checking his phone for messages to hide his surprise—no, shock—that she hadn't gone through his wallet. What woman didn't rifle a man's wallet when given the perfect opportunity? Hell, he would have checked out every card, picture, and scrap of paper in hers.

Whereas Katy MacBain was either too good to be true or . . . uninterested—the latter not boding well for a four-month-long fantasy that had, at exactly 6:25 this morning, rocketed from sensual curiosity to full-on fascination.

Or maybe she was interested. He thought about the way she met him so directly, those gray eyes challenging and full of warmth. She wasn't cowed by him in the slightest, and she might actually be—dare he hope?—flirting right now. "You're quite the racketeer, Miss MacBain," he said, unable to control what he feared was a goofy grin.

"Oh, not me, Chief. I'm the straightest arrow you'll ever find," she said brightly. Instead of leaving, she took a seat across the desk from him and treated him to a full-wattage smile. "Of course, I did hope that returning your belongings all safe and sound would help my cause."

Gunnar eyed her for several seconds, wondering if she knew what effect that smile had on men. "You can drop the chief when we're in station," he said as he also sat down. "In fact, no titles for anyone unless we're on scene. Just first or last names or both, depending on your mood."

Her smile vanished with her surprise. "Seriously?"

"Apparently Gilmore set that rule the day he formed the squad," Gunnar explained. "He told me he felt that eliminating reminders of everyone's position in the hierarchy would create a more relaxed and cohesive team."

"And does it?" she asked, clearly skeptical.

He shrugged. "I've only been here two weeks, so I don't know. And personally, I don't really care, so long as when I tell someone to do something, they do it."

"Okay." The gleam returned. "So long as you also don't care if I call Gretchen 'Sunshine.'"

Gunnar snorted and picked up his pencil. "So long as I'm not here the first time you do."

"Um, speaking of Chief Gilmore," she said, making him look up and study her. "Did he ever mention having campfires at the station in the evenings?"

Gunnar set his pencil on the desk, then clasped his hands together over his stomach as he leaned back in his chair. "There haven't been any since I showed up, and there's no evidence of a fire pit."

Katy leaned forward. "During my interview for this job, I mentioned that, in Pine Creek, I'd arranged for us to have campfires at the station and invited the towns-people to join us. The fires became so popular that we ended up having one most evenings from spring through fall, as well as several bonfires throughout the winter. And when Chief Gilmore told me right on the spot that I had the job, he said he'd like to start having campfires here, too."

For the life of him, Gunnar couldn't imagine why. "Go for it," he said, straightening and picking up the pencil again.

She shot to her feet like she'd been electrocuted. "Great. Thanks. You're going to love them," she said as she turned to leave.

"Just make sure there's a water hose nearby if the tones go off."

She stopped at the door and beamed him another smile. "I have a brother who's an amazing metalsmith, and before I left for Colorado, I asked if he would make another fire pit like the one he made for Pine Creek Fire & Rescue. Only this time, he added a thick dome cover that pivots out from the bottom to smother the flames if we have to leave the station empty."

Gunnar recalled seeing a website showcasing Brody MacBain's metalwork when he'd been checking out her family. The ex-Marine was four years older than Katy and one hell of an artist. Which was no small feat, considering the man had returned home two years ago carrying a Purple Heart in place of the body parts he'd left in Afghanistan.

"Any preferences on where I set the pit?" she asked.

He waved her away without looking up. "Put it wherever you want."

Gunnar waited until she was gone, then leaned back in his chair again and stared at the empty doorway. He still didn't know why the woman had fallen off the radar for two entire weeks, but judging from what he'd seen of her so far, whatever had sent her into hiding couldn't have been overly traumatic.

Only enough to make her break a promise to her very best friend, a quiet voice whispered, but he dismissed it. Women had their own logic, and he'd long ago accepted his faulty comprehension.

He grinned then, recalling Katy's disbelief when he'd ignored her complaint about Gretchen stealing her patient, and his grin broadened as he remembered her expression when he'd asked for his wallet and cell phone after their little water rescue. No doubt, this woman wasn't like anyone he'd ever met. Even more surprising, he couldn't imagine being bored in her presence, a thought he'd never had about any woman.

And Aunt May wondered why he still wasn't married. Was having to watch her brother's insidious, nearly decade-long suicide not explanation enough? Because spending his formative years with someone trying to numb a broken heart with booze certainly had the poor bastard's son questioning the sanity of anyone who handed over that kind of power to another person.

And Gunnar liked to think he was at least intelligent enough to not turn into his old man.

He became aware of voices coming from the parking lot. At first, he ignored them, but their increasing volume eventually drew him to the window, where he saw a white late-model pickup backed up to the patch of tree-studded lawn near the front of the station. Katy stood in the bed of the truck, arguing with four firefighters—three of whom scowled up at her, while the fourth held the tailgate closed.

Obviously believing their new team member was deaf, Captain Ike Russo bellowed as he held the tailgate with one hand while gesturing toward the opposite end of the parking lot with the other.

More curious than concerned—although quick to start in barking, Russo wasn't a biter—Gunnar decided to wait and see how Miss MacBain "handled" her first face-on encounter with her male coworkers. That is until he saw Paul Higgins reach out and forcibly stop Skip Mason from climbing up into the truck bed.

Gunnar gave a muttered curse and headed out the side entrance of his office, not the slightest doubt in his mind as to why Michael Gilmore had abandoned his precious creation. For a seemingly intelligent man, how could he not have known better than to throw a bunch of adrenaline-hyped alphas together, much less expect them to play nice? Christ, Skip Mason clearly believed there wasn't a vertical cliff he couldn't scale, a mangled car he couldn't get inside of, or a woman he couldn't charm out of her clothes.

Which was probably a good part of the reason Gilmore decided to leave before his final hire—a six-foot-one, real live suntanned goddess—showed up for work. Gilmore was adding a flame to a powder keg.

Though Gunnar would put money on the flame.

"Is there a problem?" he asked when he reached the tense assemblage.

A brightly given "absolutely not, Chief" came from the bed of the truck, at the same time, he got at least two yeses accompanied by several nods.

"I remember Mike mentioning something a couple of weeks back about having campfires," Russo said with one last scowl at Katy before turning it on Gunnar. "But I don't recall him saying anything about having them in front of the station, where anyone walking by can see us sitting on our keisters while on the clock."

"And he sure as hell never said anything about inviting townspeople to join us," Paul Higgins added. "So they can tell us to our faces what cushy jobs we have."

"Did you really say she could put it out here?" Russo asked, gesturing toward the lawn.

Had he? Gunnar recalled Katy asking if he cared where she set up the pit, but all he could remember after that were those fog-gray eyes and that killer smile. He looked up at her. "Is there a particular reason you want to place it where the good citizens of Spellbound Falls, such as that gentleman this morning, can see their hard-earned tax dollars paying firemen to sit around a campfire?"

"Precisely so they can see us," she said, her eyes taking on a familiar gleam. "We'd be better served to invite the complainers to join us than to send them scurrying down the street."

What the hell? No, she couldn't possibly be scolding him for coming to her rescue this morning. First off, he'd been protecting her feelings, and secondly, he was her chief.

"If we want the taxpayers to support us," she continued, apparently unintimidated by his scowl, "then we need to help them understand our jobs. And the best way to do that is by showing them that, even if it appears we're just sitting around doing nothing, we're usually rehashing our last training session"—that gleam intensified—"and becoming a relaxed and cohesive team." She glanced around at the others, and he wouldn't blame every man for falling in line right that moment. "Every mom who brings her kids to visit, and every person who hangs out with us waiting for the alarm to go off, will be an ally at the town budget meetings instead of an adversary."

Son of a bitch, now she was giving them civic lessons.

And Gunnar suddenly knew why she'd been hired.

"Put it exactly where she wants," he said and turned to head back inside. He broke into a grin at the stark silence dogging his footsteps.

It had bugged him that Gilmore had given the final paramedic slot to a green newbie who had no business being on such a highly skilled squad. But now he knew that, instead of an old lecher hoping to pretty up the place, Gilmore was a genius. He'd already had a station full of experienced firefighters and medics. What he hadn't had—and obviously knew he needed—was a skilled citizen liaison. And who better to get those citizens to support his costly creation than a woman who, as a real estate broker, had regularly talked people into signing away their lives on thirty-year mortgages?

That the woman also prettied up the place was merely a bonus.

Gunnar entered his office with a snort. Gilmore must have thought he'd won the lottery when Katherine MacBain showed up for her interview looking even more beautiful in person than she did on paper. After deciding she was perfect for the specialized position, the man had simply gotten around Katy's lack of experience by getting her further training. And now that he had access to the books, Gunnar had found where the determined bastard had taken liberties with several accounts to pay for the expensive wilderness school he'd somehow managed to get Katy into within a week of hiring her.

So, hell yes, she could put that fire pit on the sidewalk if she wanted, if for no other reason than he wanted to see her in action. He just wondered if Miss MacBain realized she would be trying to win over taxpayers by inviting them to hang out with a bunch of antisocial jackasses.

Including himself.

Chapter Six

Unable to make himself leave, despite having no reason to stay, Gunnar sat in his darkened office later that evening, putting a dent in the bottle of single malt scotch he'd found in a file drawer while staring out the window at Spellbound Falls Fire & Rescue's first community campfire—which appeared to be enjoyed by Katy alone.

He still couldn't decide what he thought about the woman now that he'd finally met her. On the one hand, he could see Katy and Jane being best friends, bonding over growing up in a small mountain town, both of them appearing a bit . . . parochial. Jane he could understand, seeing how she'd been raised by nuns. And he supposed growing up in an equally sheltering clan might make Katy somewhat naive for her age.

But on the other hand, the two women were polar opposites. Jane topped out at five-foot-five. She was only

now starting to shed some crazy "I'm just a nobody orphan" image of herself, and her idea of a good time appeared to be sticking her nose in other people's business.

Katy, however, didn't seem to have any doubt who
she was, to the point she'd gone after a job for which she
hadn't been even remotely qualified. Probably it had
surprised her that she'd gotten it, just as much as it
had her family.

It had certainly surprised everyone on SFF&R, having been repeatedly warned in the last two weeks to be
ready to pick up the slack when the new rookie hire arrived. Which could explain Gretchen's behavior, though
he also assumed the woman was never easy, even on a
good day. Gunnar smiled at the thought of Katy calling
the older medic "Madame Sunshine." More like Madame Thundercloud.

Still, Gilmore might have been well-intentioned, but
he hadn't done Katy any favors by making it seem like
she was hired for reasons other than her competence, at
least based on the quiet whispers he'd heard around the
station today.

Of course, the joke was on them. After telling them
to put the fire pit exactly where she wanted, he'd gone
back inside and stood at the window again, half expecting the men to simply walk away. But to his amazement,
Russo had opened the tailgate, and every last firefighter
had scrambled into the bed of the truck—causing Katy
to scramble out of their way—and wrestled that heavy
steel monster to the ground and over to the spot on the
front lawn she'd indicated.

It had to be that damn smile. He didn't doubt that, the
moment he'd left, Katy had given the men the exact same

smile she'd given him not five minutes earlier. It would have been just as sincere, too. Warm. Killer. And he would bet the title to his Lear it had been accompanied by a gleam in those fog-gray eyes.

Oh yeah. He might have gone a bit overboard in prepping the crew for Katy's arrival, but at the end of the day, Michael Gilmore was a freaking genius.

And Gunnar was beginning to worry that chasing halfway around the world in search of a wilderness angel had instead landed him in the realm of a beautiful, beguiling enchantress.

Although he probably should reserve judgment until he found out if that smile also worked on women. He lifted his glass to his mouth with a snort. He doubted it would win over Madame Sunshine, as he'd never seen the battle-hardened medic so much as crack a grin, not even once, since he'd been here. No, Conroy was more a smile killer.

Gunnar chewed his cheek as he watched Katy pivot on the tree stump she was using for a seat, one of five she'd dragged out of the back of her truck and set in a half-circle around the pit. She looked toward town for several minutes before turning back and taking a poker to the roaring fire she'd built an hour ago. After a while, she set down the implement and rested her chin on her knuckles, staring into the cavorting flames, which sent ember fireflies up into the black night.

Now that they were out of reach of that smile, the men—and Gretchen, of course—showed their apparent disapproval of Katy's little scheme by boycotting her campfire. Even Welles was conspicuously absent, which proved how determined the kid was to be accepted as part of the team, as the overenthusiastic intern hated missing anything that involved actual flames. About the only time the boy wasn't underfoot was when he was chasing after his little sweetheart of a girlfriend.

Gunnar hoped the young couple managed to keep at least some of their clothes on this summer, so that instead of having to tell his parents he wouldn't be the first recipient of the Bottomless Forward Bound Scholarship because he was going to be a father, Welles would be heading off to the University of Maine in Orono the first week in September. And rather than wondering how she possibly could have gotten pregnant, Jaycee would be happily ensconced in a nearby dorm as the second recipient of the dozen full scholarships some anonymous citizen had generously offered to underwrite every year in freaking perpetuity.

Gunnar drained the remains of the scotch in his glass, dropped his feet to the floor, and stood up with a dog-tired groan. He figured he had two choices: he could drive twenty miles to the campground he was calling home and sleep on a thin pad, or he could walk twenty feet to the private quarters that came with his new title and collapse onto a comfortable bed. He just sure as hell wasn't sauntering out to that campfire, wanting to think he was at least as smart as his crew when it came to staying out of reach of killer smiles. Especially when his head hadn't touched a pillow in thirty-six hours.

The problem was if he slept at the station and the alarm went off, he couldn't very well not respond, because, hell, in the two weeks he'd been here, he'd been on a sum total of five calls. And based on the records he now had access to, in the four months since its inception,

SFF&R had averaged one structure fire, two false alarms, and eighteen medical runs a month. Vehicle accidents averaged 3.4 a week, most of the personal injuries too minor to transport. And up until last night, there had been zero actual rescues, because Michael Gilmore apparently felt that helping a man down off his camp roof didn't count. They hadn't even gotten to use any of their fancy equipment, as they'd simply reset the camp owner's own fallen ladder.

Gunnar figured the only reason he'd even found an open position on the squad was because his predecessor had quit out of sheer boredom. In fact, it had been at supper during his second shift that he'd foolishly asked if anyone had checked to see if the alarm might be broken. Once all the men quit laughing, Russo said Gilmore kept assuring them calls would pick up once tourist season got into full swing. But despite it being the first week in June, apparently even hardcore backcountry hikers didn't like sleeping under the stars when temperatures regularly dropped into the upper forties at night—that party of inexperienced hikers on Fraser Mountain obviously not getting that particular memo.

So it was little wonder the locals were disgruntled about paying for the upkeep of a multimillion-dollar facility crammed full of expensive equipment and staffed around the clock with three rotating crews of firefighters and medics, all of which they saw sitting idle the majority of the time. Hell, at last night's hastily called council meeting, several rather vocal female citizens (he'd heard them referred to as the Grange ladies) suggested that instead of hiring any more people, they should fire the entire lot of them, sell all the equipment except for the big truck that had a bucket on its ladder (any logger or some guy named Grundy could probably figure out how to run it), and turn the station into a community rec center everyone could use.

That was when Officer Sheppard should have drawn his weapon. Who in their right mind turned a brand-new, state-of-the-art fire station into a rec center?

With what could only be described as amazing patience, Duncan MacKeage had quietly settled the matter by reminding the ladies that all the councilmen, backed up by a citizen vote last year, had promised the anonymous benefactor who had paid for the building and equipment that the town would keep the station maintained and fully staffed. They hadn't, however, apparently agreed on a reasonable budget to back up that promise, thus precipitating an understandably worried fire chief's search for a citizen liaison. And if that liaison happened to be a tall, beautiful Mainer with a killer smile . . . well, maybe the true genius was the person who'd hired Michael Gilmore in the first place.

Which reminded Gunnar that he should probably find out who in town was wealthy enough to be funding safety buildings and full scholarships to the tune of millions of dollars. Because one, he couldn't resist a mystery; two, he didn't like not knowing who indirectly signed his paychecks; and three, past experience had taught him that, if things suddenly turned nasty, it was damn hard to choose a side if he didn't know all the players.

Not that he expected trouble, because how dangerous could chasing after angels be, anyway? It's not like they ran around the woods carrying guns and shooting at—

Well, okay. Jane happened to have been holding a shotgun when Markov crashed his floatplane into a pond she'd been walking past, and she apparently hadn't been the least bit shy about firing off several rounds at his assassins when they'd flown overhead again. And he recalled Markov mentioning something about a fist-sized hole getting blown in a lobster boat when Jane took offense to being dragged off to Shelkova against her will.

So maybe he'd just stick with his motto of better prepared than dead.

Unable to stifle a yawn, Gunnar lifted his arms over his head, only to stop in mid-stretch when he caught a glimpse of movement down on the sidewalk. He stepped to the edge of the window just as a man walked up the station driveway, dressed like a tourist and carrying what appeared to be two cardboard restaurant cups.

Jake Sheppard.

Coming fully awake when he recognized the bastard, Gunnar strode to the door leading to his private quarters. He'd anticipated having to drive off a few rival males. He just hadn't expected to find himself dealing with a world-class Lothario who thought stealing other men's girlfriends and wives should be an Olympic sport.

Why some enraged husband hadn't killed the idiot by now was anyone's guess.

Gunnar walked into the bathroom and splashed water on his face, ran his wet fingers through his hair, then grabbed a towel and dried off as he strode back to the bedroom. He pulled off his T-shirt, tossed it and the towel on the bed, then rummaged through his duffel bag for something non-duty to wear. He'd stopped into the L.L. Bean outlet in Bangor to buy camping equipment because he hadn't been able to find a decent rental on-line, and figuring he should dress like a local, he'd also grabbed a couple of fleece vests, several chamois shirts, and a pair of the store's famous hunting boots. He pulled out a deep green flannel shirt and slipped it on, then tucked it inside his station pants as he walked back in the bathroom and eyed himself in the mirror—because, dammit, the bastard was a world-class womanizer.

Deciding he should hunt down a barber tomorrow, Gunnar walked back in the bedroom and over to the mini fridge serving as a nightstand, pulled out two of the domestic beers he'd inherited from his predecessor, studied them a moment, then put them back and grabbed one of the energy drinks. Giving a resigned sigh as he glanced at the bed, he strode through the station, exited through one of the open bay doors no one had bothered to close, and casually sauntered down to Spellbound Falls' first community campfire.

He just barely stifled a snort when he saw that, instead of taking a seat next to Katy, the smooth bastard had chosen a stump at a diagonal, so he could look her directly in the eyes. "I hope you're not sneaking my crew alcohol in coffee cups, Officer Sheppard," Gunnar said, choosing a stump right beside her.

"No, it's hot cocoa," Katy rushed out with a soft laugh. She pulled off the plastic cover and tilted the cup to show him its steaming contents. "Jake said he was almost to the campfire when he saw I was the only one here and decided to run back to the Drunken Moose and get us both hot cocoas. Wasn't that sweet of him?"

"As sweet as apple pie," Gunnar said, returning the bastard's smirk while popping the tab on his energy drink. "So, Shep, how's your jaywalking conspiracy coming along?"

Katy leaned closer and nudged Gunnar just as he was taking a drink, making him spill some on his shirt. She smelled of campfire, sea, and vanilla. Intoxicating. "Shep is the dog," she whispered. "This is Jake." She used her cup to gesture at the now grinning bastard. "He was about to tell me how those children ended up in the water this morning."

Three-to-one Jake had pushed them in out of sheer boredom. "Do tell," Gunnar drawled.

"Oh, I don't know," Jake drawled back. "It's a rather long story, and you look a bit . . . haggard. Why don't you turn in, Chief, and I'll catch up with you tomorrow?"

"Oh no, Jake," Katy injected brightly. "We don't use titles here. Just first or last names or both, depending on your mood."

Okay, he needed to tone it down, because either Katy understood the male ego far better than she let on and had caught the undertone in both their voices, or—

Or else she was a completely oblivious airhead. He really couldn't believe it was the latter.

"And I'm sure Gunnar," she continued to Jake, "is used to functioning on very little sleep, considering his former line of work."

Gunnar stilled with his drink halfway to his mouth, even as he saw Jake nearly choke on the sip of cocoa he'd just taken. "My former line of work?"

The firelight reflected off a sudden gleam in Katy's eyes, which Gunnar began to realize meant—hell, he was fairly certain it meant he didn't have a clue what was about to come out of that lovely mouth.

She glanced in Jake's direction, then leaned closer again. "What you did during all your world travels," she whispered, "back when you lived in—on the island."

Good God. He definitely hadn't been expecting that. How in hell could she possibly know where he was from? Unless she'd spent those two missing weeks on some library computer in freaking Idaho researching the idiot her best friend was trying to hook her up with.

Even though Jane had sworn she'd never mentioned his name?

Katy fired off one of her smiles at Jake, who'd obviously heard the whole exchange and seemed as confused as Gunnar. "So, Jake, how did those children end up in the water this morning?"

"Children?" Jake repeated, his eyes appearing to be locked on her mouth.

Oh yeah. The woman definitely knew what was going on.

Which meant Miss MacBain was likely the only person at this campfire in full possession of their faculties at the moment. Which also told Gunnar that apparently the only weapon an angel or enchantress—he was pretty sure there was a difference—needed to take down a world-class Lothario was a killer smile, which was why he was sitting beside her. Hell, the way the firelight danced in those beguiling eyes, there was a good chance even Grouchy Gretchen would crack.

"I assume the girl fell in," Gunnar said, "and the older boy jumped in after her." Let's keep this moving, he thought. The sooner Jake got the story out, the sooner the man could be on his way.

"That's mostly what happened." Jake frowned. "Except

Evan kept insisting they'd seen a large bird. From his description, I'd say it was a bald eagle."

"Evan?" Gunnar repeated.

"He's the older boy."

Katy had gone as still as a stone, not a smile or gleam in sight. What was that about? "Did Evan say the eagle was responsible for his sister falling in the water?" she whispered, clearly disturbed by the notion.

Jake shook his head. "No. Evan said he and his little brother were over by the park trail leading up to the viewing platform when he heard a loud screech and a large bird swooped down out of nowhere at him. He didn't get that welt on his shoulder from scraping a rock in the water; he got it when one of the bird's talons snagged his shirt." Jake's gaze slid to Gunnar, then back to Katy, and he shook his head again. "Evan said he thinks that, instead of attacking him, the eagle had been trying to get his attention. He told me the bird continued flying toward the pool, then dove into the water and latched on to something just below the surface."

"Ohmigod, it was the girl," Katy murmured, the firelight illuminating her distress.

Jake nodded. "If she screamed when she fell in, Evan wouldn't have heard it because of the noise of the falls. He said the bird flapped its wings, trying to fly off with what he finally realized was his sister, but she was too heavy. Evan started running, calling back to his little brother to get help, and jumped in the water." Jake took a sip from his cup, his expression sobering. "Evan told me the bird looked like it was trying to drag Clara—that's his sister; she's seven—toward him, but the current kept pulling the three of them toward Bottomless."

Gunnar couldn't quite stifle a snort. "Really?" he said. "Either Evan or you are aspiring fiction writers. That eagle was dragging its meal to shore."

Katy turned startled eyes on him. "Are you saying that, with all you've seen and done in your lifetime, you don't believe the eagle was trying to save Clara?"

"Yes, do tell us, Wolfe," Jake drawled, "just some of what you've seen and done."

Gunnar shot the bastard a glare, finally remembering why he never was the bigger man. "So, did Evan have to fight off the eagle when he reached his sister?"

Jake eyed him for several seconds then shrugged. "He said the bird let go of Clara the moment he got to her and then flew up to a nearby tree."

Katy gasped. "That's why he kept looking toward the falls. I thought he was embarrassed by all the people watching on the bridge, but he was looking for the eagle. I wonder if it stayed around long enough to see that Clara regained consciousness."

Okay, Gunnar was back to worrying he'd just spent the last four months obsessing over a dunce. Katy might not be all that naive about men, but anyone with half a brain knew better than to believe a wild bird of prey would try to save a drowning child.

And what was up with all that talk about his former life, anyway? Exactly what did she think he'd seen and done in it?

"Oh, the popcorn!" she said, pivoting on her stump. "We can't have a campfire without snacks."

Jake blatantly ogled her, watching Katy's backside dancing in the firelight as she bent over a large canvas bag.

Hell, Gunnar figured he also might as well enjoy the view. And he did until he saw Katy surreptitiously pour her entire cup of cocoa onto the ground behind the stump. Odd. So the woman didn't care for . . . what? Chocolate in general or just hot cocoa?

Or maybe she'd taken a sip and discovered the idiot really had brought her a hot toddy.

She stood, suddenly. "Even better, I just remembered I have some candy I bought in Ida—in Colorado in my truck."

"It's getting late," Gunnar said. "Why don't you save it for your next campfire?" He shot her his most killer grin. "With more advanced notice, I'm sure you'll get a bigger crowd."

"If that candy's still in my truck in the morning," she said with a laugh, heading around the pit, "there won't be any left for the next campfire." She stopped at the edge of the parking lot and looked back. "Jake? Did you tell Niall what Evan told you about the eagle?"

"Just as soon as I returned from the hospital," Jake said with a nod.

"And what was his reaction?" she asked with a sidelong glance at Gunnar.

Jake also glanced at Gunnar, then cocked his head at Katy and grinned. "Niall's finally getting the hang of cussing in French without slaughtering the language with his heavy brogue." Jake sobered when she didn't return his grin. "We both went to the park and looked around for Evan's eagle, but if it existed, it was long gone."

"And is little Clara going to be okay?"

"The doctor said she didn't seem to have any ill

effects from her swim, but he wanted to keep her overnight to make sure." Jake grinned again. "The family's staying in one of Sam and Ezra's rental cabins, and I'm betting that'll be the last time those kids sneak out while their parents are sleeping to do a little sightseeing on their own."

"Thank you for telling me." Katy lifted the empty cup she was still holding and pretended to take a sip, tilting it as if it were still half full, then licked her lips as she used the cup to gesture at Jake. "And thanks again for the cocoa. Better drink yours before it gets cold. I'll only be a minute," she ended as she turned and disappeared into the darkness of the parking lot.

Gunnar couldn't tell if Katy was encouraging Sheppard's attention or if she simply didn't want to hurt his feelings. "Get lost, you horny bastard," he quietly growled.

Jake spit out his mouthful of cocoa. "What?"

"And don't come to any more campfires. In fact, I catch you even talking to Katy in passing, I will take out ads in every newspaper in Europe saying Jayme Sheppard can be found in Spellbound Falls, Maine."

"Are you insane?"

"Katy," Gunnar said, nodding toward the parking lot while holding eye contact with the bastard, "is off-limits to you and Wyatt."

Jake looked down and casually brushed at the cocoa he'd spit on his pants. When he looked up again, the idiot was grinning. "Why would I want to get lost after risking life and limb asking for permission to date Miss MacBain?" He arched a brow. "Or maybe the better question is whether *you* got permission?"

"How many of those hot toddies did you drink while lurking in the bushes before making your move? Permission from whom?"

"Niall MacKeage, my boss and her cousin."

"Christ, you are drunk. Nobody asks anyone if they can date a twenty-eight-year-old woman except the woman herself. And I'm pretty sure you've never asked permission to do anything in your life."

Jake shrugged. "It's your funeral." He eyed Gunnar for several seconds, then suddenly sighed. "Okay, look. I've heard you referred to as a Renaissance man more than once over the years, so I assume you probably know a little something about Scots. How come you don't know how protective they are of their women?"

"Because I live in the twenty-first century," Gunnar said, dryly.

"But the MacKeages and MacBains," Jake said, using his cup to gesture at the parking lot, "don't." He shook his head with a grin. "I'm not sure what century Niall and Duncan and Alec MacKeage believe they're living in, but they act and talk and think like Highland warriors from a thousand years ago. Nobody messes with them, or their wives, or their children. And if they happen to have a pretty cousin living in town, nobody better mess with her, either, if they value their lives."

"You're serious."

Jake nodded. "And smart enough to ask my boss for his blessing to date Miss MacBain."

"Then why wasn't your boss smart enough to say no?"

Jake brushed at his pants again. "Because Niall likes me." He looked up, still stone-cold sober. "And because he knows I can protect Katy just as well as any of them."

"Protect her from what?"

"Men like you." Jake snorted. "And me."

Gunnar chugged the last of his energy drink, wishing he'd dumped it down the sink and refilled it with the rest of that single malt scotch before he'd come outside. From the onset of this crazy odyssey, he'd assumed Jane had embellished her tales about Katy outmaneuvering the men in her extensive family in order to pique his interest. And he believed the MacKeages and MacBains still held to many of the old clan ways, but surely not to the point that a guy needed to ask permission just to date one of their women. Talk about handing over one's personal power. Why would an obviously intelligent, fully grown woman put up with that bullshit, anyway?

But then, who was to say how archaic he might act if he had a beautiful cousin running around tossing out smiles like Mardi Gras favors.

"Christ, Sheppard," Gunnar snarled to cover the fact he hadn't anticipated this particular problem. "Katy's at least two inches taller than you."

"So I noticed," Jake drawled, amusement lighting his sharp brown eyes. "But then, it's been my experience height doesn't matter to women nearly as much as . . . length."

Forget the goddamn newspaper ads; Gunnar would call this bastard's enemies personally.

"What's the matter, Wolfe?" Jake drawled on, openly grinning. "You rethinking your choice of sabbatical hidey-holes now that you've sized up your competition?"

And he was starting with his list of cuckolded husbands.

"I might put in a good word for you to Niall," Jake

added, the sudden seriousness in his eyes contradicting his casual tone, "for the name of that snitch in Brussels last year who—"

"Fworry," Katy said as she walked into the light of the fire, chewing while also licking her fingers. "I cwouldn't find the cwandy, but—" She stopped talking and finished chewing while wiping her hand on her pants, then stopped in front of Jake and held the bottom half of a plastic box in front of him. "I found the home-made cookies my mother made that I kept smelling all the way up the interstate last night. Go on, take two," she said, tilting the box enough for him to reach inside. "They're chocolate chip and have been the grand champion cookie three years running at the Pine Creek Artisan Festival."

Gunnar frowned, even more confused. According to the evidence on her chin and lips, Katy apparently liked chocolate.

"Thank you," Jake said as he took two of the cookies. He bit into one and grinned up at her as he chewed. "I can see why," he said. "Did your mother by any chance give you the recipe? Because the house I just bought, which happens to be right on Bottomless, has a fully equipped gourmet kitchen if you ever feel like baking up a batch."

She turned away with a laugh. "I hope it's also equipped with smoke detectors, because I usually set them off just boiling water."

Gunnar couldn't believe the bastard was continuing to dig his own grave.

Katy walked over and held the box down to him. The firelight accentuated the curves of her body. "Take three," she whispered. "Heroes who jump into cold rushing streams to save children deserve extra."

What the—did she just wink at him?

Well, hell. Gunnar decided there must be Scots blood someplace in his family tree, because he was thinking any male over the age of ten should have to ask permission just to talk to Katy—him being the one exception, of course.

Having gotten pretty good in the last three weeks at distracting her mind from trying to fill in what her memory obscured, Katy scowled up at the ceiling of her cubicle and decided that, for tonight's entertainment, she would give herself a good scolding. Because really, what could have made her bring up Gunnar's former occupation in front of a non-Atlantean? And if that hadn't been enough of a blunder, she'd almost mentioned Atlantis by name.

She may have gotten blindsided this morning, but forty-eight hours away from the gorgeous hunk of a man should be enough time to get used to her sudden and powerful attraction to him. Somewhere deep within, a tiny warning light flashed, but Katy scowled and turned her attention elsewhere. Officer Sheppard, for starters. What in the world should she do about him?

She smiled, remembering how she'd almost burst out laughing when Jake and Gunnar had started in on each other like two roosters who'd just discovered a new hen in the coop. She couldn't help being flattered by Jake's obvious interest, but she'd shot straight into giddy schoolgirl mode at the realization that Gunnar had been acting rather . . . territorial.

But then her scowl returned. She knew only too well what could happen when two males found themselves attracted to the same woman. Heck, when her brother Brody and Greg Lane had both gone after Betty Miller their senior year of high school, the posturing idiots had been so busy one-upping each other to impress the girl, it had been mid-July before either of them realized Betty had moved to Texas a week after graduation.

But unlike Betty, Katy didn't need boys—or in this case, men—fighting over her in order to feel feminine and desirable.

It certainly helped soothe a badly bruised ego, though.

So how in heck was she supposed to discourage Jake? Because she'd never really been in the position of having to deflect a man's interest, since her brothers and cousins usually scared them off—usually before she even knew the obvious cowards were interested.

Now, though, she was officially all grown-up and lived a hundred crooked miles away from her watchdogs. Well, except for Duncan and Niall and Alec. But she figured they were too preoccupied with their own lives to be interfering in hers. When Duncan wasn't chasing after his youngest twin boys, who'd just started walking, he was busy keeping his and Peg's other five children in line while also running a construction business. And when Alec wasn't putting the finishing touches on the monster of a house he and Carolina were building at the far end of the fjord, he was racing after Lachlan when-ever the magical little toddler decided it would be fun to jump in the Bottomless Sea and go for a swim with his orca buddies.

And Niall? Katy smiled again. Even though he'd been born in the twelfth century, Niall was actually the most modern-minded of the three. But then, his understanding of how important it was for a woman to be independent probably had a lot to do with the love of his life, Birch, who happened to run the local women's crisis center. Still, Katy was worried Niall's ancient Highlander genes were about to make an appearance, seeing how last week Birch had finally admitted she was three months pregnant. Openly living with a woman was definitely a modern thing to do, but having a baby without their being married would likely prove more than Niall's big old Highlander heart could handle.

Come to think of it, maybe she should ask Birch how to discourage Jake, since both Birch and her mom, Hazel, had had plenty of practice discouraging men when they'd lived in Canada—even if the con artists had been more interested in their trust funds than in them.

Too lazy to lift a hand to cover her yawn, Katy finally felt it was safe to close her eyes now that she'd replaced the looming nightmares with dreams of getting up close and personal with her handsome new boss. Which better happen soon, she decided, because she didn't know if she'd survive three whole months waiting for a permanent chief to be hired. In fact, if she couldn't find a way to get Gunnar to kiss her within the next week, there was a good chance she truly would embarrass herself by kissing him first.

So, it was settled then. Exactly forty-eight hours from

7:00 a.m. tomorrow morning, she was officially starting her completely in control but subtle pursuit of Mr. Wolfe. And on that note, and with images of the sexy mythical warrior kissing her in the moonlight reflecting off the magical Bottomless Sea, Katy fell into the first truly refreshing sleep she'd had in three weeks.

Chapter Seven

Feeling much like the proverbial moth being drawn to a flame, Gunnar followed his nose toward the open bay doors of the station, willing to bet the only restaurant in town serving breakfast had fan-powered vents running from its ovens directly out to the street. Because every day from 6:00 a.m. to noon, hapless tourists and locals alike inevitably found themselves following the unmistakable aroma of cinnamon-laced buns straight to the Drunken Moose.

Having learned his lesson yesterday morning, Gunnar stopped short of stepping outside and slowly leaned forward enough to see the bench, only to straighten back up with a silent curse. Was there a reason Miss MacBain was still here? Hell, he'd waited in his private quarters a whole thirty minutes past shift change to avoid running into her.

He peeked again, this time straightening with a frown. Aside from the matter of why the woman was still here, why was she wearing skintight britches and riding boots?

Gunnar knew Katy was an accomplished equestrian, having found several old articles online accompanied by photos of her and a delicate-featured, long-legged horse—Quantum Leap, he thought the mare's name was. Her older half-brother, Robert MacBain—who for some insane reason went by Robbie, even though the man towered over just about everyone on the planet—had been in several of the photos, most of which had been taken at various equestrian events throughout New England. But the articles, each fueling speculation the teenage girl from Maine was Olympic-bound, had suddenly stopped around eleven years ago. And if he recalled correctly, the last article had included a photo of Michael MacBain—who no one called Mike, apparently—proudly posing with his youngest daughter and her horse after they'd just placed first in the dressage segment of a three-day meet in upstate New York.

Gunnar had scoured the Internet looking for why Katy had suddenly stopped competing, expecting to find where she'd taken a bad fall during the grueling cross-country segment. But the Olympic contender had simply vanished from the equestrian world.

She obviously hadn't stopped riding, though. But thanks to the fire pit out front, he knew Katy hadn't ridden a horse to work yesterday. So why was she dressed in britches and boots and still freaking here, sitting between him and two fat, gooey, icing-covered cinnamon rolls with his name on them? After having to wait twenty minutes for another batch to finish baking last Thursday, he'd been smart enough to call in his order this morning while hiding in his room like a prepubescent schoolboy.

Suddenly, Katy gave a whoop, shot to her feet, and bolted down the driveway. Stepping through the door to see what had her so excited, Gunnar saw a tractor-trailer rig set up for hauling horses stop in front of the church diagonally across from the station driveway.

A towering man with shoulder-length dark hair climbed out of the driver's door, and even from where he stood, Gunnar could see Robert MacBain's grin as Katy ran across the road without slowing down or bothering to look for traffic. Hell, he was even able to hear the man's grunt when she slammed into his chest, as well as Katy's squeal of delight when the giant caught her up in a fierce hug that lifted her off the ground.

Gunnar slid his gaze to the trailer, guessing that solved that mystery.

Only to create a new one—where was Miss MacBain planning on keeping her horse? Because he was fairly certain Katy's campsite, which happened to be within rock-throwing distance of the cabin—more like a wooden tent, if you asked him—he'd been calling home for the last two weeks, wasn't large enough to fit a full-size pickup, a horse trailer, and a horse. And wouldn't her more immediate neighbors have a problem with sitting around their campfires in the evening swatting flies and smelling manure instead of the sweet aroma of burning pine?

Another wave of cinnamon-laced air wafted past his nose on the breeze blowing in off Bottomless, prompting a resigned sigh as Gunnar headed down the driveway toward the happy reunion. Sheppard might think he had the upper hand by having his boss' permission to date Katy, but Gunnar had a feeling Robert MacBain's blessing was the one that really mattered. He reached into his pocket with a snort, pulled out his fire chief's badge, and clipped it on his belt, figuring he might as well put the ill-gotten asset to work.

"Come on, Robbie," Gunnar heard Katy say when he was halfway down the four-vehicle-wide driveway, her plea more demanding than cajoling as she tried to drag her half brother toward the trailer. "I haven't seen her in over two months."

"Then two more minutes won't matter," the giant said as he held his ground and watched Gunnar walk toward them. "While ye introduce me to your new boss."

"My what?" Katy said, stopping in mid-tug to look toward the station, only to frown when she spotted him. "But how do you know he's—"

Gunnar saw her gaze drop to his belt and sighed again when he saw the amusement in her eyes as she lifted them back to his. Nope, definitely not an airhead. In fact, he was starting to worry Katy might understand the male mind a little too well. Oh wait, of course she did; the woman had spent twenty-eight years perfecting the art of outmaneuvering the men in her family, on the chance she might want to : . . say, maybe vanish off the face of the Earth for three entire weeks without any of them being the wiser.

Checking for traffic, Gunnar seized the opportunity of having to wait for a motorcycle and stretch limo to pass to size up Katy's sizable half brother. He stifled a grin as he pictured Sheppard craning his neck to ask Robert MacBain's permission to date Katy—assuming the lengthy bastard even found the nerve. Although Gunnar was tempted to ask, because he was pretty sure he never wanted to find himself on the wrong side of this particular Scot.

What in hell was in the water in Pine Creek?

"Robbie," Katy said when he finally reached their side of the road, "this is our fire chief, Gunnar Wolfe. Gunnar, this is my brother, Robbie. He's brought my horse, Quantum Leap."

"Chief Wolfe," MacBain said, extending his hand.

"Oh, no, Robbie," Katy drawled while looking directly at Gunnar. "We don't use titles at SFF&R, because we want to be a relaxed and cohesive team."

"My predecessor's idea," Gunnar said as he broke the handshake and looked at Katy again. "May I ask where you intend to keep your horse?"

"At the Inglenook resort. Olivia Oceanus was kind enough to—"

"P-papa? Papa, I need help."

"Angus?" MacBain growled over Katy's gasp. They rushed to the high open window on the trailer. "What are ye doing in there, son?"

"I-I was bringing a surprise for Aunt Katy," the young voice said on a sob. "But I . . . he's dead, Papa. We need to hurry and go back to Gram's so she can heal him."

"Who's dead, Angus?" Gunnar heard Katy ask as he chased MacBain down the length of the trailer and around the back.

"I swear that boy's going to be the death of me," the man muttered as he stopped at a door halfway up the other side. "Christ, he rode in there all the way from Pine Creek."

Gunnar undid one of the latches as MacBain undid the other.

"He must have snuck in during one of my trips to the barn to get another horse," MacBain continued as he lowered the ramp and vaulted up it before it even touched the ground.

Gunnar followed, only to have to duck a large equine nose reaching for him and then bump into a second nose when he straightened, making him step back in surprise. Good God, they were drafts. Percheron, possibly mixed with Clydesdale or . . . hell, he wasn't sure what they were other than huge.

He knew Robert MacBain was a logger by trade, but he couldn't imagine harvesting timber with horses would be lucrative enough to support the man's household along with his horse-breeding hobby. And he'd swear he'd seen skidders and tree harvesters on the MacBain Logging website he'd found while researching Katy's family. But then Gunnar remembered clicking a link that had taken him to MacBain Mounts, even as he also remembered wondering at the time if there was much call for draft horses bred exclusively for riding.

The beasts were definitely drinking the same water as the humans.

"It's m-my fault, Papa," a quivering voice said as MacBain dropped to one knee in the narrow aisle between the two front horses, letting Gunnar see a young boy clutching a black and white—and definitely dead—cat to his chest. "I . . . I killed Timmy."

"Angus," Katy called out as she ran up the ramp and bolted past Gunnar, then slid to a halt behind her brother. "Oh, honey, what happened?"

Deep gray, tear-soaked eyes lifted to hers. "W-we need to take him to Gram. She can make Timmy all better. But we gotta go now."

"Son," Robert said gently, reaching out and palming the boy's head. "Ye know Gram can only help people and animals that are alive. Here, let me take him."

"No!" Angus cried, stepping back. "That's not true! She can help Timmy. I don't want . . . I didn't mean to kill him," he ended on a whisper.

"Angus, you know I'm a paramedic," Katy said, softly. "Not a doctor like Gram, but I can help people and animals, too. It's a good three-hour drive back to Pine Creek, and I'm right here. Why don't you let me see if Timmy has a heartbeat? There's an ambulance right up the driveway, and I have a stethoscope in it that'll let me hear if he's breathing."

"You . . . you can heal him?"

"I can try," Katy said gently, holding out her hands. "Let me have him, honey. I promise to do everything I can to help Timmy."

Angus looked down, causing several huge tears to fall on the motionless cat—its wet fur implying the boy had been clutching it for some time—and sucked in a shuddering breath. "He . . . he's gonna be a year old next month," Angus said as he looked up, his uncertain eyes stopping on his father before lifting to Katy. "I told him that Papa was taking Quantum to you, and Timmy said . . . he told me he wanted to go, too." Another shudder wracked the boy's body, and he finally passed the cat to Katy. "The tack box fell over on him when I climbed on it to look out the window. I smelled salt air, and I wanted to see Bottomless. Ye gotta heal him, Aunt Katy, because he was looking forward to living with you after I told him how much fun you are."

"I promise to try," Katy said hoarsely, carefully cradling the cat's lolling head and pressing its limp body to her chest. "But you need to know, Angus, that it might be too late. Timmy might not want to . . . he could be—"

"No!" Angus shouted. "He wants to live!"

"Ah, son," MacBain murmured, sweeping the boy into a fierce embrace. "Go, Katy," he roughly commanded over his shoulder.

Katy turned to leave, only to stop short when she nearly ran into Gunnar, her own tear-filled eyes widening in surprise. Apparently, she forgot he was there. "Nay," she snapped when he turned to exit the trailer ahead of her. "I mean, I prefer ye stay here," she said more evenly, the hint of a brogue thickening her words.

Gunnar nodded and stepped aside to let her pass.

"Angus, ye know we must accept what we cannot control," MacBain said as Katy disappeared down the ramp. "And Timmy's living or dying is his decision, not Katy's or Gram's or yours." He leaned away to tilt his son's head up. "And ye must respect that."

"But . . . but he didn't decide anything, Papa. I killed him."

"Nay, son. Ye merely climbed up on a heavy trunk in a moving vehicle and it fell. So who's to say the bumpy road's not to blame? Or me, for driving the truck? Or even Timmy himself, for not getting out of the way in time?"

Gunnar lifted his hands and scrubbed his face. That cat definitely hadn't gotten out of the way in time, as its tiny neck was clearly broken. He absently petted the nose nuzzling his arm and looked out one of the windows to see Katy running up the station driveway, only to frown when she suddenly veered left and ran in the patch of wooded lawn. He could see through the trees that she stopped at the fire pit and sat on one of the stumps, then saw her scan the parking lot, the front of the station, and even look toward the road before she bent at the waist and pressed her cheek to the cat.

"I hope you're prepared for the consequences of your actions today," MacBain said, drawing Gunnar's attention. "You're probably scaring ten years off your mama's life right now as she searches for you," he went on as he stood and led his son down the narrow aisle between the horses—all four of which seemed more concerned with chomping their hay than with the tragic little drama playing out around them.

Gunnar realized MacBain had also forgotten he was there when the man's step faltered slightly before giving him a nod on his way past.

"But Mama's not scared because she doesn't know I'm missing," Angus said, having to run to keep pace as his father strode up the outside of the trailer with him in tow. "I told her I was getting up when you did this morning and riding my bike to Aaron's so we could work on our treehouse before he had to leave with his dad. But I planned to call once I'd given Aunt Katy my surprise so Mama wouldn't worry when I didn't come home for lunch. Only instead of going to Aaron's, me and Timmy waited behind the chicken coop, and when ye went in the barn to get Buttonhole, we ran in the trailer and hid up front behind the bales of hay." They rounded the front bumper of the truck—Gunnar following despite knowing this was absolutely none of his business.

But he was rather interested in how MacBain intended to handle the situation. And he was intrigued by Angus' obvious lack of concern about being in trouble, evidenced by the fact the boy was blithely explaining how he'd lied to his mother and snuck past his father despite knowing he'd be found out. Hell, the kid actually sounded proud of himself.

Which meant one of two things: Either this was Angus' first serious transgression and MacBain was trying to figure out how to deal with the boy, or it was just another one of many stunts his son had pulled, and the man had simply given up trying to rein him in.

Nope, neither. Because when MacBain finally stopped beside the driver's door and dropped to one knee to look his son level in eyes, the glare he gave Angus actually made Gunnar wince. "Then you'll be spending the next month mucking out stalls for scaring ten years off my life for riding in that trailer all the way from Pine Creek. And," he quietly growled when the boy started to protest, "for deceiving yer mother, you'll not go near any electronics until all of next winter's firewood is split and neatly stacked in the shed."

"But Papa! That'll take me all summer!"

The man's features softened. "You're lucky ye're going to have a summer, Angus," MacBain said, thickly. "That heavy trunk could just as easily have fallen on you, and ye could be just as dead as Timmy."

"He's not dead!" Angus cried, looking toward the station only to suddenly gasp. "See! Papa, do ye see!" he shouted, pulling away and running up the edge of the road until he was even with the station driveway. "Timmy, stop! Ye can't go near the road!"

Gunnar had to grab the bumper of the truck to steady himself when he saw a gangly, black-bodied, white-footed cat darting back and forth down the driveway chasing after a leaf caught up in a swirling breeze. He glanced over to see MacBain appeared just as stunned, the man now fully kneeling as he stared, not at the cat, Gunnar realized, but at Katy as she followed her miraculously recovered patient at a more leisurely pace.

Nope, not possible. Gunnar looked back at what had to be a doppelganger, because the cat Katy had carried out of the trailer had had a broken neck.

"Sweet Christ," MacBain softly murmured.

Yeah. That. What he said.

Except the man still stared at his sister.

Angus looked both ways for traffic and ran across the road. "You healed him, Aunt Katy! I told you Timmy wanted to live!"

"That you did," Katy called to him with a smile. "Turns out Timmy only had the wind knocked out of him, so all it took was for me to breathe some air back into his tiny lungs."

Gunnar had to grab the bumper again, because honest to God, Markov's wilderness angel—aka Jane Abbot—had saved the future king from drowning nearly the same way, only she had entered his submerged plane and given him air by way of a kiss.

Angus scooped up the still dodging and darting Timmy with an excited whoop, then continued up the driveway at a run. "Here's your surprise, Aunt Katy," he said, stopping and thrusting the miracle cat out to her.

Gunnar was able to hear Katy's sigh as she accepted the robustly given gift, because despite it still being none of his business, he was striding up the driveway right behind MacBain—partly because he wanted to find out why the man was obviously upset with his sister, but mostly because he wasn't going anywhere until he touched that cat.

"His full name is Tuxedo Tim," Angus continued in full presentation mode, "because Nora says his white paws and chest and mustache make him look like a groom at a wedding."

Gunnar had no idea who Nora—wait. MacBain had married a woman who already had two children, a boy and a girl. Nora must be the girl, because Robert and Catherine had only had boys together. Three, he recalled, thanks to his nearly photographic memory, further recalling Angus was the oldest. He saw Katy nudge her nephew along, continuing right past her brother and boss as if she didn't even see them. Well, or else she'd definitely seen something in MacBain's eyes that she didn't want to deal with.

Gunnar turned and fell into step beside her. "Angus?" he said, looking around Katy to smile at the boy. "I happen to love cats, and I wonder if I might hold Timmy."

Angus lengthened his stride enough to look at him. "Tuxedo Tim is Aunt Katy's cat now, so it's up to her who holds him." He then looked up at Katy and veered closer. "But I don't think you should be letting strangers hold him," he whispered.

"Mr. Wolfe is the fire chief here in Spellbound Falls and Katy's boss," MacBain said as he caught up with them.

Katy silently handed Timmy to Gunnar without looking at him, then broke into a jog as she crossed the road and disappeared around the front of the truck.

Gunnar cradled the squirming, surprisingly strong cat against his chest and gently pressed one of his fingers along its neck from its shoulder to its head. He'd heard a few years back about a man smashing into a tree while skiing in Europe and being declared fine by the local hospital, only to keel over dead in the resort lounge that very same night when he'd tossed his head back taking a drink of beer and a vertebra in his neck had snapped in half.

Gunnar definitely didn't want Timmy's neck to finish breaking on his watch. So he stood on the lawn of the church holding his now purring excuse to still be there, and watched MacBain open the truck's passenger door and hoist his son inside. He handed the boy a cell phone and told him to call his mother, then walked to the trailer just as Katy led a delicate-featured, long-legged horse down the ramp.

Gunnar knew riding horses, and this one was a beauty for its age, which he estimated to be early twenties, even though it appeared to have the physique of a teenager. Katy silently handed the lead line to her brother, then ran back up the ramp and reemerged one minute later with a bridle tossed over her shoulder and carrying a well-worn English saddle.

If finally dawned on Gunnar that brother and sister weren't talking because he was there.

Yeah, well, tough. He wasn't leaving until someone told him what in hell had just happened. Because he was pretty sure dead cats shouldn't be loudly purring or licking a young boy's tears off their paws. And he also wanted to know why MacBain appeared to be angry at his sister.

Gunnar glanced over his shoulder, then walked up the slight knoll and sat down on the church steps, figuring a little distance might make them forget he was there again. He absently brushed pieces of hay out of Tuxedo Tim's fur as he watched MacBain take off the wrappings protecting Quantum's legs while Katy saddled her horse and then slipped off its halter and put on its bridle—the silent dance revealing the duo had done this often over the years.

MacBain tossed the leg wrappings into the trailer, lifted the heavy steel ramp as though it were made of plastic, walked over to Katy, and grabbed her raised leg and lifted her onto Quantum's back, then quickly grabbed hold of the horse's bridle. "I'm dropping off the two geldings at Inglenook, then helping Duncan ferry the mare across the fjord to his house. When I'm done, I'll swing by and give ye a ride back here to your truck."

"Thank you, but I have too much to do today to hang around Inglenook. I'll get a ride with someone headed to town," Katy said, urging Quantum forward.

MacBain held fast. "I'll pick ye up in four hours."

"You'll be wasting your time, because I won't be there."

When her second attempt to leave merely resulted in Quantum's hind end sweeping in an arc as its head stayed in place, Gunnar heard Katy's sigh all the way from the church steps. "Leave it be, Robbie," she said, her eyes pleading. "And don't ye say anything to Mum. I don't want . . . I can't . . . please, just leave it alone."

MacBain studied her face for nearly a minute, his

features drawn, before he simply let go of the bridle and silently stepped away.

Immediately, Katy urged Quantum into a trot up the side of the road, checked over her shoulder for traffic, then crossed just beyond the station driveway. MacBain moved to the front of his truck and watched as she broke into a canter the moment she reached the recreational trail, which Gunnar knew ran past the turnoff to Inglenook some six or seven miles north of town.

So nope, he wasn't the reason for their silence. He didn't know what Katy wanted her brother to leave be, but the woman obviously had no intention of discussing it with him now or later. Nor her mother, apparently.

It never ceased to amaze Gunnar the personal stuff he could learn about people on the Internet. Then again, he'd learned something just as interesting in person today. Even though these Scots were undeniably protective of their women, the women weren't afraid to stand up to them. At least Katy wasn't.

As soon as she'd ridden out of sight, MacBain walked around to the driver's door, climbed in, and said something to his son, then started the truck and pulled onto the road also heading north.

Without Tuxedo Tim.

"Hey, miracle cat," Gunnar said, gently grasping its chin in mid-lick to make it look at him. "Besides rising from the dead, can you really talk? Only to Angus or to anyone? Because I was wondering if you could tell me what in hell just happened here."

When the cat's only response was to lick Gunnar's finger, he stood with a sigh and headed across the street to hunt down Welles. What good was having an intern if not for sending him to the Drunken Moose to pick up the chief's breakfast? After, that is, the kid ran to the mercantile for kitty litter and cat food.

"So, Tux," Gunnar drawled as he sauntered up the station driveway. "Could you at least tell me if Katy's lips are as soft and sweet as they look?"

Once she was out of sight of town, Katy surrendered control of both her horse and the turbulent emotions swirling inside her. Quantum took advantage of the freedom by instantly surging into an energy-efficient gallop, and the tears Katy had been holding at bay finally burst free to splatter across her face and hair like wind-whipped raindrops. She let them come, knowing they carried the heartbroken energy of this moment and so many others of the past month, and knowing that, no matter how much she just wanted to run to her mum and let it all out, this was her only option. There was just too much she couldn't risk sharing.

Honestly, for all the times she had tried to create a miracle, why had she succeeded this time?

And of all the people who could have witnessed it, why Robbie and Gunnar?

Timmy hadn't been dead, but he'd been close. Hearing his tiny, oxygen-starved heart struggling to beat when she'd pressed her ear to his chest, Katy had immediately sent her mind's eye racing through his limp body to find the most immediate area of trauma. Two of Timmy's neck vertebra were broken but miraculously hadn't severed his spinal cord. Several crushed ribs were pressing on his tiny lungs, restricting his breathing, and one of his hind legs was shattered.

But Angus had obviously known what he was talking about when he'd shouted that Timmy wanted to live, because as Katy raced through the cat's battered body, swirling tendrils of white light reached out from each wound, trying to grab her, seemingly pleading for her to stop and help. The ferocity of his need outsized his tiny body.

It was then Katy realized she'd had the missing piece of the puzzle since she was seven, when she'd snuck out of bed late one night to hide the last two cookies from Brody so she could have them the next day after school. As she'd crept to the stairs, instead of her parents being asleep in their own bed like she'd thought, she'd heard them talking in whispers in the living room below. So, of course she'd sat down on the top step to listen, because everyone knew whispering meant secrets. For hadn't she overheard Papa just the week before telling Robbie in the barn that knowing a man's secrets gave you power over him?

Except she hadn't been able to grasp the secret her parents were whispering about. All she'd heard was her sobbing mother complaining that it wasn't right she could heal a cranky old man dedicated to plaguing his family, but she couldn't save a teenager who, because he was too young to see past his present circumstances, had tragically given up on life.

Katy hadn't understood then, but she did now. Whoever—or whatever—she was trying to heal had to want to heal. That unless the determination to live was there, she could do nothing more than ease their final moments.

Sweet little broken Timmy had desperately wanted to live, and that had made all the difference. Katy smiled ruefully. Maybe he hadn't known he was supposed to have nine lives.

The day after she'd overheard her parents, the talk at school had been about a really bad accident just outside of town where a pickup truck crammed full of teenagers slammed into a tree at eighty miles an hour. A bunch of ambulances and fire trucks and police and sheriff cars had been there with all their lights flashing, according to a third grader who lived right across the street from the tree. The girl had noticed Katy listening with the other kids and had announced she'd seen Doc Libby there, too, but apparently not even a big-time doctor from some big-time hospital in California could save that poor boy.

Katy had wanted to shout that it wasn't her mum's fault, that the boy had given up. But she'd merely turned and walked away, remembering her papa telling her that trying to reason with a bully or explain anything to a braggart was like spitting into the wind, with her likely coming out the loser. She might have been only five or six when he'd shared that particular bit of wisdom, but she'd gotten the message.

And that was why she'd never missed any of the self-defense lessons her papa had given her and her older sister, Maggie, every Saturday morning. If you couldn't reason with bullies, sometimes you had to fight, she figured. It was also why, instead of leaving after, she used to sit on the Christmas tree bailer and watch Brody's lessons.

But when she'd asked if she could take both, complaining all she and Maggie got for a weapon was a stick while Brody got to wield a sword, her papa had scooped her up with a laugh and plopped her on top of his tall, broad shoulders.

As he strode to the barn, he explained he was teaching his two beautiful daughters how to use anything that was straight and stout as a weapon, because in all likelihood they wouldn't have a sword handy if they ever needed to defend themselves. He'd then promised Katy that, by her early teens, and wielding nothing more than a common broom, she would be able to trounce a grown man—including, he'd added with a tug on her leg, Brody.

Katy felt a fresh surge of tears at how much she missed those Saturday morning lessons, and her being so sure that by the time she left home, she could even trounce the world.

Except three weeks ago, the world had trounced her instead.

And in doing so, had turned her into a murderer.

Chapter Eight

Closing in on twenty minutes of searching upstairs and down and even the parking lot and fire pit area for his missing crew, Gunnar finally reached the end of his patience. None of the six squad members—one of whom was Katy, whom he hadn't seen in three days—was responding to his texts or in-house pages. Even Welles was suspiciously absent.

By God, manually setting off the alarm should bring the delinquents running.

Gunnar reentered the station through an open bay door and strode down between the aerial and main engine, only to stop when he came to the empty slot where their rescue truck usually sat. He slowly turned in a circle. Both ambulances were here, as well as engines one and two, the aerial, and the on-duty captain's pickup. Only 987 was out.

He couldn't have missed an alarm. Christ, the few times it had sounded on his shift, every cell in his body had screamed in pain. And the one time it had gone off at night, he'd bolted out of bed ready to punch anything that moved, only to grab his pounding chest when he realized where he was, certain he was having a heart attack. How in hell did these people survive entire careers of constant adrenaline spikes? He'd been here barely three weeks and had already lost the ability to sleep through an entire night, even away from the station.

Hell, maybe Conroy was grouchy because she hadn't slept in twenty-five years.

Gunnar cocked his head when he caught the muffled sound of snickering, then strode toward the utility room again. He stopped just short of the door and peeked around the corner to see his four missing firefighters and Conroy lined up along a large open window, their attention fixed on something outside.

Silently, he walked over and stood behind Gretchen because she was the shortest—calling herself five-foot-one was a bald-faced lie—and looked out the window to see what was so fascinating. But the only thing out there was their rescue truck, backed up at an odd angle against the thirty-foot wall of granite that had been cut out of the mountain to make room for the station. Then he heard voices coming from a fairly good height and leaned forward slightly to see the top of the cliff.

"The windshield," Russo whispered from the side of his grinning mouth, keeping his eyes trained out the window while gesturing with his head.

Gunnar dropped his gaze to the truck's windshield at the same time he heard a distinctly feminine snort, then stiffened when he saw the reflection of Katy hanging some twenty feet down from the top of their hose tower—leaving her another twenty feet above the ground—with Welles hanging from his own rope just off to her right.

"Listen," Russo whispered.

"Well, I guess now we know," Gunnar heard Katy mutter, "why they insisted on using the hose tower instead of the cliff."

"Why?" Welles asked, frowning over his shoulder at the cliff some thirty feet away.

"Because they knew we could have found enough toeholds in the granite to climb up on our own." She kicked the brick wall she was braced against, then started gently swaying. "No chance of that happening here."

"Oh, wait, I have my phone!" Welles cried as he bumped into the wall while twisting to get past his harness to reach his pocket. "We can call someone to come get us down."

Katy stopped swaying. "And just who are you going to call?"

Welles abandoned his pocket to grab the rope and brace his feet on the building again. Even from this distance, Gunnar could see the reflection of the kid's scowl. "I don't know about you, but this sure feels like an emergency to me. I say we show them by calling 911."

Katy chuckled. "And who do you suppose dispatch will tone out?"

Welles went motionless. "Cripes," he said, thumping his helmet against the bricks with a clearly audible groan. "Every last one of them knows I don't like heights. 'It's only half as high as the aerial,' they said. 'MacBain won't suspect a thing if you play the victim,' they said.

'It'll be fun,' they said." He rolled his head to look at Katy. "They didn't say they were pranking me, too," he muttered as he rolled back. "I thought they were finally treating me like one of them."

Gunnar saw several of the squad members shift uncomfortably, including Gretchen.

"They are," Katy said as she crab-walked sideways and playfully punched his shoulder, making Welles lift his head. "They wouldn't have involved you at all if they didn't consider you a full member of the squad. They would have just come up with another prank."

"If that's true," the kid said, his jaw cocked defensively, "then how come everyone always calls me Welles?"

"For the same reason we all call each other by our last names," Katy said, letting herself swing away. "It's a passive-aggressive sign of affection. Like another way of saying 'I've got your back, buddy; just don't ask to borrow my truck or date my daughter,'" she explained in a perfectly delivered male voice.

"Then why don't they—and you—call me Ingersoll-Hoffenmyer?"

Yes, Miss Citizen Liaison, Gunnar silently drawled. Why?

Even though the reflection had grown distorted from the sun's angle changing on the windshield, a blind man could have seen Katy's surprise. In fact, it was a good thing she wore a helmet, because the chin strap was likely all that kept her jaw from hitting the ground.

"Welles is your first name?"

The kid nodded. "Welles Ingersoll-Hoffenmyer. My mom didn't want to give up her maiden name when she got married, so they hyphenated," he said as if by rote, apparently having had a lot of practice explaining why his name kept running into the address box on forms.

The entire team of eavesdroppers leaned forward as a single unit, trying to hear what Katy muttered, only to all flinch when the alarm suddenly sounded five freaking feet away.

"Attention Spellbound Falls Fire & Rescue. Spellbound Ambulance One is asked to respond to 624 Crabtree Lane for a fifty-two-year-old male, breathing but not responsive, with probable insulin reaction. Copy Spellbound Ambulance One: 624 Crabtree Lane, fifty-two-year-old male, probable insulin reaction. Piscataquis out, fourteen-twenty-three."

"I'm on it!" Gretchen shouted—likely because she couldn't hear her own voice—as she shot toward the door. She turned and gave everyone the once-over. "Higgins, it's time you put all those pretty muscles to use," she called out as she spun back to the door while gesturing for him to follow.

"Hey! Don't leave without us!" Katy yelled from her lofty perch.

"Come on, guys!" Welles added frantically. "Don't make me miss a call!"

"Dammit, you idiots," Katy shouted, "get out here and untie these lines!"

Grinning, Russo slid open the screen, leaned out the window, and twisted to look up at the hose tower. "It's only a forty-two-car pileup just north of East Podunk," he called up to them. "Conroy and Higgins have it covered." He pulled back inside, his grin widening at Katy's colorful response, then leaned out the window again. "If you haven't made it down by the time we're done with supper, we'll send up any leftovers," he added, only to jerk back inside one second before a helmet bounced off the window jam. He'd been bluffing with the supper line, fully intending to help her if she struggled much longer, but if the woman was going to start chucking equipment at him, she could find her own way down.

Russo turned his grin on Gunnar. "You been looking for us?"

For the life of him, Gunnar couldn't remember why. "Just wanted to know who's fixing dinner tonight and what we're having," he said, striding off. He stopped at the door. "I assume you made sure it wasn't MacBain's turn before you set her up?"

Russo sighed. "Higgins was supposed to make his firehouse lasagna." He grinned and gestured at the window. "The dashcam in the truck is on and Wi-Fi enabled, so we'll intervene if it looks like they're getting into trouble. If MacBain hasn't figured it out by sunset, we'll get them down in time to enjoy at least some of the campfire."

Gunnar merely arched a brow, making Russo's grin turn a bit sheepish. "My wife's bringing our two sons and an outdoor popcorn popper she found at the Trading Post." He shrugged. "She's also bringing the elderly couple that lives next door."

Gunnar slid his gaze to Bean and Mason.

"My landlord stopped by our house yesterday," Bean said with an equally sheepish shrug, "and asked if it's true that our campfires are open to the public. I told him that he and his wife should come hang out with us for a while tonight."

"I met two hot little divorcées from New York City at the Bottoms Up night before last," Mason said, his grin lecherous, "who used their divorce settlements to go halves on a vacation home right on Bottomless. And when they mentioned they've been trying to mingle with the locals, I invited them to swing by tonight."

The poor unsuspecting bastards hadn't even lasted a week. "And that, gentlemen," Gunnar drawled, "is why Gilmore waited for someone with very specific skills to come along before making his final hire." Fighting his own grin when all three of theirs disappeared, he headed for the door again. "You might want to ask around town if any loggers have butt ends they'd like to donate, because it appears we're going to need more seating."

And he intended to carve *chief* into the top of one of those stumps, so he'd be sure to have a front row seat from which to watch Miss MacBain charm the good citizens of Spellbound Falls out of their hard-earned tax dollars one beguiling smile at a time.

Hell, maybe he'd even pin his badge on his chest and toss out a few grins of his own.

Katy scowled down at the purring diesel engine using her leg for a scratching post. "Don't think I didn't see you napping on the chief's windowsill earlier," she scolded. "Even though I specifically told you to pretend you're just a stray town cat who enjoys visiting the station," she added, hoping no one noticed it only visited every third day. But she couldn't very well leave Tux at the campground all by himself for twenty-four hours straight. Heck, she wasn't even sure she was supposed to have a cat unless it was on a leash, and she really did not see that happening.

She dropped a piece of butter-soaked popcorn on the floor, then sighed when, instead of gobbling down the treat, Tux batted it around the station kitchen. "Everyone's been feeding you all day, haven't they?"

The morning she'd ridden Quantum to Inglenook, Katy returned to her truck in a far better frame of mind than when she'd left, thanks to Shiloh's infectious joy when the kid spotted her cantering up the resort road and ran out his cottage driveway hollering and waving. Katy had stopped and dismounted, lifted Shiloh onto the saddle, and led him to the stables. She'd continued around the paddock a few times to cool Quantum down as the boy continued talking about how wonderful Inglenook was, then boasted how he'd boldly asked Mrs. Oceanus about the chickens when she'd greeted them in person when they'd arrived. But, he'd admitted with a sly grin, he'd asked after mentioning he was best friends with her friend Katy MacBain. Mrs. Oceanus had told him to send her an email explaining his business plan—which is what he'd been working on when he'd spotted Katy—and they would have an official meeting to discuss it in a few days.

Once Quantum was settled into her new quarters, Katy had kissed her horse on the nose, hugged Shiloh good-bye with the promise she'd be back the next day to give him his first official riding lesson, then hitched a ride to the station on one of the resort vans shuttling guests to town.

Honest to God, she'd completely forgotten she now owned a cat until she'd opened the door to her pickup and found a note propped on the steering wheel from Gunnar saying Tux (no tomcat worth his kibble was going to answer to Timmy, he'd explained) was locked in his office. He'd be out doing fire chief work most of the day, so Katy was free to retrieve her new pet.

She'd found Tux curled up on a fleece inside an open drawer of a file cabinet, sleeping off what appeared to be a cinnamon bun hangover, judging from the dried icing on his ears and the smell of cinnamon on his breath. Their first night together had been . . . interesting, as apparently any tomcat worth his kibble was nocturnal.

Tux wasn't all that impressed being stuck inside their cabin, either, when there were wonderful sounds and smells and softly scurrying critters on the other side of the thin material. Oh yeah. Not only did her roof leak, it now also let in mosquitoes thanks to the hole he'd clawed in the door screen.

But despite nearly dying in a moving vehicle, the cat apparently loved riding in her pickup, sprawled on top of the back seat with his nose only inches from the side window she'd opened a crack. He also liked riding in boats, Katy had discovered when she'd met up with Peg MacKeage at the marina. Tux had sat on the pontoon's raised back deck with his nose in the air and his eyes half closed in pleasure as they'd cruised up the fjord to Peg and Duncan's house, where he'd then found a virtual army of kids to play with and a barn full of new cat buddies.

Katy had actually thought about leaving Tux at Peg's, but the little imp had already purred his way into her heart. And really, he acted more like a dog than a cat. She didn't even have to mess with litter boxes, because apparently no tomcat worth his kibble would even think about doing his business in a silly plastic box filled with fake dirt.

Seeing Tux had decided the popcorn was finally dead enough to eat, Katy tossed down another piece, then snapped the cover over the large tub and set it inside the canvas bag she'd brought for carrying snacks out to the campfires. Lord, she hoped someone showed up tonight, having made a point to tell everyone she knew in town to tell everyone they knew that the firehouse campfires were open to the public. Heck, she'd even told people at the campground.

She'd felt so foolish sitting all by herself for nearly an hour at the first one and could have hugged Jake when he'd walked up and handed her a cup of cocoa—that is, until she'd realized why he was there and that she hadn't had a clue what to do about it. And then she'd nearly jumped up and hugged Gunnar when he'd come out and sat down beside her—that is, until she'd realized why he was there and turned into a giddy schoolgirl. In fact, the real reason she'd gone to her truck was to take off the turtleneck she'd had on under her flannel shirt, she'd been so hot and bothered.

"I hope you know those campfires are going to bite us all in the ass."

Katy turned with an armful of snacks she'd purchased at the Trading Post to see Gretchen standing beside the table peering into the canvas bag. Sighing, she said, "Yeah? And why is that?"

"Every Tom, Dick, and jag-off in this community already feels free to butt in on what we do. But don't let our jobs interfere with your coffee klatch."

"I'm sorry," Katy said, deciding to get to the bottom of the lady's problem. "Have I said or done something to offend you?"

"Yeah, you got hired."

"And that offends you because . . . ?"

Gretchen scooped up Tux when he started twining around her legs, then cuddled him to her chest and slowly smoothed his fur—the woman's gentleness in stark contrast to her obvious disdain for his owner. Or maybe occasional roommate and meal ticket was a more accurate take on their relationship.

"I started in public and private stations over twenty-six years ago," Gretchen said in an acidic tone, "in what was then a male-dominated profession. I've been kicked, spit on, punched, and even stabbed, and it's cost me backaches, heartaches, an untold number of friends, and two husbands to finally get on a squad of this caliber in a station this well-equipped. And you come bouncing in here with your long legs and perky boobs and big, bright smile, some volunteer experience and a piece of paper from a four-week rescue course, and not a clue what the women who came before you had to endure just to be considered competent." Gretchen walked to the window and stared outside. "You bet I'm offended." Her voice thickened. "Because right now, there's an overworked, underpaid, highly skilled female medic out there still having to prove every damn day that she's just as capable as any man, because Gilmore passed over her application to give the final slot to you."

Ouch. Definitely hadn't seen that coming. "I wasn't aware," Katy murmured, "that states have different training and licensing for volunteers as opposed to full-time paramedics."

Gretchen turned in surprise. "They don't," she snapped. "Schooling doesn't make a good medic, experience does.

So," she added in a sneer, dropping her gaze to the snacks Katy was still holding, "tell me, bright eyes, just how these campfires are going to help us be better firefighters and medics."

Katy started to snap back an equally derisive response but stopped when she saw Gretchen rub her chin in Tux's fur and realized the woman wasn't nearly as angry as she was threatened. Katy suspected Gretchen had been defending her position to younger, quicker, stronger men and women for so long that she didn't know how to stop.

Katy smiled. "Thank you."

Gretchen's eyes narrowed. "For what?"

"For your backaches and heartaches and lost relationships and all you endured so that when I show up at a scene on the worst day of someone's life, they don't look past my shoulder and ask when the paramedic is arriving."

Gretchen stared at Katy for several heartbeats, hugging Tux a little tighter, then suddenly headed for the door. She stopped in the hall and looked back. "I suggest you bring that bright smile along when you ask the chief to transfer you to one of the other shifts, because, Katy, I only work with people I trust to have my back if a scene turns ugly."

Like this one just did? Katy listened to the rushed footsteps fading down the hall. Well, she'd asked. And Gretchen had not-so-delicately confirmed what Katy had known even as she'd dropped her application in the mailbox all those months ago, which was that she really had no business being here.

Except she did. Because no way did she take women

like Gretchen for granted, knowing full well that without them fighting the big fight, she never would have been able to come bouncing in here with her bright smile and perky boobs and minimal experience. Katy finally lowered the snacks into the canvas bag and decided that, just like Gretchen had been doing for twenty-six years, she would keep right on proving her worth every damn day.

But hopefully without a chip on her shoulder.

"Funny how some people love to dish it out," Welles drawled as he sauntered into the kitchen grinning like a Cheshire cat, "but they can't take it."

Oh, yeah. Russo and Mason and Bean hadn't liked it when, less than half an hour after they'd left their new medic and intern dangling off the hose tower, they'd walked in the kitchen arguing over who was cooking to find Katy and Welles sitting at the table eating peanut butter and jelly sandwiches. She hadn't even gotten to ask the slack-jawed trio what they were having for dinner, since the men had nearly tripped over their own feet rushing back out. Katy and Welles had given each other conspirator's smiles as they'd heard two sets of footsteps running down the stairs and the squeak of one set of hands sliding down the pole to the first floor. Welles had gone to the window, then relayed the news that all three men were storming the rescue truck, with Mason climbing in to get the SD card from the dashcam.

"Are you still rubbing it in their faces?" Katy asked, trying but failing to give the boy a stern look. She couldn't help it; it tickled every last funny bone to think of those pranksters finding the video erased. "I told you the real victory is in acting as if you do that sort of thing every day." She arched her brow higher. "You didn't tell them how we got down, did you?"

Welles held his hands up in surrender, although he couldn't stop grinning. "Not even when Bean and Mason threatened to lock me in the hazmat room for the entire campfire." He suddenly sobered. "I, ah . . . I may have embellished what happened today when I called Jaycee, my girlfriend. So when you meet her tonight, could you maybe not mention that I kind of panicked when I realized the guys had left us?"

Katy gasped in mock horror. "Are you serious? The only reason I didn't panic was because you were so calm." But then she also sobered. "You did excellent today, Welles, and you're going to be an amazing firefighter." She went back to smiling when he ducked his head to hide his flush. "Aren't you breaking rank by coming to the campfire tonight?"

He looked up, his chin rising defensively. "I think they're a great idea. And so is encouraging parents to bring their kids to the station." His grin returned. "Whenever we went to cities or a town big enough to have a full-time fire department, I used to throw a fit until Mom or Dad took me to visit the fire station." He moved to the table and toyed with the handles on the canvas bag, suddenly serious again. "Ah, speaking of Jaycee," he said, two flags of red darkening his cheeks when he looked up. "Can I ask you a sort of personal question?"

Not sure how they'd jumped from fire stations back to girlfriends, Katy merely nodded.

Welles suddenly strode to the door, looked down the hall, then turned and looked in the general vicinity of

Katy's feet. "I was wondering if you could tell me how to . . . if you could give me some pointers on . . ." He took a deep breath and lifted his gaze to hers. "Look, I'm a virgin, okay, and I want to make love to Jaycee," he said rather aggressively, his entire face and neck now crimson. "But I need for you to tell me how."

Katy wasn't sure she'd heard right, but from the mortified expression etched on the kid's face, she probably had. "Excuse me—what?"

"I'm a virgin," he repeated. "And I only have nine weeks left before I leave for college."

"What's college got to do with it?"

"I can't show up there still a virgin. So, what do I do?"

Good Lord, he couldn't possibly be serious. "Why are you asking me?" Katy asked, fighting to tamp down the wave of anxiety building in her gut. Heck, she was certainly no expert. "This is something you should be asking a guy. Ask Chief Wolfe or Russo or Mason." She shook her head. "No, not Mason. Ask Gunnar or Ike."

Welles glanced down the hall again then walked back in the kitchen. "I can't tell any of them I'm a virgin. I . . . it's embarrassing."

And this isn't? Katy wanted to shout. "Then ask your father."

"Cripes, no!" he yelped, taking a step back. "I don't need a two-day sermon on being our family's last chance to have a kid go to college because I didn't get a girl pregnant." He eyed her for several seconds, then blew out a sigh. "Look, I just need a few pointers on what a girl likes during sex is all. And you've got to be what . . . nearly thirty?"

"And just what does my age have to do with it?" Katy

whispered—again so she wouldn't shout. Honest to God, this was the first time she wished the alarm would sound.

He shrugged, apparently as deaf to the warning in her voice as he was clueless. "I figured by now you've had sex with lots of guys."

"Welles!"

His eyes widened, and he held up his hands. "I didn't mean that like it sounded. I don't think you're a—that you sleep around or anything."

Katy sucked in another calming breath. "Okay then, let's start with my pointing out that girls don't like being used for practice."

"No, it's not like that. In fact, losing our virginity before we leave for UMaine was Jaycee's idea. She doesn't want to look like a backwoods hick to her roommate any more than I do."

"Contrary to popular belief, Welles, there's going to be plenty of female and male virgins arriving at colleges all over the world in September."

"Were you?"

"That's none of your business," Katy said softly, this time to keep from smacking him. Come on, you stupid alarm—ring!

"Never mind," he muttered as he turned away. "I'll just ask some of my buddies."

Well, cripes, indeed. "Oh, no you don't," Katy said as she stepped forward and spun him around, not about to leave a bunch of horny idiot seniors in charge of his sex education. "Give me a minute, will you? You can't just spring this on me without warning and expect me to start rattling off ways to get in a girl's panties."

"Getting in isn't the problem," he said, dryly. "I'm

asking about what to do once it's a go. Cripes, Katy, you're not only a woman, you're a paramedic. How hard can it be to give me a few pointers?"

"What's my being a para—wait, Dr. Bentley. You should be talking to him about this."

Welles was shaking his head before she'd finished. "I already know the mechanics. And when I sort of brought it up at the physical I took last month to join the department, all Bentley did was give me a ten-minute lecture on safe sex, along with a brochure on STDs and a pocketful of condoms." He brightened. "So, you're not saying you won't help me, only that you need time to think about it?"

No, she needed time to find Jaycee and smack some sense into the girl. "Yeah, give me at least until my next shift, okay?" So I can Google books on pleasing women and give you a list of them, she refrained from adding. Because honestly? If all she had to go by was her own experience, she was afraid Jaycee was going to be equally disappointed.

"All right, then," Welles said, grabbing the canvas bag off the table. "I can't wait for you to meet Jaycee." He stopped in the hallway when he realized Katy wasn't following. "I told her how cool you are when I called and invited her to the campfire. And my dad dropped off some firewood and we stacked it between some trees near the pit." He glanced toward the window. "The sun's not setting for a couple of hours yet, so my mom sent a bunch of citronella torches with Dad in case it doesn't cool off fast enough this evening. She said if we stick them in a circle outside the sitting area, they should help with the mosquitos until it gets fully dark."

"You go ahead and start setting them up," Katy said, waving him away. "I need to stop by my cubicle and grab a fleece, and then I'll be right out."

Katy listened to his running footsteps fade to rhythmic thumps down the stairwell, then pulled out a chair and sat down, propped her elbows on the table, and dropped her head into her hands with a groan. He hadn't really just asked her how to make love, had he? She'd always thought guys talked about that kind of stuff between themselves. Heck, that was practically all she and Jane used to talk about in high school.

The two of them would sit for hours in the tiny hunting shack at the far end of the Christmas tree field, devouring articles on what boys liked in a girl, how to make them notice you, and how to keep them interested. And once she'd worked up the nerve to plop *Cosmopolitan* and *Marie Claire* on the counter, she and Jane had graduated to reading what men liked in a woman, how to make them notice you, and how to keep them interested. Then they'd spend hours discussing what traits a boyfriend needed to have to be considered for the role of husband.

They'd actually made lists. Long lists, Katy remembered with another groan.

But she'd stopped sneaking into Brody's room and stealing his *Playboy* and *Penthouse* magazines when she'd realized that seeing all the beautiful women, airbrushed and lens-filtered to perfection, had started depressing Jane.

Katy snorted. Either Jane had forgotten she had a deformed foot and noticeable limp, the self-esteem of a salamander, and the sexual prowess of a nun, or else the man she'd saved from drowning last fall was simply more stubborn than she was. Because Miss Orphan Nobody Jane Doe Abbot was right now happily married to a real live king, making her a freaking queen and mother of a princess, and living in an honest to God palace.

What were the chances of that happening to a small-town Maine girl who had still been a virgin at twenty-eight?

Katy lifted her head and smiled. The next time she went home, she was finding their old lists and sending Jane's to her. A sharp pang rattled her chest, reminding her that she should actually call her best friend instead of just dropping something in the mail. She sure had enough to tell her.

Darkness surged, a rush of cold sadness like dirty floodwater, but she jumped to her feet and shook off the chill. Pulling up some memories didn't have to mean all of them. Biting her lip, she fought to distract herself.

Maybe it would be worth taking a gander at her own list to see how Mr. Gunnar Wolfe measured up to her teenage ideal of a perfect husband. The thought made her blush and shake her head. Heaven help them both if the man didn't even meet her criteria for boyfriend.

Chapter Nine

Not wanting to miss Katy's reaction when she came out to SFF&R's second community campfire, Gunnar sat on a stump next to the stump holding her canvas bag, keeping an eye on the open bay doors while also conversing with guests stopping by to welcome him as their new fire chief.

His vigilance finally paid off when Katy came rushing out of the station and actually stumbled to a halt at the sight of what had to be thirty people sitting and standing in small groups around the blazing campfire. They talked and laughed and drank what Gunnar hoped to God were nonalcoholic beverages. Noticing Katy's wide-eyed gaze slide to her left, he looked over to see another dozen people walking up the driveway, most all of them carrying folding chairs, bags of food, and small coolers. He looked back just as she finished taking a long guzzle from her metal water bottle, then watched her take a deep breath, smooth down her shirt, plaster her signature smile firmly in place, and casually saunter toward the monster she'd created. Gunnar turned when he heard a snort to see Jake—decked out in his crisp blue uniform and weighted down with various police toys—drop the stump he carried on the other side of the one holding the canvas bag and then sit down.

"Looks like we might have to start calling ahead for reservations," Jake said.

"Unless you've got a mouse in your pocket, there is no we."

"You ask permission yet, or you waiting to grow a bigger pair first?"

"I'm waiting to see what kind of response I get from the ads I took out all over Europe."

Jake stood with a grin broad enough to be seen from space and plucked the canvas bag off the stump. And then the bastard moved in front of it and gestured for Katy to take his stump. "I've been saving a seat for you."

She hesitated a couple of heartbeats, then stepped around him and sat down where her bag had been. "Thank you, but I believe it's better if I sit between you two."

It was all Gunnar could do not to laugh as the thwarted bastard sat on his old stump.

"Feeling pretty proud of yourself this evening, I suppose," Gunnar drawled to Katy.

She looked at him in surprise. Or maybe that was horror. "I never dreamed all these people would show up," she said—in yup, definitely horror—as she gestured at the crowd. "Ten or twelve people were the most we ever had at one time in Pine Creek."

"I imagine it will settle down here once the newness

wears off. But I was actually talking about your little victory this afternoon."

A big, bright smile replaced her horror. "I will cherish the look on everyone's faces all the way to my grave."

"So, when did you realize you were being filmed?"

That smile turned smug. "When I realized where our safety lines were tied off and found myself wondering why they'd parked the rescue truck at such an odd angle." She chuckled. "Someone forgot to put a piece of black tape over the little red light on the dashcam."

Gunnar leaned closer. "If I promise not to tell, will you tell me how you got down?"

She glanced over at Russo and his wife and two sons sitting across the fire, then flashed a mysterious look. "By magic." She laughed when he scowled at her. "Okay," she said, leaning his way. "We went up."

Gunnar straightened with a snort. "Hell, you should be proud of yourself," he said, knowing it would have required far more upper-body strength than anyone on the squad thought the new rookie possessed. Damn, he wished she hadn't erased that video.

Katy took the canvas bag from Jake when she noticed him rummaging through it, then pulled out a plastic tub and set it on her lap as she looked around at all the people again, her gaze occasionally stopping on a group before moving on. She looked down at the tub and sighed. "I only popped a pound of popcorn."

"Buttered, I hope," Gunnar said, plucking the tub off her lap just as Jake reached for it. He pulled off the top and grabbed a fistful of popcorn but stilled with it halfway to his mouth when Katy arched a delicate brow at him.

"Didn't I just watch you devour two large helpings of lasagna and half a loaf of garlic bread, then wolf down a quarter of a pie?" she said, only to laugh. "Sorry, no pun intended."

"Do you know how many calories a six-foot-three body needs every day just to maintain itself?" Gunnar asked, stifling a grin when Jake snorted again. "Wait. Never mind. I met your brother." He leaned forward. "Have you met Robert MacBain, Shep—I mean, Jake?" Gunnar slid his gaze to Katy. "He's gotta be what? Six-six? Six-seven?"

And there was that gleam. "Robbie's six-foot-seven-and-a-half in his stocking feet."

Like shooting fish in a barrel. Gunnar straightened and shoved the handful of popcorn in his mouth to keep from laughing out loud. Hell, not only was Katy fully aware of what was going on, the little minx was even helping him throw Sheppard under the bus!

Which was kind of scary, actually. Katy MacBain was an overly astute, mischievous, bona fide celestial being who could also magically scale brick walls, apparently.

He heard her softly gasp. "Ohmigod, Welles just bumped into Titus and made him spill some of his drink, and the kid never even slowed down."

Gunnar followed her gaze to see Welles weaving toward them with Jaycee in tow, but he had no idea which of the men in the young couple's wake was Titus. He studied the group, trying to decide which of them seemed to fit the name, when a small figure with shining silver hair passed behind them, face blocked by the crowd. Heart pounding, he peered harder, waiting for what he thought—based on height—was a woman to emerge, but she seemed to evaporate from his view.

"I wonder how Welles would feel," Katy continued dryly, "if he knew he'd just assaulted the person funding his entire college education."

Nearly choking on the second mouthful of popcorn he'd managed to grab before she'd snatched the tub away, Gunnar quickly took a large guzzle of his energy drink to wash it down. "Who's funding it?" he asked, giving all the men a longer look.

She leaned closer. "We can't really tell Welles," she whispered. "The Oceanuses insist on remaining anonymous."

He definitely recognized the name Oceanus but had yet to meet the owners of the two biggest resorts in town. "Are both Oceanuses here? I thought their names are Mac and Olivia?"

Katy blinked at him, then frowned. "Not Mac—Titus. He's here with Rana. His wife?" she clarified at his blank look. "Your former boss, who also happens to be—" She stopped and straightened away. "Oh, I'm sorry. I forgot you've only been here a few weeks and don't know everyone yet," she added with a glance at Jake, who didn't even try to pretend he wasn't blatantly listening as he chewed his own mouthful of popcorn.

Gunnar went back to studying the men as he tried to recall anyone named Titus Oceanus ever hiring him. He sighed, guessing it must have been in his former line of work, when he'd seen and done . . . something that had involved a lot of travel.

Katy surreptitiously pointed at a small group of people twenty yards away across the campfire. "Titus is the tall white-haired gentleman talking to Duncan MacKeage." Her eyes lit with amusement. "I believe Duncan introduced himself to you before I arrived?"

He definitely recognized Duncan, only this evening the Scot had a one-year-old boy sitting on his shoulders—with what looked to be its identical twin held by a pretty blonde woman standing beside him—as well as a four- or five-year-old boy tugging on his hand while pointing at a group of children of varying ages sitting at a—

Gunnar stiffened. Where in hell had the picnic table come from? And when? No, two tables. What he'd thought were people sitting on benches made of planks and stumps when he'd come out earlier were actually picnic tables, each one at least ten feet long and painted bright red. Then he noticed all the lights strung overhead in the trees, casting a soft glow over the small patch of woods now that the sun had dropped behind the mountain.

"Son of a bitch," he muttered as he stood and slowly turned in a circle. "They've turned this place into a rec center." There were even two rope swings hanging from a pine branch up toward the parking lot, and nearly a dozen blazing torches stuck in the ground all over the lawn. Gunnar kept turning, then stilled when he saw a . . .

No, there was no way they could have moved in a concession stand—Spellbound Falls Grange painted on its side in big bold letters—without him knowing about it. But people lined the sidewalk in front of— Christ, a little old lady just leaned out the window, took the money out of some guy's hand, and replaced it with two hotdogs and a longneck bottle of beer. "How in hell did they get that trailer wedged in between those trees?" He looked over when Jake started laughing. "It's not funny, Sheppard.

Instead of stuffing your face, you should be arresting them for selling booze on town property. The council wouldn't give them the station, so they took over our freaking yard."

"That's what the Grange ladies do," Jake said through his laughter. "If they can't get something they want through normal channels, they just wait until no one is looking and take it. How do you think the town got the recreational trail? When the train stopped running years ago, the women simply claimed the railbed as town property, tore up the tracks from ten miles north of here all the way down to Turtleback, and built the park at the base of the waterfall."

"And nobody ever tries to stop them?"

Jake snorted. "Five of the seven councilmen are married to Grange ladies."

Which explained why Duncan MacKeage had been the one to shoot down their attempt to get the fire station at the meeting. Gunnar gestured at the quarter-acre of woods that now had at least fifty people scattered around it. "They can go set up shop in the park they already have, because unlike the railroad bed, the fire station is still in operation."

"The way I heard it," Jake drawled, his amusement growing in direct proportion to Gunnar's obvious indignation, "they didn't want to spoil the aesthetics of their park."

"But they don't mind cluttering up a multimillion-dollar working facility?" Gunnar grabbed Katy's hand and pulled her to her feet. "I want you to introduce me to Titus," he said as he led her around the fire pit. He snagged Welles on his way by, cutting off whatever the boy was saying to someone. "Come on, Ingersoll-Hoffenmyer, you have an apology to give."

"Wolfe."

Gunnar stopped and turned to see Jake standing and holding a hand to his ear, only to flinch when the station alarm suddenly blasted from the speaker just inside the middle bay door. Everyone froze, their startled cries drowned out by the long series of tones that followed. Jake was the only one moving, listening to dispatch on his earpiece as he cut through the trees toward town and immediately broke into a run when he reached the sidewalk.

"Attention Spellbound Falls Fire & Rescue. You're asked to respond to 355 Sunrise Point for unknown number of patients in and out of consciousness, possibly drug related, with at least two people unresponsive at this time. Law enforcement already en route. Acknowledge Spellbound Falls Fire & Rescue; 355 Sunrise Point, unknown number of patients, at least two unresponsive. Law enforcement en route. Piscataquis out, nineteen-forty-nine."

The ensuing silence was shattered by Captain Russo barking orders over the sudden wail of a police siren coming from the center of town. "Everyone rolls!" he shouted as he ran toward the station, the other three firefighters, Katy, Welles, and Gunnar following. "Mason on Engine One; Higgins and Conroy in Bus One; Bean and MacBain in Two," he continued as Gretchen ran forward from the rear of the station. "Welles, you're riding with me."

Russo stopped in the center bay doorway facing in. "Hey!" he snapped, making everyone freeze beside their respective trucks and look at him. "Nobody leaves their vehicle until I give the okay," he ordered, even as he stared directly at Gretchen. "Got that, Conroy?"

"Sure do, Captain."

Russo then turned to face out. "Clear the driveway!" he shouted, even as Gunnar saw several firefighters from other shifts already herding people onto the grass. "Grindle, put out that—" Russo stopped when a second siren suddenly sounded nearby.

Gunnar looked through the trees to see Niall MacKeage's black pickup with flashing blue lights pull out of the camp road on the other side of the church and head toward town.

"Grindle, put out that fire before you leave!" Russo repeated to one of the off-duty firefighters. He then looked over and flashed Gunnar a grin. "You're welcome to tag along, Chief," he said before turning and running to the captain's pickup parked in the end bay.

Deciding he didn't need to add another vehicle to the parade, Gunnar ran to Engine One and climbed in the front passenger seat, not about to miss a chance to ride in a speeding, light-flashing, siren-blaring fire truck.

"Buckle up," Skip Mason said with a laugh as he hit the lights and siren and rolled out of the station to fall in behind the captain's pickup.

Gunnar glanced over at the still stunned crowd, seeing some of them cover their wide-eyed children's ears when Mason sounded the air horn as he pulled onto the main road toward town. Yup, nothing like making every cell in their bodies scream to let the townspeople know exactly where their hard-earned tax dollars were going. Hell, if he didn't know better, he might think their new citizen liaison had called in a false alarm merely for effect.

"I just realized this is MacBain's first official run," Skip said loudly over the blaring siren as he tailgated Russo, apparently trying to push the captain down the road faster.

"Yup," Gunnar grunted more than said, rather occupied pressing both feet down on the imaginary brake on the floorboard. He shot Mason a tight grin. "Assuming Conroy doesn't run around touching all the patients and calling dibs."

Mason grunted back.

"Do you know where we're going?" Gunnar grabbed the door handle as they took a sharp curve at—hell, he was pretty sure the gauge with the needle pointing slightly past fifty was the speedometer.

"That's Russo's job," Skip said as he gestured out the windshield. "My job is to follow that pickup straight into hell, then do whatever the captain tells me to do once we get there." He snorted. "There's not a piece of equipment I can't run or a fire I can't read, but I've never made captain because apparently nobody wants to follow a guy into hell who gets lost driving to an apartment he's lived in for three years." He flashed Gunnar a grin. "I blame getting dropped on my head as a kid for screwing up my sense of direction."

"Back off my ass, Mason," Russo snapped over the radio. "Okay, boys and girls, we're turning left in half a mile onto a camp road. Our scene is a quarter mile in on our right. It appears this might be quite a party, so if things turn ugly, you get the hell out of the way and let the guys with the guns be the heroes. Cut the sirens when we turn," he added as they rounded a curve to be greeted by flashing blue lights in the opposite lane. A deputy sheriff stood beside his cruiser, holding back oncoming traffic while directing SFF&R to make the turn.

Gunnar reached over and flipped off the siren, then braced himself again when the large engine swung onto the dirt road. He still bumped his head on the side window when the truck violently rocked back and forth over a series of large, shallow potholes. Mason added his own curse to Gunnar's at the sound of tree branches scraping along both sides and the top of the truck, only to slam on the brakes with another curse when they heard a loud thump half a second before an overhead branch snapped with the force of a gunshot.

"This is logging country, for chrissakes," Mason snarled. "Doesn't anyone on this road own a freaking chainsaw?" He reached for the radio mike at the same time he glanced at his side mirror. "Higgins, you stop and pick up whatever that goddamn tree knocked off my engine."

"Don't have to," Paul Higgins returned with a chuckle. "I'm pretty sure my roof strobes caught it. Looked like one of your rear floodlights."

Mason let go of a heavy sigh and reached forward and patted the dash. "There, there, Lucinda, don't you fret none. Skippy will make you all pretty again before he turns in tonight."

Gunnar looked out his side window to hide his grin, noting the low-hanging sun filtering through the trees now that they were out of the shadow of the mountains but quickly sobered when Mason bought the engine to a full stop.

"You'll fit," Russo said over the radio, causing Gunnar to look beyond the pickup to see half a dozen vehicles parked on either side of the road at staggered intervals, leaving a crooked, even narrower path to the flashing blue lights a hundred yards ahead. Hell, a couple of people had plowed down small bushes and driven straight into the woods to park.

"If we'd brought the rescue truck instead," Mason said as he expertly threaded the engine through the obstacle course, his eyes constantly darting from one outside mirror to the other, "we could have plowed some of them out of our way. For chrissakes, what moron drives a Mercedes into the bushes?" He stopped his darting long enough to shoot Gunnar a grin. "They must be handing out some really good shit at the party."

"Most of the license plates are from out of state."

Mason snorted. "About the only Maine plates I've seen on any vehicle costing over twenty grand belong to that fancy resort on top of Whisper Mountain. The locals don't like spending money on anything potholes and road salt are just going to eat. The day after I moved here from Dallas, there was a two-foot snowstorm in freaking April. Where'd you say you're fro—"

"Slide the engine in that open driveway this side of MacKeage's truck," Russo said over the radio. "You buses can have the road but pull beyond our party driveway." The mike keyed off then back on again. "Remember, unless we see flames coming out of windows or kittens stuck in trees, this is law enforcement's rodeo. And wait on my go."

Gunnar unfastened his seat belt when Ike pulled in across from the two police pickups parked on either side of what he assumed was the party driveway—leaving it clear. Mason pulled Engine One into the driveway on the left, then undid his own seat belt and jumped out. Gunnar scrambled out his door and ran to the back of the engine to find the firefighter already standing on the bumper checking out the tree branch damage.

"That's going to leave a permanent mark," he muttered, jumping down. He grabbed the backpack he'd set on the bumper—which Gunnar recognized was one of the triage kits all the trucks carried—then walked to the end of the driveway.

"Sure is quiet for a party," Skip said when Gunnar walked up beside him, both of them looking toward the flashing blue lights and red strobes of their ambulances. Russo was speaking with Niall MacKeage in the driveway as Katy and Gretchen stood beside the rear ambulance with jump bags slung over their shoulders. Both women appeared ready to bolt the moment the captain said go, along with Bean and Higgins, who stood beside them.

Mason glanced over at Gunnar. "You got any medic training or at least up to speed on administering Narcan? 'Cause I'm thinking everyone's passed out." He squinted through the trees at Bottomless and chuckled. "Or they heard the sirens and are swimming for it."

"I'm pretty sure I can jab a needle into someone," Gunnar said, returning his grin, "as long as they aren't moving."

"So long as you're moving after. I've had some guys wake up throwing punches." Mason shook his head. "It apparently pisses them off when you bring them back from the brink of death."

"We're good to go, people!" Russo called out as he walked back to the road, freeing Gunnar and Mason to jog over to him. "Conroy. MacBain. You've got an unresponsive man and woman on the far side of the camp. A deputy is giving CPR to the man beside the shed, and the woman is down on the beach!" he hollered to their backs as they hurried down the driveway.

Ike sighed and turned to his firefighters. "We've got Chief MacKeage on scene, along with Jake Sheppard and an off-duty cop from Turtleback in plain clothes, and two county deputy sheriffs—one here and the other one out at the main road. Niall said there appears to be a wide variety of drugs; anything from alcohol and good old-fashioned weed to heroin likely cut with fentanyl—which would explain the two possible overdoses. He also said there were maybe fifty partiers here twenty minutes ago, but most of them left either by boat or on foot through the woods when they heard someone had called 911. So our job is to search the grounds and interior of the camp as well as the neighboring yards and any outbuildings for anyone else that may be passed out. If you come across anyone merely high on weed, tell them there's a blond guy wearing a Spider-Man T-shirt on the porch handing out cookies. If you find anyone drifting in and out of consciousness or acting confused, escort them to the porch and leave them with Spider-Man. He's Cole Wyatt, the off-duty cop. He'll keep everyone corralled until Conroy or MacBain can check them out."

Gunnar clenched his jaw. He'd managed to go for

weeks without seeing that son of a bitch Wyatt, but now wasn't the time to chew on old grudges.

Ike squinted at the darkening woods. "Higgins, grab some flashlights out of the engine because I think we're going to be here awhile." He looked at Mason. "You're not licensed in Maine yet to do more then put a Band-Aid on anyone, so take that jump bag to Conroy or MacBain. They may need an extra Narcan kit. Okay," Ike added with a grin, rubbing his hands together, "let's go hunt us down some stupid people. And whoever finds the most gets a prize." He slid that grin to Gunnar. "Anything you want to add, Chief?"

"How does eight hours of comp time sound for a prize?"

"Works for me," Skip Mason said, grabbing a flashlight from Higgins and heading down the driveway, followed by Bean. Higgins handed out the other flashlights, then jogged after them.

"Whoa," Russo said, grabbing Welles when he started following. "You're with me."

"Aw, come on, Captain."

"Rule number one," Ike said, slapping a hand on Welles' shoulder and guiding the kid down the driveway, "never question a captain's orders on scene. Ever. You got a gripe, you take it up with him after."

Chapter Ten

Gunnar clicked on his flashlight and swept the powerful beam back and forth through the woods as he ambled along the driveway, reminding himself not to go anywhere near the porch. It wasn't that he expected he could put off seeing Wyatt indefinitely. He simply preferred not to have any witnesses to their . . . happy reunion.

Keeping an eye out for both vertical and horizontal partiers, he went on to wonder if he could mark this down on Gilmore's stats sheet as multiple runs, since they had multiple patients, or did he have to list it as a single call? Because he was pretty sure the more runs he could show, the easier it would be to justify their worth to the good citizens of Spellbound Falls. Not that it was any of his business, since he didn't intend on being around for next year's budget meeting.

That brought him to an abrupt halt.

So where exactly did he intend to be a year from now? Or even three months from now? In another dark alley or stinking jungle chasing power-hungry assholes? Or maybe trying not to die from a gunshot wound in some third-world hospital that never even heard of antibiotics? Honestly, none of that sounded appealing anymore. And he knew he couldn't count on another Markov Lakeland coming along and pulling him out of the ocean the next time he got run over by an aircraft carrier while fleeing for his life.

He sighed and resumed looking for partiers. Some Renaissance man. Even Sheppard and Wyatt had enough intelligence to get out of the game before someone permanently took them out.

Gunnar really couldn't see himself being a cop, though. Hell, he'd probably spent more on jet fuel just getting here than they now earned in a year. Not that he was worried the bastards were living paycheck to paycheck, figuring they hadn't kept exact records of all the contraband they'd handled. In fact, he wouldn't be surprised to learn Jake had paid for that well-equipped home right on Bottomless with solid gold ingots.

So was there a reason he hadn't made plans beyond meeting Miss MacBain? Such as what he intended to do if he actually liked her? Not liking her was as simple as jetting back to Shelkova to throttle Jane, then going to hang out with Anatol and his womanless tribe of nomads until he gained back at least some of his faculties.

Except half the men were no longer bachelors. Markov had also told him that Anatol, with his rusty manners, freshly barbered hair, and weatherworn but still manly physique, was still trying to charm Irina into leaving behind family, social stature, and most of the trappings of civilization for the elemental freedom of nomadic life. The really scary thing was Markov had said that even though his aunt was leading Anatol on a merry chase, it appeared the old bear was actually making progress.

So, what was up with everyone he knew all of sudden pairing up, anyway? Hell, when he'd called last month, even Aunt May had prattled on about some handsome widower who'd just purchased the house at the end of her street. Gunnar hadn't bothered to check out the guy, though, because he was pretty sure that within a week of moving in May had known more about her new neighbor than the handsome widower knew about himself.

Gunnar chuckled, guessing that should teach him for introducing May to the World Wide Web eight years ago. What he'd only intended to be a means for them to keep in touch when he was hunting down bad guys had damn near started a small war when the neighbors had realized their Internet access was unusually slow because May was hogging the bandwidth. So, he'd flown back to Reykjavik and quietly persuaded—and paid for—the cable company to run a propriety fiber optic cable directly to May's house. And the woman still complained it was too—

Gunnar stilled at the sound of an angry shout, immediately followed by a distinctly feminine scream that ended abruptly, both having come from somewhere beyond the two-story camp—which, if he remembered correctly, was where Russo had sent Gretchen and Katy.

Gunnar tore off at a run, catching sight of Niall and Jake and Ike and Welles rushing out of the woods from various directions as they also headed toward the unmistakable sound of a solid object repeatedly hitting flesh, followed by pained grunts. The obvious assault made Gunnar's heart pound in dread as he envisioned the unresponsive male patient rising up from near death and beating the crap out of Katy or Gretchen.

He rounded the corner of the building three strides behind Jake, only to find Niall MacKeage planted in place. "Nay," Niall snapped, snagging Jake's arm and then Gunnar's, effectively bringing the other men also rounding the camp to a halt. "If we don't want to find ourselves on the wrong end of that rake," Niall said calmly over everyone's heavy panting, "I suggest we let the lass finish."

Gunnar actually dropped to his knees in relief when he realized that Gretchen was safely out of the fray, that the grunts came from a large, wild-eyed man, and that the solid object triggering them was the handle end of a garden rake, which Katy used to repeatedly knock the guy to the ground every time he rolled away and tried to get to his feet again.

"Stay down," she told him.

"Go to hell," the man growled as he struggled to his feet.

Once again, Katy applied rake to rib cage, and the man went sprawling.

Gunnar couldn't tell how tall he was, since the stupid bastard never made it any higher than rising to one knee, but he had the shoulders of a linebacker and looked to outweigh Katy by at least a hundred pounds.

No, all he could do was stare at the surreal scene, remotely aware of more men arriving only to find themselves equally transfixed by the sight of Katy MacBain relentlessly driving the cussing, combative guy farther away from—

Gunnar shoved at Russo's leg. "Gretchen," he said, nodding to their right.

"Shit," Russo muttered, heading to their downed medic sitting slumped against a tree. One hand clutched her throat and the other held something to her face as she also stared wide-eyed at the one-sided battle.

Gunnar looked over at Katy again as he tried to reconcile the fact he'd been rushing to her rescue only to find himself thinking he should probably rescue the idiot. "Ah, I'm pretty sure we're supposed to be saving people," he said to no one in particular, "not beating them up."

Niall crouched to his heels between Gunnar and Jake, who had also dropped to his knees in either relief or disbelief or both. "When Michael MacBain would have been schooling his daughters on how to defend themselves," Niall said, "he'd have taught them the importance of not letting up until their assailant could no longer get up."

Well, Katy obviously hadn't missed any lessons. Less than a minute had passed since Gretchen's scream, but it felt to Gunnar like time had slowed to a crawl. And he'd swear that, instead of a battle between a drug-hyped gorilla and a woman armed with only a garden rake, he was watching a precisely timed, perfectly choreographed, and strangely beautiful . . . dance.

He stiffened when Katy suddenly backed off enough for the guy to make it to his feet, peripherally aware of Jake quietly drawing his weapon and aiming it at the visibly weaving, still wild-eyed, still combative idiot.

And then the fine hairs on Gunnar's neck rose when he heard a soft, feminine growl. Katy swung the business end of the rake in a low, sweeping arc that ended with the tines snagging the back of the idiot's ankles one second before her left boot slammed into his chest.

"Holy sweet Jesus," someone whispered.

Yeah. That. What he said.

The ensuing howl came out in a whoosh as the gorilla shot backward, his disappearance followed by a series of heavy thuds that ended with a muted splash. Katy walked to the edge of the shallow bluff and looked down, then dropped the rake, turned, and ran past her stunned audience on her way to Gretchen.

Gunnar made a mental note to remember that, in the hands of an avenging angel, a garden rake could be just as lethal as a shotgun.

"And that, gentlemen," Niall said with quiet pride as he stood and headed toward the bluff, "is how Scots women deal with contrary men."

Jake slipped his gun back in its holster as he looked over at Gunnar and grinned. "I think we're asking the wrong gender for permission."

"Have you given that mouse in your pocket a name yet?" Gunnar asked as he stood to go check on Gretchen and turned straight into an oncoming fist.

His head snapped back in an explosion of pain, and even as he dropped like a stone, Gunnar at least had enough brain cells left firing to remember to stay down once he hit the ground. Except Cole Wyatt apparently hadn't been schooled by Michael MacBain, and the bastard gave Gunnar a couple of kicks, then landed on top of him and pummeled his ribs.

Time slowed again as Gunnar heard the surprised shouts of his crew, footsteps rushing forward, and even Jake Sheppard's heavy sigh before the punishing stopped and the weight lifted away. He rolled onto his side and cradled his ribs as he tried to catch his breath through spasms of coughing.

Oh yeah, he really needed to stop being an ass.

"Holy cripes, Chief," Welles said, dropping down beside him. "Are you okay?"

Hearing more grunts and growls and fists hitting flesh, Gunnar rolled onto all fours then straightened to his knees in time to see Niall and Ike rushing into the free-for-all and attempting to gain control of their respective men. Because, of course, the firefighters took offense to someone beating up their chief, and, of course, Jake had taken offense to them beating up his longtime partner. Gunnar made a grab for Welles when the kid suddenly charged straight into the fray, then hissed out a curse when the wasted effort made him fall to all fours. He took several slow breaths as he stared at the ground, then cursed again as he staggered to his feet—partly because this wasn't their fight, but mostly because he was worried Katy would show up holding that rake.

"Hey!" he roared, albeit too late to save Skip Mason from taking a blow to the jaw when Jake didn't even bother to pull his punch. He was also too late to save Paul Higgins from getting tossed through the air just as the firefighter's fist was about to connect with Wyatt's face, although Paul only flew a couple of yards when Niall MacKeage let go in mid-toss and turned in unison with everyone else.

"Leave him alone. Wyatt's, uh, he's an old buddy of mine."

"Where I come from," Mason said gutturally, holding a hand to his jaw, "buddies don't sucker punch buddies."

"Oh, I don't know," Gunnar drawled to cover up the fact he could barely breathe as he looked directly at Wyatt. "They might if the last time they saw each other a misunderstanding landed one of them in the hospital."

Wyatt stared at him for several crawling seconds, then silently turned and walked away.

Gunnar sighed, deciding that had actually gone better than he'd expected, seeing how he was still alive. And for payback that had been so long coming, he'd gotten through it pretty fast.

He looked around the dusk-darkened yard at the mess of lawn chairs, coolers, towels, various items of clothing, and even a few hastily abandoned purses; at the smoke wafting up from the charred remains of something on a charcoal grill; and at the picnic table loaded down with enough liquor bottles to fill the backbar at the Bottoms Up. "Has anyone noticed we seem to be the only ones at this party?" he asked, even as he wondered if he could still mark this down on the stats sheet as a call.

Then again, with the exception of Katy and Niall—coincidently the two Scots—most everyone else could probably be considered patients. Hell, even Welles had the start of a shiner.

Ike Russo dabbed at his swollen lip, scowled at the blood on his fingers, then glanced around him. "We better make sure we haven't overlooked any stupid people before we clear the scene. Besides us," he clarified, bending over to swipe a flashlight off the ground, then flicking it on as he walked away.

Jake headed toward the porch, where Wyatt sat on the

steps with his arms resting on his knees, spitting blood on the ground between his feet. Niall walked over to the deputy sheriff, whose badge dangled from a torn shirt pocket, the two of them then heading toward the bluff where gorilla man was lying on his side in handcuffs . . . napping.

Higgins and Bean and Mason, all sporting their own various battle wounds, each walked to one of the lit flashlights illuminating the grass where they'd been dropped. Gunnar heard each of the firefighters mutter a curse as they headed off in different directions—Mason limping while gingerly probing his temple, Higgins sucking on his knuckles, and Bean wiping his mouth with the back of one hand while cradling his ribs with the other.

"You okay, Chief?" Welles asked.

"I'm good."

The boy walked over and picked up one of the two remaining flashlights, then turned and faced him again. "Can I ask you a question?"

"Yeah, go ahead."

"How come you didn't fight back? I saw you," he rushed on. "You just let that guy beat on you without even defending yourself." He took a step closer. "I bet you could have taken him, but you didn't even try."

Gunnar started to respond but stopped. "There are times when not fighting back can be a silent form of apology, and I . . . well, tonight was one of those times."

"But wouldn't it be easier to just say you're sorry?"

"Not when you know it's going to fall on deaf ears. Go catch up with Ike."

Gunnar waited through Welles' hesitation, and then for the kid to enter the woods, before hugging his rib cage and slumping over with a groan as he looked around for a relatively soft place to land.

"I've got you," an avenging angel said, lifting one of his arms and carefully tucking her shoulder into his armpit while wrapping her other arm around him and grabbing his belt. "Your choice," she continued as she took some of his weight. "You want to lie flat on the ground or semi-sitting on the edge of the table?"

"Upright."

She guided him over to the picnic table, turned them both around, then backed up until he felt the table. "Wait," she said over the sound of several bottles crashing onto the ground. "Okay, sit on the edge and then straighten until you find a comfortable position."

"How's Gretchen?" he asked to keep from hissing at having to support his own weight again.

"Angry. Stubborn. Embarrassed." Katy gently clasped his jaw and turned his head slightly, then leaned in to squint at his cheekbone. "And delusional enough to actually thank me." She dropped her hand with a snort and dug in a pocket on her cargo pants. "And apparently far more charitable than I am, considering her patient woke up and backhanded her head hard enough to send her flying, then started choking her."

Her hand emerged with a small penlight, which she clicked on while using it to gesture toward the bluff, where he could see Gretchen kneeling beside gorilla man. "She has a cut on her brow that needs to be sutured, and her neck's already so swollen she can barely talk, yet she insisted on tending the bastard when I told her I don't patch up people I beat up."

"Speaking of which, what happened to letting the guys with the guns be the heroes?"

"The thing about heroes," she murmured while gently opening his swollen eye, "is that you can't always count on one being around when you need them." She aimed the beam at his pupil, moved it away, and brought it back, then slid it to his cheekbone. "So every Saturday morning from the time we could walk, our father taught me and my sister, Maggie, how to save ourselves by using anything we could get our hands on for a weapon." The tiny beam gave enough light for him to see her smile. "He told us that men will expect a woman to struggle, but not for her to become the aggressor. So the element of surprise, along with a stout stick and calm mind, should get us out of any trouble we might find ourselves in."

"You must have thought my warning the other day was rather patronizing, since you're obviously more than capable of handling your teammates." He chuckled, only to immediately regret it when a sharp pain spiked through his chest. "Not that any of them will be in any hurry to bother you after today—including Gretchen."

Her smile vanished as she dropped her gaze, but not quickly enough for him to miss the flush in her cheeks. "I have to lift yer shirt," she said rather huskily as she stared at his chest. "And see if any ribs are broken."

Then again, maybe she wasn't so much embarrassed as aware—as in her realizing they were alone, in the dark, and she was about to run her wonderfully feminine hands all over him. Gunnar bit back a groan that had absolutely nothing to do with his injuries. His five-month fantasy was about to come to life.

Not wanting her anywhere near the lower half of his body, he pulled his shirt out of his pants and gathered the material high enough on his chest to expose his ribs, only to flinch when her delicate fingers gently brushed over his skin—making every drop of blood in his body rush straight to his groin anyway.

"Sorry," she murmured with a throaty chuckle as she shut off the light. She shoved it in a pocket, then positioned herself in front of him and looked him level in the eyes. Well, in the eye that wasn't swollen nearly shut. "I'm going to have to poke and prod to the point it may hurt a bit," she said as she splayed her hands on both sides of his torso just above his belt. "So, I'd appreciate ye not taking a swing at me."

Oh yeah, definitely aware, if that hint of a brogue was any indication.

"Trust me, I excel at learning from other people's mistakes," he drawled—the last part coming out in a gasp when her fingers slowly walked up his sides. "Your hands are really hot. Their temperature," he added lamely, even as he wondered if he could reach down and tug on his pants without her realizing why he needed to adjust them.

Except she didn't appear to be listening, much less worried about what his hands might be up to, as he was pretty sure her eyes were closed while she focused on him, on moving her hands over him. His ribs—on feeling his ribs. Wait, was that a smile?

So was the woman checking out his injuries or bringing her own fantasies to life?

Her fingers nearly scorched him now, making each rib they touched feel . . . funny. Sort of shivery, as if they were moving inside him. In fact, he felt hot and shivery all over. The way it felt before two bodies came together in bed—sharp and bristling with energy. But different, somehow. Soothing.

He'd swear the higher those fingers climbed, the easier it was for him to breathe and the less he hurt. Hell, even his cheekbone quit throbbing.

Guess lust was an effective painkiller.

If he leaned forward just a few inches, he could kiss her. She wouldn't even see it coming because her eyes were closed. And with her being so tall and him semisitting on the table, their mouths were at the same level. And she couldn't call him out on it, because he was hot and shivery and not really thinking straight after taking a sucker punch to the head.

They might have met only a few days ago, but he'd been imagining this moment since the first time Jane mentioned her very beautiful, very best friend in an email—thoughtfully including a photograph—nearly five freaking months ago. Except he hadn't been beaten up in his fantasies, so he couldn't exactly relive them by sweeping Katy off her feet and carrying her off . . . someplace private.

Even if he felt her lips for only a second, it would be enough.

Hell, he didn't care if she slapped his face; he just wanted to taste her.

Gunnar froze in mid-lean when her eyes suddenly opened, appearing unusually bright considering it was totally dark now. "Nothing's broken."

Yes. Yes, it was. He was broken. And he'd spent all this time and energy and traveled thousands of miles looking for a wilderness angel handing out life-saving kisses.

She reached up and cradled his face in her hot, delicate hands, and even though he couldn't see it, he could hear the smile in her voice when she said, "I'm sorry. Were ye hoping for a couple of days off from work? Because I could go find that rake if ye want."

"I need a bus!" a voice croaked from the bluff. "Welles! Higgins! Somebody! We're transporting!" the croaking continued, moving closer. "Where in hell is everyone?"

The hands cradling his face disappeared, the accompanying sigh echoing his own. But then she leaned down and placed a tender kiss on his cheek, light as air but somehow still scorching. "You stay put while I go help her," Katy said as she headed off.

"Excuse me." Gunnar cleared his throat when he realized he sounded rather hoarse himself. "Are the medics in Pine Creek in the habit of ordering their chief around?"

He saw her silhouette stop. "They do when he's the patient. Stay put."

For a long moment, Gunnar felt the kiss on his cheek, drank in her scent—vanilla and campfire—and wanted to dive into it. Then his cheek cooled, and the kiss faded into the night.

A drawn-out crash came from near the shed, the cacophony of banging metal laced with a croaked string of very unladylike and quite inventive curses.

"I'm right here," Gunnar heard Katy say at the same time he saw her penlight click on, faintly illuminating Gretchen sitting in a tangle of lawn chairs. More powerful flashlight beams arched through the darkness just as a vehicle started out on the road, the relative silence of the abandoned party shattered by the overloud beeping of an ambulance backing up.

The beeping finally stopped, and the yard turned to day when the floodlights on the rear of the ambulance came on, making Gunnar realize he still held his T-shirt up under his armpits. He pushed away from the table, then began tucking in his shirt with another sigh. Just a few more inches and those luscious lips would have been on his. Then he would have—

What the hell? Either he was a lot tougher than he thought or Wyatt had grown soft in retirement, because not only did his ribs barely hurt anymore, he felt surprisingly . . . energized. Much like he imagined Tuxedo Tim had felt after Katy breathed life back into his tiny lungs. Gunnar snorted, half tempted to look for a blowing leaf he could dodge and dart after as he headed to the ambulance.

"You should start slowing down," Gretchen said in a raspy whisper, gesturing at the road ahead. "It's that sign on the—"

She stopped talking when Katy drove past the entrance to Moose Point Condominiums. "I told you I'll pick up my car tomorrow," Gretchen continued. "I shouldn't be driving with a painkiller in my system."

"Then I guess you'll have to stay at the station tonight."

"I don't need to be babysat," she snapped hoarsely, "for a sore throat and three tiny stitches on my brow."

"And a possible concussion," Katy added, "as well as a couple of bruised ribs."

"I am perfectly capable of taking care of myself."

"And you can go right back to taking care of yourself tomorrow." Katy flashed her a smile. "But tonight, I'm afraid you're stuck with me."

Her passenger fell silent and stared out the side window. Katy felt her smile fade. She didn't care how much Gretchen groused. Nobody should be alone after being so brutally attacked. And something told her a good part of Gretchen's protests had to do with her not wanting the firefighters to see her all beaten up; Katy remembered—all too well—feeling perversely embarrassed and ashamed at finding herself a victim four weeks ago. She also knew the sense of absolute aloneness could be even more wounding than the attack itself.

"The men need to see for themselves that you're okay," Katy said into the silence. "You have to realize they're going to feel responsible for your getting hurt."

Gretchen looked over in surprise. "They were busy doing their own jobs."

"I heard Ike say he should have known better then to send us to tend drug overdoses all by ourselves."

"He was told there was a deputy sheriff giving CPR to one of them," Gretchen rasped. "Ike knew we weren't alone."

"Where was the deputy? When I heard you scream, I only saw you and your patient."

Gretchen dropped her gaze to her lap. "I . . . ah, I told him I had it covered and sent him to go find you. What happened to your patient?" she asked in an obvious attempt to redirect the conversation.

"I found a teenage girl down on the beach with her boyfriend." Katy chuckled. "Both of them scared to death their parents were going to find out they'd been smoking pot. Apparently, it doesn't agree with the girl, so the boyfriend took her away from the crowd, and she fell asleep waiting for the dizziness to pass." Katy shrugged. "My guess is whoever called 911 saw them and thought the girl had also overdosed. The kids started apologizing when I showed up, thinking they were the reason we were there. And when I assured them they weren't, the brats took off down the beach. I didn't bother chasing them, figuring anyone that agile didn't need a medic."

"Probably right."

"I was just climbing up the bluff when I heard you scream." She smiled again. "And as luck would have it, I happened to notice a rake leaning against the side of the shed as I ran past."

"Where did you learn to fight like that?" Gretchen whispered. "One minute, the bastard was choking me, and the next minute, you showed up and kicked him hard enough that I swear I heard one of his ribs crack. Who taught you to do that?"

"Every Saturday morning when we were growing up, our father gave me and my older sister lessons on how to defend ourselves."

There were several heartbeats of silence. "Could . . . do you think you could teach me to fight like that?"

Score! Katy smiled out the windshield. "Funny you should ask. I've been planning to talk to Birch Callahan, the lady who runs the crisis shelter here in town, about starting a self-defense class for women."

"Then consider me your first student."

"Oh, I won't be teaching it," Katy explained. "I'm

hoping to get Niall and my other two male cousins to collectively teach it."

"But wouldn't the women be more comfortable learning from you? Why even bother involving men?"

"Because it's most likely a man they'd ultimately be defending themselves against. And if women only spar with other women, they might lose their confidence if they ever found themselves facing an angry, aggressive brute." She shot Gretchen a sinister grin. "Trust me, it's quite empowering to know you can trounce a 250-pound man with nothing more than a broom or garden rake."

Gretchen snorted. "I felt empowered just watching you go after that bastard. My God, you were relentless."

"That's because Papa taught Maggie and me to never hesitate or back down or we'd lose the advantage of both surprise and momentum."

Gretchen straightened her shoulders as far as her sore ribs would allow. "I want to help set up the classes. We'll ask Chief Wolfe if we can hold them at the station, and I'll handle the paperwork and scheduling and make flyers to post around town." She looked over at Katy. "That is, if you want my help."

"I'd love it."

"I . . . ah, I'm sorry," Gretchen whispered, her shoulders slumping again.

"For what?"

"For being a bitch to you earlier."

That made Katy laugh. "Do you honestly believe you're the first person to judge me on my looks alone?"

Gretchen sighed. "I suppose not."

"I've been underestimated most all my life." Katy shot

her another smile. "Sometimes it works to my advantage, but most of the time, it's just a pain in the ass." She rolled her eyes. "You think I have a hard time being taken seriously as a paramedic; imagine a New York businessman shopping for a million-dollar Maine vacation home believing a long-legged, perky-boobed, twenty-two-year-old knows anything about septic systems, artesian wells, snow loads, and shoreland regulations."

Gretchen hid her face in her hands. "I can't believe I actually called you that."

"Too late. I'm not letting you take back your compliment."

Gretchen dropped her hands and blinked at her. "What?"

"Every girl likes to hear she has perky boobs," Katy drawled, laughing again when Gretchen's gaze dropped to her chest.

Katy let off the gas as they approached town, only to spot their huge aerial set up down in the park near the base of the waterfalls, its rear floodlights illuminating the bucket extended high into the trees. She checked her outside mirror to make sure no one was behind her, then slowed the ambulance to a crawl as she idled across the bridge. "What do you suppose they're doing?" she said, gesturing toward the fire truck.

"That looks like Matt in the bucket," Gretchen rasped. "Now why would he be stringing lights in the town park at—" She looked at her watch. "Good Lord, what are they doing out here at nearly one in the morning?"

Katy pulled the ambulance across the road and stopped next to the sidewalk. "I know what they're doing," she said, shutting off the engine. "You missed it earlier, but when we rolled out of the station, did you notice all the people in the side yard?"

"Yeah, I did. I couldn't believe the crowd. Paul told me a steady stream of people had been showing up since around seven."

"That's because the Grange ladies have apparently decided Spellbound Falls needs a community rec center." Katy chuckled. "I wish you could have seen Gunnar. He was so offended when he realized they'd hijacked our campfire, he wanted Jake to arrest them for selling beer on town—" She stopped talking when she saw Skip Mason in the fire chief's pickup, which was towing the concession trailer behind it, turn off the road onto the park path, only to stop when he spotted the ambulance.

"What is that?" Gretchen asked.

"That would be the Grange's concession stand. They had it set up in our woods near the sidewalk. And see those two red picnic tables?" Katy added, pointing toward the two tables a few yards from the aerial. "They were set up beside our campfire pit. And all those lights Matt is stringing through the trees had been strung through our trees."

"That still doesn't explain what they're all doing here at one in the morn—"

Gretchen's door opened, and Ike Russo leaned into the cab far enough to unclip her seat belt, then gently guided her down to the ground. He held her by the shoulders as he gave her a visible inspection, his worried gaze stopping on the small bandage on her brow. His eyes turned distressed, then he blew out a sigh and enfolded her into a careful hug.

"Knock it off, Ike," she sputtered. "I'm fine."

"You're not the one to decide such things," he grumbled.

Gretchen eased out of his grip and ducked her head, likely to hide the blush in her cheeks, Katy decided. She moved past Ike, and out of Katy's sight, muttering as she walked. "Way too much fussing going on around here."

Katy chucked and slipped out of the cab. "Should we go check out what's happening down at the park, Gretchen?" she called.

Gretchen appeared on Katy's side of the bus and flashed a relieved smile. "Yeah, I could use some air."

Together, they crossed the bridge and headed for the park. By now, the lights were up and glowing, and most of the team had gathered at the picnic tables. The sight made Katy smile, a microcosm of the good will she'd been longing to create in her new town. So funny what a little nudging could do.

"MacBain, Conway, nice of you to join us," Gunnar called out. "Leave it to you two to show up when the work's nearly finished."

"Guess we're the smart ones," Katy said with a grin. She found her way to one of the tables and took a seat, then glanced around her at the transformation. "Looks fantastic, guys."

Nods and smiles appeared all around her, and she nearly chuckled at their pride. Where were those guys who got so up in arms about her fire pit? Not that she missed them, of course.

"Here you go, ladies." Skip Mason placed a bottle of water in front of each of them. "Join the party," he said with a wink.

Katy's whole body went clammy, and she dropped her

gaze to the ground. He's a good guy, she told herself.
Nothing to fear here. You're fine.

But the tension only pressed down harder, made her
head throb and her mouth go dry. She looked at the bottle of water, desperate for a sip, but knew there was just
no way. Lifting her eyes and forcing her mouth into a
smile, she scanned the group. They talked and laughed,
calling out to Matt as he lowered the bucket.

Seizing the moment, she took her bottle, opened it in
her lap, and then lowered it until its top stood even with
her knee. Glancing around one last time, she poured it
out, then closed it and put it back on the table. She stared
at the empty bottle and her body relaxed. Crisis averted.

"You want us to go get the fire pit, Chief?" Welles
asked, catching Katy's attention.

"No!" all the firefighters—and even Gretchen—said
in unison.

"That work of art is ours," Ike added in a growl.

"Yeah," Paul Higgins injected. "The campfires are
our community service."

"And if the Grange ladies try to have their own campfire here in the park," Ike went on, "they better make
sure they get a permit first." He suddenly grinned. "And
after we do a safety inspection on their pit, maybe we'll
write them one."

Raucous laughter broke out, echoing between the
trees. Katy joined in, once again thrilled that her fire pit
had become so inarguably theirs. As her head went back,
her eye caught Gunnar's, and the expression on his face
killed her mirth. He held her eye for several seconds,
then glanced, ever so slightly, at the empty bottle in front

of her. Finally, he looked away, every bit of the interest she'd just seen now erased.

It's not a crime to pour out water, she told herself, knowing deep down that had nothing to do with it.

At shift-change the next morning, Katy walked into chaos in the station kitchen. She stepped inside and found everyone clustered around the television, hooting and hollering like they'd discovered a second sun.

"What's going on?" she asked Welles, who stood nearest the door.

"Canada has a new island," he said and pointed to the television.

Katy frowned. Why was that such a big deal? She peered up at the TV, mystified by the fuss over an ordinary—albeit stunningly beautiful—blue-green land mass, teeming with lush flora and soaring mountain peaks. Then she saw the headline. This wasn't some re-named or reclaimed piece of land. Instead, according to the stunned newscasters, this island literally appeared in the center of James Bay in Canada, rising up out of the water overnight.

She smiled, realizing she was more in the loop than most. Of course. This was Atlantis. The rumors about Titus' plans were true. He'd actually done it, and he'd thrown the world on its ear in the process. Good for him, she thought, her grin widening.

And then it faded as Gunnar popped into her mind. She glanced around the kitchen, found him standing near the corner, his expression deep and unreadable. She waited for him to look at her, wanting to at least give him some sign of concern. How devastating it must be to know he could never go home again. She couldn't even imagine how she'd fall apart if Pine Creek suddenly disappeared.

When he finally looked her way, she tried to say all of that with her smile. He smiled back, looking a bit like he didn't quite get the joke, but maybe that had something to do with him cutting those ties—to the Oceanuses, to Nicholas, and to magic in general—a long time ago. Whatever the reason, he seemed to interpret her smile as an invitation, and he navigated through the others and made his way to her.

"Pretty crazy, huh?" he said, leaning casually against the wall.

"Depends on your perspective, I guess." Katy thought about giving him a wink, then thought better of it.

"So this doesn't surprise you?"

"Not especially. Does it surprise you?"

"As much as anyone, I guess."

"Got it." If he could downplay it, so could she.

He studied her for a moment, the quizzical look returning, and then it cleared. "So, I've been meaning to ask if I could go riding with you sometime."

Katy felt her eyes widen. Well that was a lovely idea. Why hadn't she thought of that? "I didn't know riding interested you."

"I happen to love horses."

Ahh. That make perfect sense. He might have to give up Atlantis, but he'd always be a mythical warrior. And what did warriors need? Horses.

In fact, she realized, maybe a renewed relationship

with horses might be his way of dealing with his other losses. He might have to give up some things, but he didn't have to give up everything.

"Gunnar Wolfe, I would be thrilled to take you riding," Katy said. "In fact, if you'd be willing to help me turn a young friend into a capable rider, there'll even be a kiss in it for ye."

His eyes widened, a bit like a kid getting his first glimpse of Christmas morning abundance, then he nodded like a bobblehead. Chuckling softly, she gave him her brightest smile, immensely pleased with the way things were shaping up. Not only did she get to spend time riding her beloved horse with this hunky man, she also got to help him hold on to his essence in the process.

Chapter Eleven

Gunnar peered up at Katy, painfully aware of how hard she was trying not to be amused at his compromised state. What a bust this adventure had been. And she'd planned such a lovely day, too, a chance for them to spend time together and, as fellow horse lovers, help Shiloh get over his fear of riding. And now, here they sat, Gunnar perched on one big rock with his injured leg stretched out on another, and Shiloh likely terrified of horses for life.

Of course, he had saved the boy, he told himself, hoping he'd looked pretty damn heroic doing so, leaping off his horse as it bucked and flailed and catching the kid in a tuck and roll right before he hit the ground. A slight shiver rolled across Gunnar's shoulders at the memory of that bear, how fierce the creature had looked and how quickly it appeared, barreling toward their little riding party in a rush of grumbly roars and glinting teeth. At least the horses' terror seemed to panic the bear, or at least made it rethink its plan and flee. Thank heaven for small—very small—favors.

But now, after the drama had passed and the horses had fled, even the kiss Katy offered as reward wasn't going to lighten his mood. Gunnar sighed heavily. His leg hurt like crazy, and they were stranded in the woods. A lovely day, indeed.

"The brats. We specifically train our horses not to desert their riders," she muttered as she gently probed his knee. "That's why I chose them for our trail ride today."

"You actually set up scenarios where a bear comes charging out of the woods at your horses so you can teach them to . . . what, go hide behind a tree until the coast is clear?" Gunnar arched a brow. "What I'm really interested in knowing is how you train the bear."

She stopped probing, and if she'd scowled like that when all hell had broken lose, they'd be halfway to Inglenook by now and the bear would have a wrenched knee. "It doesn't feel like anything's broken," she said, gesturing at his leg as she stood up.

Hell, he could have told her that. But he'd been hoping she would . . . do something to make it all better like she had his ribs two days ago, or better still, like she had Tux last week. Because he really wasn't looking forward to what he estimated was going to be a five-mile hike with a bum knee.

"I guess we might as well make ourselves comfortable until help arrives," she continued as she scanned the area. "Shiloh can gather some dry branches and I'll get a fire going before we lose the sun behind the mountain."

"Since there doesn't seem to be any cell phone service out here, can I assume you have a satellite phone in your pocket?"

She gave him a strange look, then rolled her eyes and picked up a nearby branch.

"Then may I ask how you plan to contact the help we're going to comfortably wait for?"

She apparently found that question more humorous than his first one. "Those bratty horses will do it for us." She arched a brow, outright mimicking him. "You think that when three riderless horses show up at Inglenook, someone's just going to take off their saddles and put them in their stalls?" She snorted. "Trust me; these woods will be crawling with men mounted on anything from horses to ATVs to boats scanning the shoreline within an hour. And both of Nova Mare's helicopters will be airborne within minutes of being called."

"Sorry to burst your bubble, but I heard one of the barn hands say those horses have been at Inglenook a sum total of six days, so they've probably not been this far out on the trails before. Who knows how far away whatever barn they know to run back to might be?"

Katy blinked at him, then hung her head. "Crap. That means it'll be after dark before anyone realizes we're missing." She hugged herself and glanced toward Shiloh. "I'm just sorry for putting Margo through the horror of spending all night wondering if her son's hurt."

"This isn't your fault, Katy," Gunnar drawled, deciding to borrow a line from Robert MacBain's book on parenting. "In fact, I say we blame the bear."

He saw her jaw slacken, and his grin widened when she spun on her heel and strode off.

Gunnar tucked his hands behind his head as he leaned back against the tree and watched her put Shiloh to work gathering dead branches, then closed his eyes on a sigh. Other than having a wrenched knee and Margo having to worry about her son, he kind of liked the idea of being stuck in the woods with Katy. Because it still got pretty chilly at night, and the best way he knew for two unprepared people to stay warm was to snuggle.

Okay, two and a half people. But even with the kid snuggled between them—which he didn't doubt Katy would insist on—Gunnar figured his arms were still long enough to make respectable contact.

He snapped open his eyes two minutes later when Katy dropped to her knees beside his leg. "Give me your knife and T-shirt," she ordered, holding out her hand.

"Why?" he asked, even as he reached down and unsheathed his multi-tool.

"Because we can't just sit here doing nothing all night." She snatched the tool out of his hand, then used it to gesture at him. "I need that shirt you're wearing under your fleece."

"Why?"

She opened the serrated blade. "To make a bandage for your knee."

He grabbed her hand as the knife descended toward his ankle. "Why?"

She sat back on her heels and took a calming breath. "Because Shiloh apparently watches a lot of nature shows, and he's not real keen on spending the night in a forest he knows for certain has bears. The kid's truly scared," she continued with a sad smile. "He's a house hermit, and before he moved here, the biggest patch of woods he'd been in was half an acre of scrub brush on an abandoned lot down the street from his house."

"So, you're expecting us to walk out of here?"

"We've still got about four hours of daylight and it can't be more than . . . what, two or three miles to In-glenook?"

"Try five." Dammit, he wanted to snuggle, not hike five miles up and down a mountain on a bum knee. If he rode out of here on an ATV, he'd be back in business in two days, tops. But if he had to hike out, his knee would be the size of a football tomorrow morning and he'd be laid up for a week.

She looked down at his knee, which already was swollen enough to show through his jeans, then looked up and—Christ, was that a gleam in her eyes?

"Man up, Wolfe. I'm sure you've been on much longer marches with significantly worse injuries when you were a . . . in your former life." She pulled her hand from under his, gestured at his chest with the knife, then grabbed the hem of his pant leg and pierced it with the blade. "If you're shy, I won't peek while you strip."

For the love of God, what freaking former life?

Gunnar unsnapped the buttons on his fleece and pulled it off over his head, grateful he hadn't tied it to his saddle when they'd stopped to let the horses drink. Because the only thing worse than hiking five miles with a bum knee would have been doing it half naked in Maine in the mountains in June.

Katy stopped slicing the pant leg, sat back on her heels, and looked around. "Shiloh," she called when she spotted the kid a few yards off the trail across from them. "Forget the firewood and try to find a fairly straight, stout branch that's about as long as Mr. Wolfe is tall." She glanced down and turned the multi-tool over in her hand, then looked in Shiloh's direction again. "If you can't find any you think would work as a hiking stick, then look around for a young tree about as thick as your wrist and I'll cut it down."

"We're gonna walk home?" Shiloh shouted, dropping his armful of branches and running to them. "So we won't have to sleep in the woods?"

"That we are," Katy said cheerily.

Gunnar saw the light leave Shiloh's eyes when the kid glanced at him then back at Katy. "But I thought Mr. Wolfe hurt his leg and can't walk. We . . . we can't just leave him out here all by himself with a bear around. It'll be dark before anyone can come get him."

"That's what the hiking stick is for, Shiloh. Mr. Wolfe is coming with us. It might take a bit longer, but we should still be home before dark."

Gunnar pulled off his T-shirt to cover his sigh, only to stop with it halfway over his head when he heard Katy say, again quite cheerily, "See that, Shiloh. You start spending more time outdoors, and when you grow up, you'll have a big broad chest just like Mr. Wolfe."

"So much for not peeking," Gunnar muttered from inside his shirt.

"Sorry," that still-cheery voice said. "I forgot."

He finished pulling off his shirt to see young Shiloh staring at his chest, the kid's eyes widened in . . . hell, he couldn't tell if the boy was impressed or horrified.

"Am I gonna have hair all over me like that, too?"

Nope, definitely not impressed. Gunnar drove his arms into both sleeves of his fleece, only to freeze with it halfway over his head when he heard, "If you're lucky you will," at the same time he felt the knife blade slicing his jeans precariously far up his thigh. "Because I happen to know that girls like boys with hair on their chests," she continued, giving Gunnar a wink when he finally popped his head out of the neck opening.

Lovely. Now the kid looked like he was about to puke. "You might not think what girls like is all that important right now," Gunnar said dryly as he snapped the snaps on his fleece, "but trust me, Mr. Fox, you will in a few years."

"So, how's that hiking stick coming along?" Katy asked.

Shiloh eyed Gunnar another couple of seconds, then turned away. "I'm gonna find myself one, too. And I think I'll have you whittle a point at the end of mine— no, on both of them," he mumbled as he headed a short distance down the path. "So me and Mr. Wolfe will be armed if that bear comes back."

"Does Margo know what a bad influence you are on her son?" Gunnar asked as Shiloh, still mumbling to himself, gave a sapling a little shake before moving to another one.

Katy glanced over her shoulder at the kid and smiled. "From what little I've spoken with Margo this last week, I got the impression part of the reason she left Arizona and, as Shiloh would say, 'dragged her son clear across the country almost all the way to Canada,' was to expose him to more outdoorsy, manly men."

"They don't have manly men in Arizona?"

"Not like we have here, according to Margo. She told me that after spending a few hours looking around town before her interview with Olivia, she was willing to do whatever it took to get that job." The hint of a gleam popped into those vivid gray eyes. "She also told me Shiloh wasn't the only reason she wanted to move to the land of handsome giants." She picked up the T-shirt. "Margo's been divorced for three years, and I get the impression she's lonely."

"So, Shiloh hasn't been around very many men since he was four?"

Katy looked up in surprise. "He'll be nine next month. And I think he used to visit his father . . . occasionally."

It was Gunnar's turn to be surprised. "Nine? Wait, how old is your nephew, Angus?"

"He just turned eight."

"But he's nearly half a foot taller and has to weigh twice what Shiloh does."

She snorted. "That's because Angus is a Highlander and Shiloh is . . ." She shrugged. "I'm guessing his mother's people aren't a brawny lot." She started cutting the T-shirt into wide strips. "I don't know what Shiloh's father looks like or how tall he is."

Gunnar took advantage of her being busy to do his own examination of his now exposed knee, gently poking and prodding and trying not to wince.

"It's going to be uncomfortable." She stopped shredding the T-shirt long enough to shoot him a crooked smile. "Okay, it's going to hurt like hell, but walking on it shouldn't do any more damage."

"Is that a professional diagnosis or a guess?"

She arched a brow. "Would you prefer to get a second opinion from Gretchen?"

"No offense," he muttered when she set down the

knife and gently lifted his knee. "But the only patient I've seen you work on seems to have mysteriously vanished. Or haven't you noticed Tux is missing?" He grinned when she looked up. "Maybe you should bring along your barn cats when you're training your horses not to run away."

Instead of the cute, sexy scowl he'd been going for, Katy merely rolled her eyes again. "Tux is a teenager. He didn't want to come to Spellbound Falls to live with Angus' fun aunt; he was looking for a new crop of girl cats to chase that he wasn't somehow related to." She started wrapping the material around his knee. "He'll turn up in a day or two and scoff down two pounds of food, sleep for five days, and be chasing girls again next week."

But then she sat back on her heels, her expression suddenly guarded. "What were you implying when you said Tux mysteriously vanished after I worked on him? Do you think he spends most of his time at your cabin because . . . I scare him?"

"Nah," Gunnar drawled. "He just likes that I dig out beer and popcorn when he comes over. So, am I going to live?" he asked, gesturing at his leg.

She studied him for several heartbeats, clearly trying to decide if she believed him or not, then turned her attention back to his knee without answering. Finally getting it trussed up to her satisfaction, she just as silently grabbed his multi-tool and got up and walked a couple of yards down the trail.

Gunnar decided not to broach the subject of Tux's miraculous recovery again—at least not in the foreseeable future.

Ten short minutes later, and with all three of them

heavily armed with pointy sticks, the ill-fated riding expedition turned hiking adventure was headed down the trail—which was uphill at the moment. Shiloh had insisted Katy also needed a sharpened stick, rushing to assure her it was only for backup in case one of theirs broke, because he and Mr. Wolfe would protect her if any more bears crossed their path. Or moose or bobcats or coyotes or raccoons—the latter being quite vicious, he'd explained to Gunnar, if they happened to be rabid.

Figuring a pointy stick could be just as lethal as a garden rake in Katy's hands, Gunnar didn't have the heart to tell Shiloh that if that bear showed its ugly face again, they would be hiding behind the nearest tree while Miss MacBain kicked its sorry ass.

But the kid's bravado had thankfully gotten Katy smiling again, as well as her shoulders shaking in silent laughter when Shiloh told her not to be afraid, that he'd be right behind her. She would be in the middle, he'd proclaimed, and Mr. Wolfe would be in front. Because, he'd informed Gunnar, in wolf packs the weakest wolves always took the lead and set the pace, so they wouldn't fall behind without the others noticing—only to point out to Katy that he'd just made a joke because Mr. Wolfe was injured.

But the pace Gunnar set was apparently too slow, as Katy called a halt to the forced march less than an hour later. He immediately stopped, not about to argue when he saw the trail rose steeply up ahead.

"Okay, this isn't working," Katy said as she guided him over to the edge of the trail. "Sit," she ordered, all but shoving him onto a low boulder. She dropped to her knees in front of his legs, the left one fully exposed since he'd cut off the flapping material from where she'd thankfully stopped slicing halfway up his thigh. "Your limp has been getting progressively worse," she continued, partially unwrapping the bandage and pressing her finger to the engorged flesh above his kneecap, then watching its reaction. "You're blowing up like a balloon."

"Yeah," he agreed, glancing back then leaning against the tree behind the boulder. "Wrenched knees have a tendency to do that when you ignore their screams."

She lifted her gaze to his, her eyes distressed. "I'm sorry, I know it hurts. But I don't know what else to do." A hint of a smile suddenly lifted one side of her lovely mouth. "If you were ten pounds lighter, I could probably piggyback you out."

He reached up and slowly unsnapped his fleece while holding eye contact, glad to have her smiling at him again. "I'm pretty sure I could shed ten pounds if I stripped off."

She slapped a hand over his with a laugh. "But you'll gain twenty pounds of blackflies piggybacking on you the minute they see your big, broad, naked—"

"I sure am thirsty," Shiloh said, hopping up on the boulder beside Gunnar.

Katy pulled her hand away, plopped down on the ground with her back to them, and stretched her legs out in front of her, then slowly rolled her feet with a groan. "Riding boots are not designed for walking." She glanced over her shoulder at Shiloh. "We could all use a drink. I'll go see if I can find a nearby source of water in a minute."

Gunnar would rather she found a nearby source of beer.

"We can't drink out of a stream," Shiloh said. "It could have bacteria in it that'll give us diarrhea. Or it could have gra . . . giar . . ." He looked at Gunnar. "It could have a parasite that comes from beavers and other animals pooping in the water." He looked at Katy again. "We can only drink from a spring, and then only from where it bubbles out of the ground."

Gunnar wanted to know if there was a reason the kid always looked at him when he was explaining something.

"It's giardia," Katy said, rolling to her knees and standing up. "And I promise to find us a nice clean spring, hopefully close by."

"Or," Gunnar said, "you and Shiloh could find that spring on your way to Inglenook, while I have a little nap waiting for you to come back and get me—preferably on something that has four wheels and isn't afraid of bears."

"But you can't stay here all by yourself," Shiloh said in alarm. "It's gonna get dark soon. Do you know how many predators come out at night to hunt?"

Okay, the kid really had to stop watching nature shows and spend more time actually in nature. Although Gunnar guessed having a real live bear charge out of the woods at them more or less reinforced those television-induced fears.

He noticed Katy wasn't voicing an opinion, instead scanning the trail in both directions before plopping down on the ground again with a heavy sigh. "I've been half expecting we'd come across the horses by now." Her gaze darted between Shiloh and Gunnar, until she suddenly threw back her shoulders. "Okay, Mr. Fox," she said brightly, belying the worry Gunnar could still see in her eyes. "I think it's time we call on some divine help. So why don't you ask that big shiny angel of yours what we should do."

Shiloh gasped hard enough that he nearly fell off the rock. "Katy," he hissed, darting a quick glance at Gunnar before leaning forward. "You promised not to tell."

"It's okay. Mr. Wolfe is one of us. Go on," she added with a nod. "Ask your buddy if he knows of a clean spring nearby, and if we should leave Mr. Wolfe here or press on together."

One of us, Gunnar silently repeated. One of us what?

"He can see angels, too?" Shiloh whispered, eyeing Gunnar suspiciously out of the corner of his eye. "Then tell him to let me see his."

Katy blinked, clearly flummoxed. "I . . . I'm not sure mythical warriors even have angels, because . . ." She shrugged. "Because they're mythical." She looked at Gunnar. "Do you have a guardian angel, Mr. Wolfe?"

Well, damn. "I, ah, have always assumed I do."

"I don't even know what a mythical warrior is," Shiloh whispered.

Hell, neither did he.

He did have a firm rule about not lying to kids, though, even for the sake of calming their fears. He could be an ass to adults because they usually deserved it, but kids . . . well, one, they never forgot—or forgave— an adult who lied to them, and two, they deserved better. Besides, kids usually handled the truth better than adults. Instead of wallowing in worry, the not-yet-jaded little optimists often started looking for silver linings— and usually found them.

"Have you ever heard of the lost island of Atlantis,

Shiloh?" Katy asked, apparently deciding to further compound her lie.

The kid gasped again. "I just saw it on the news! Only it's not lost anymore because they found it yesterday morning. Mom got me out of bed to watch what everyone is calling a historical event."

More like hysterical, Gunnar was thinking.

"The newscaster said a huge land mass the size of Rhode Island," Shiloh continued, "just suddenly appeared right in the middle of James Bay overnight." He stopped and looked at Gunnar. "That's in Canada, at the bottom of the Hudson Bay." He looked at Katy again and frowned. "All the scientists are baffled because there wasn't even an earthquake that would have made it rise up from the ocean floor." He leaned forward again. "You know, like the one that happened here five years ago," he whispered, "and moved all the mountains and turned Bottomless Lake into a sea."

Gunnar inwardly snorted. Another hysterical event that still had scientists baffled. But at least there'd been an earthquake to account for the mountains . . . moving.

"Geologists from all over the world went to see the land mass," Shiloh continued, "and last night, the news showed a video they took of all the towns and villages they found scattered all over the island. There was even a palace. They said the buildings looked like they were being lived in up until about a year ago but that it appeared the people just left for no reason. They're saying that even though there's an advanced infrastructure—" He stopped and looked at Gunnar. "That's the roads and water and sewer systems and stuff."

Hell, maybe the kid felt hairy chests and intelligence

were mutually exclusive. "Thank you for explaining that."

Shiloh looked back at Katy. "Anyway, they said it seemed like an advanced civilization even though they didn't have electricity or any modern technology, but in other ways, it appeared ancient. In fact, the scientists think that carbon dating—"

He stopped again but Gunnar held up his hand. "Thanks, but I actually know what carbon dating is," he drawled.

Shiloh shot him a scowl then looked at Katy. "They think carbon dating is going to show that the buildings are thousands of years old, and that's why people started calling the place Atlantis." He frowned. "But what's that got to do with Mr. Wolfe being a mythical warrior?"

Gunnar caught himself actually leaning forward in anticipation.

"Because Mr. Wolfe is from Atlantis," she said, beaming Gunnar a bright smile.

That was the island in the northern Atlantic she kept talking about? Wait. So, did that mean the former life she kept talking about was him being a mythical warrior?

"It's okay if Shiloh knows your secret," she assured Gunnar. "He can see and talk to angels, and you used to travel through time and kill demons with your sword."

Yeah, well, he hoped the kid didn't want to see his sword, because he couldn't for the life of him remember where he'd left it. And if he could travel through time, then why wasn't he zapping back to . . . oh, three hours ago and killing that demon bear with his sword? He cocked his head at Katy. "You told Shiloh I was one of you. So, what's your magical claim to fame?"

That made her smile vanish and her gaze drop to her lap.

"Katy sees other stuff," Shiloh piped up, only to frown at her again. "But the day we met on the plane, you never told me what you see."

"I see . . . I can see what's wrong with people," she murmured.

"You mean you can see their auras?" Shiloh said. "Like if they're sick, the energy around them looks all angry and red or something?"

"No, I can see—in my mind—exactly where they're injured." She looked directly at Gunnar, her chin rising defensively. "And because I'm trained as a paramedic, I can help them."

That was a big, bold . . . half-truth if he ever heard one.

Then again, it was her lie, so he guessed the woman was entitled to make it as outrageous as she wanted. The only thing he couldn't figure out was why she'd started telling it to Shiloh over a week ago on the plane. Well, unless she hadn't wanted to hurt the boy's feelings when he'd told her he could see and talk to angels.

So, did he break his rule about not lying to kids and play along, or did he . . . what? Destroy Shiloh and Katy's budding friendship, which the boy obviously needed? That wouldn't exactly advance his relationship with Katy, now would it?

"So how come you don't just look in your mind to see what's wrong with Mr. Wolfe's knee and fix it?" Shiloh asked. "Then he won't hurt, and we can get out of the woods quicker."

"I did look," Katy said. "And because his knee is only bruised, there's really nothing for me to do. Our bodies are quite good at healing themselves, Shiloh, and I've discovered that sometimes it's better not to interfere." She looked at Gunnar again, her eyes lighting up like a fogbank at sunrise. "And sometimes all it takes is a kiss."

Gunnar dropped his gaze to her mouth. Dammit, he didn't know if she was talking about her reviving Tux or the kiss she'd promised to give him for saving Shiloh. Hell, forget dodging and darting down the trail chasing a leaf; if Katy kissed him right now, he could probably fly the three of them back to Inglenook just like Superman—another hero of mythical proportions.

Okay; he might finally be getting a handle on Miss Katherine MacBain, in that she was a beautiful, capable, compassionate, and occasionally avenging angel and a beautiful, lying, flirtatious enchantress. And he liked that. In fact, the next time Robert MacBain was in town, he just might ask the man for permission to date both of her.

Suddenly, Shiloh gasped so hard Gunnar had to catch the kid from tumbling off the rock. "Look at that," Shiloh whisper-shouted, pointing up the trail before Gunnar had even finished righting him. "That's a bald eagle."

Katy turned to look and also gasped.

Gunnar straightened and peered ahead, seeing what was definitely a bald eagle perched as bold as brass in the center of the trail not fifty yards from them. Hands down the largest bird he'd ever seen, Gunnar's body stilled in the creature's magnificent presence. Every detail of the eagle's body seemed to stand out—majestic mahogany feathers; crisp white head; sharp, all-knowing, ebony gaze—in a way that permitted only veneration and respect.

He sighed when he heard Katy whisper in awe, "Evan's eagle," only to frown when she scrambled to her feet without taking her eyes off the bird and said, "Ohmigod, it's him."

She looked at Gunnar and beamed him another big bright smile. "It's Telos." But then she scowled. "Telos?" she repeated. She slid her gaze to Shiloh, who was still staring at the eagle, then back to Gunnar. "Our new mythical god?" she whispered. "Oh," she huffed more than said, turning to face up the trail. "I swear sometimes you look at me like you don't have a clue what I'm talking about."

That was because most of the time he didn't.

The scary—if slightly disturbing—thing was, that's probably what he liked most about her. Because he'd much rather be confused by all her talk of mythical islands and warriors and gods than be bored to death rehashing celebrity gossip, critiquing fashion trends, and fending off tedious attempts to get him to talk about himself. Yeah. How could he not like a woman who simply made up an entire identity for him that she liked?

God, he'd love to spend a few hours inside that creative mind of hers.

"Do you think it's hurt?" Shiloh whispered as he stared at the bird staring back at them. "It's not common for eagles to be on the ground when they've got all these trees to perch in, unless they're after prey. Did you see where he came from?" he continued, looking up at the treetops then over at Gunnar.

"No," Gunnar said, also scanning the treetops. He reached out when Shiloh started to slide off his rock. "Stay here," he gently ordered, remembering Evan's eagle had actually tried to grab the kid. "Katy," he added firmly when she slowly walked toward the bird.

"It's okay," she said without looking back. "The only times I've heard of Telos showing up is when people are in some sort of trouble, so he must be here to help us."

Oh, for the love of— "Okay, enough," Gunnar said, the edge in his voice making Katy stop and turn and blink at him. "The sooner you and Shiloh get going, the less time I'll have to sit here fighting off blackflies and mosquitos." He nudged Shiloh off the rock. "And thanks to the—to Telos," he added with a tight grin at Katy before looking at Shiloh, "I won't be alone." He set his walking stick across his thighs. "And if any bears or rabid raccoons come sniffing around, I'll be well armed."

Including the small pistol he had strapped, thankfully, to his right ankle.

"But—" Katy started.

"No buts," Gunnar said, cutting her off. "Unless your eagle buddy can fly the three of us out of here on its back, the two people who can walk out will, then send someone back to get the person who can't."

Now what in hell was she smiling at? Didn't she realize he had just taken over her little misadventure?

"Hey." Shiloh moved to stand between them and shot Gunnar a glare. The kid obviously realized what was going on and obviously did not like it. "Katy's in charge of this trail ride because she knows what she's doing."

Gunnar arched a brow to keep from grinning. Hell, the kid held his stick like he intended to take a swing at him. "This stopped being a trail ride," he drawled, curious to see what the boy would do, "the moment we found ourselves walking."

"It's okay, Shiloh," Katy said with a laugh, walking up and turning the still glaring boy around to face her. "Mr. Wolfe is just doing what mythical warriors do when circumstances turn dire, which is to get all manly and bossy." Gunnar saw her eyes take on a sparkle as she smiled down at Shiloh. "Exactly like you did just now. Thank you for defending me."

She leaned away slightly while still holding the kid's shoulders and slowly moved him back and forth as she gave him a visual inspection. "Why, Mr. Fox, I do believe your chest just grew an inch broader," she said, laughing again when Shiloh snapped his head down to look at himself.

Katy started up the trail. "Come on, my little warrior. You can look for chest hairs when you put on your pajamas tonight." She turned and walked backward, making sure Shiloh followed, then actually saluted Gunnar. "We'll get right on that, big warrior sir." She suddenly stopped, and even from twenty yards away, he could see the gleam in her eyes. "Should I have SFF&R make the rescue? I hear Gretchen is covering Ray Strout's shift today."

"Just bring something to eat when you come back to get me. On an ATV," Gunnar added in his best mythical warrior voice. "And also grab the small insulated bag out of my truck." He shot her a grin. "If you make it back here before the mosquitos come out, I might even reward you with a beer."

Katy's gaze dropped to his mouth and her cheeks flushed a lovely pink. "Yes, sir," she said rather huskily, giving him another salute as she caught hold of Shiloh's hand and started jogging up the trail.

When the eagle saw them headed its way, it turned
while spreading its massive wings and took to the air
with a whistled screech, then flew up the trail about ten
feet above the ground ahead of Katy and Shiloh—the
boy still carrying his stick, Gunnar noticed.

He leaned back against the tree with a sigh of relief
and studied his definitely ballooning knee. Yup, letting
Katy be in charge was going to cost him at least two days
on crutches and a week of hobbling around like an old
man. But he really hadn't wanted to steal her thunder,
figuring she had enough take-charge men in her life already. Besides, it had been kind of nice being mothered
by someone other than Aunt May. And although he'd had
a lot of women wanting to kiss him for a lot of reasons,
he'd never had one offer to kiss him for being a hero.
Apparently, some Scots females didn't know what century they lived in, either.

Gunnar twisted to scan the woods behind him. When
Katy returned without Shiloh, maybe after they
shared a couple of beers and he got his kiss . . . well, maybe
the ATV wouldn't start when they were ready to head back.

Did Katy know anything about small engines, such as
that fuel lines had shutoffs? Or that spark plug wires
needed to be attached to the spark plug for the engine to
run? Hell, maybe he'd show Miss MacBain she wasn't
the only one who could bring something back to life
when he helped the ATV miraculously recover—in the
morning, after a night of snuggling.

Well, assuming they made it through dusk. Because
even worse than hiking five miles on a bum knee half
naked in Maine in June in the mountains was getting

stuck outdoors anywhere in Maine in June, July, and August at sunset. Hell, even after buying his own screening and duct-taping it on the inside of his cabin windows, he still found himself itching in places he couldn't scratch in public.

But the bloodsucking little bastards usually disappeared once it was fully dark, so if he kept a smudge going until then, he should be free to focus on Katy the rest of the night.

Gunnar perked up when he caught the sound of muted footsteps pounding toward him and wondered if maybe they'd found the horses, then slumped back against the tree when he spotted Katy and Shiloh and no horses running down the hill, only to perk up again when he figured they'd left the giant scaredy-cats tied to a tree.

But then he slumped again with a sigh, realizing they would have brought at least one horse with them, so he wouldn't have to walk up the goddamn hill.

"The eagle told us what to do!" Shiloh shouted as he barely avoided ramming into Katy when she stopped in front of Gunnar. "We're going . . . to the fjord," the boy continued in huffs and puffs, "so we . . . can flag down a boat!"

"The eagle told you," Gunnar repeated to Katy, watching her already flushed face darken.

"He didn't really talk to us," Shiloh said, his gaze darting between them before landing on Gunnar. "He just wouldn't let us . . . go past the turnoff to the trail." The boy took a deep breath. "He was perched on a signpost that said it's point-two-five miles to the fjord. That's a quarter of a mile," he thoughtfully explained. "And every time we tried to keep going on the regular trail, the eagle spread its wings and hissed at us." He grinned proudly. "Then Katy remembered the fjord is busy in the afternoons with tour boats and fishermen and scientists and stuff, and she thinks we can flag down one of them and see if they'll take us to Inglenook."

"How far is the trail from here?" Gunnar asked.

Shiloh frowned up at Katy.

"Maybe a quarter of a mile," she said with a shrug.

"So, on the advice of an eagle, you think I should hobble a quarter of a mile up a hill and a quarter of a mile down a trail to the fjord so we can flag down a boat that may or may not pass by close enough to see or hear us?"

She canted her head as though trying to read his mood. "That's the plan," she said quietly. "And fishermen usually troll close to the shoreline, and this is about the time of day they start making their way back to the marina."

"Then we need to get going," Shiloh said, starting up the trail walking backward. "It's gonna take us a while because you can't run, and we don't want to miss any of them."

"Is it that you don't trust Telos because he's a modern mythical god?" Katy asked once Shiloh was out of earshot.

No, it's because if we do flag down a boat, then I won't be spending the night with you. Gunnar slid off the boulder with a heavy sigh to keep from groaning the moment he put weight on his knee. He shot Katy his best manly warrior grin and began hobbling up the hill—partly because he couldn't bring himself to disappoint her, but mostly because the moment she and Shiloh were occupied watching for passing fishermen, that goddamn eagle was getting a well-aimed rock upside its mythical head.

Chapter Twelve

Having been deposited safely back at his cabin, Gunnar stood at his door and watched Katy walk toward him after parking her truck. He resisted the urge to pucker up in advance. She owed him a kiss, and even if she'd forgotten, he wasn't above a gentle reminder. Who could blame him? She was an extraordinary woman and, as he'd learned today, definitely someone to lean on in a crisis. Of course, she was also a complicated woman from a complicated family and being with her simultaneously set him on fire and made him feel like he'd bitten off more than he could chew.

What, he wondered, was the clan rule if one of their women decided she was interested in a particular man? Did she have to ask her family for permission to see him? And if they said no, what were the consequences if she went after the guy anyway?

Then again, shouldn't she have to ask the guy's family for permission?

Gunnar inwardly grinned, picturing that particular conversation between Katy and Aunt May. Though he'd never in his life considered his aunt an underdog in any situation, it was possible he'd finally met someone who could at least give her a run for her money. But then he sobered at the realization that, even though the outdated concept of obtaining permission to date was no longer the norm in modern societies, it probably should be. Because Lord knows, if even one family member wasn't on board with a loved-one's choice of mates, they could make life pretty miserable for the couple.

Hell, nearly all the fights he'd overheard between his parents had eventually turned to his father once again proving his mother's family right in that Ivan Wolfe would destroy all her dreams. It had taken exactly eight years and nine months for them to get Irene to smarten up and move back to Copenhagen—without the reason for her hasty marriage. Body tightening at the appearance of his unpleasant family baggage, Gunnar forced his mind to abandon the load and, instead, focus on the gorgeous woman before him and the much-desired boon she now owed him.

"Am I going to have three burly Scots paying me a visit the minute they find out you kissed me?" he asked, stifling another grin when Katy's jaw slackened.

But then he saw the moon reflecting off one of those here-it-comes gleams. "Scare ye, do they, Mr. Wolfe?" she said in an impressively thick brogue.

He snorted, even as he cocked his head at her. "Do they scare you?"

He'd thought to make her laugh, but she looked out at Bottomless and sighed. "They certainly try." She looked back at him, her expression serious. "If you were to find yourself interested in a girl, would a little male posturing chase you off?"

"Near as I can tell," he said with a chuckle, "there's nothing little about your family, at least not your men and horses. Jake Sheppard, however," he added, not about to waste an opportunity to throw the bastard under the bus, "asked Niall for permission to date you."

That lovely, shapely jaw slackened again, just before she covered her face with her hands and hung her head with a groan. "That is so embarrassing."

"Really?" he drawled, making her look up. "You don't think having your cousins warning off potential boyfriends saves you a lot of trouble?"

"How?"

"By weeding out the weaklings." He arched a brow. "Unless you're attracted to men who scare easily."

"Which brings me back to my question; would you change your mind if a woman you were interested in happened to have a family full of intimidating men?"

"I guess that would depend on whether or not they intimidate her."

Her jaw slackened again. "Huh?"

"Do the men in your family scare you, Katy?"

That got him an outright laugh. "Not since I was eight and thought I'd never see the light of day again when my best friend and I got caught beating up Jason Biggs for calling Cindy Pace four-eyes. Jane had to say two whole nine-day novenas and missed the town Easter egg hunt."

"And what was your punishment?" he asked, since

Jane had already told him this tale, quite adamantly declaring it had been Katy's idea to teach the boy a lesson for tormenting their friend.

The gleam returned. "That was the day I learned how hard it is for a papa to punish a daughter he's proud of. I got a ten-minute lecture on beating up boys, a twenty-minute lecture on getting caught doing it, and an hour lesson on how to lay a proper ambush." She chuckled. "To this day, Jane still tries to play the guilt card for my getting off easy whenever we have an argument." But then she sighed. "My little transgression may still come back and haunt me, though, since Jason Biggs now lives in Turtleback Station and is one of the county deputy sheriffs who patrol this area."

"Our childhood transgressions do like to come back and bite us on the ass. So, I'm still waiting for your answer," Gunnar continued when he saw her move closer. "If you were interested in a man, would you be expected to ask your watchdogs if it was okay to date him?"

She apparently needed a moment to ponder his question as she wrapped her arms around his neck and leaned into him. "Probably, once I was certain he was worth the trouble my asking them was going to cause."

Gunnar in turn slipped his arms around her waist and loosely rested his hands on her lovely backside. "And how would you know he was worth it?"

"Oh, it's amazing what a woman can learn from a kiss," she said, that gleam dropping to his mouth. "Like if the guy is equally interested in her, if he's a giver or a taker, and even if he's . . . modern-minded enough to let her be herself."

"You can learn all that from a kiss?"

She nodded, her gaze still fixed on his mouth. "As well as one more important thing." Those eyes lifted to his and that gleam now burned with an intensity that compelled Gunnar to slightly widen his stance. "She can get a good idea of what kind of lover he'll be," she added in a whisper, just before she kissed him.

Finally, gently, blissfully, their lips came together. Soft skin met soft skin, pressing lightly at first, until the heat between them erupted into a delectable dance of teasing pressure, a dance led by Katy alone. He gasped, surprised by all of it, how good it felt, how hard it was to stop, and how terrifyingly awed and hungry he'd become.

Stunned, Gunnar realized he didn't know what to do. He knew what he wanted to do, but he was pretty sure sweeping Katy off her feet and carrying her into his cabin was premature. Hell, he didn't even dare take over the kiss for fear he'd mess up and never get her naked beneath him.

But wasn't he auditioning for the role of lover right now?

She broke contact—something he knew he could not have done—and leaned slightly away. "I'm sorry," she murmured, her eyes glinting in the moonlight as they locked on his. "Have I shocked your ancient warrior sensibilities with my forwardness?"

What the— Shiloh was safely tucked in his bed at home, so why was she still going on with her lie? Except she'd started talking about his former life six days ago, at the campfire. Instead of an airhead, was Katy touched in the head? Surely Maine gave its paramedics mental evaluations before letting them anywhere near people with pointy scissors and sharp need—

Oh. Wait. He got it. Rather than being delusional,

Miss MacBain obviously had a thing for sword-wielding mythical warriors from Atlantis. So who was he to rain on her fantasy? Hell, he'd just spent the last five weeks chasing halfway around the world after an angel.

And hey, it could be worse; she could have been into candlestick makers.

Gunnar lowered one hand to the small of her back and his other hand to her head and molded her body to his, then finally fulfilled his five-month-long fantasy by taking possession of her mouth. Her response was immediate and so filled with the promise of passion that he'd swear he felt the ground shift beneath his feet.

Deciding the time had come, Gunnar gathered Katy up in his arms, painful knee be damned, and took her into the cabin. He kissed her as he walked, unable to stand being away from her lips for even a few seconds. She reached up and caressed the back of his neck, her fingertips like white-hot rose petals. His desire surged, and his pace quickened. The sooner he got this woman to his bed, the better.

Laying her down as gracefully as he could manage, Gunnar stepped back and looked at her. As he watched, she loosened her braid and shook out her magnificent hair. His chest tightened, made him feel like he could either look at her or breathe, but not both. How, how, had he ended up with this stunning woman?

As if determined to drive him over the edge, Katy reached down, grabbed the hem of her T-shirt, and pulled it up over her head. Her pink lacy bra, maddeningly demure, accented breasts he was pretty sure didn't need accenting. With a slow smile, she reached behind her and unhooked the clasp, then slowly pulled the bra up and away.

Gunnar literally felt his body temperature rise, each degree ratcheting his passion into unbearable levels. With a deep groan, he tore off his clothes and lowered himself to the bed. Lining his body perfectly with hers, he gently pressed himself on top of her, the feel of her beneath him more exquisite than he could have imagined.

"You're so beautiful," he whispered and pulled his head up slightly to look directly into her eyes. What he saw stopped his heart.

Beneath him, Katy looked so panicked and desperate his first thought was that his body weight crushed her. "I'm so sorry," he gasped and rolled to her side. "You probably need to breathe."

She shook her head, shook it again and again as she scrambled off the bed. "No," she whispered, one arm shielding her body as she searched the floor for her clothes. "No, no. No, no, no . . ."

"Katy, what is it? I'm sorry." Concern and confusion played tug-of-war with his body, made him want to reach out and give her space at the same time. He sat up, then sat perfectly still, afraid to do or say anything at all.

"No . . . I'm sorry," she said, turning away to put on her bra and fight her way into her T-shirt. She turned back to him, shirt inside out and stripes askew, her eyes so full of despair he nearly leapt up and wrapped her in a hug.

But that, he knew—the only thing he knew in this moment—would have been the biggest mistake imaginable. He scooted a little closer to the edge of the bed, so desperate to understand, but she stiffened and ran to the door.

"I'm so sorry, Gunnar," she said, voice spreading

through the room like the clearest, loneliest bell he'd ever heard. And then, before the echo had even faded, she was gone.

He stared at the door, body stiff and hollow and awkward, like the moment right after a car accident, when nothing seems completely real and you wish you could back up the clock and look for signs of trouble or turn right instead of left.

Or maybe just not get in the car at all.

Chapter Thirteen

Katy ran, up mountains and down. She lifted weights, more reps than she'd ever attempted before. Then she ran some more. No matter what she did, the picture of Gunnar's shocked, disappointed, beautifully passionate face would not leave her mind. She couldn't stop seeing his eyes, the way they'd glowed with a cascade of emotions—desire, then surprise, then despair—superimposed over every single thing she'd tried to look at since.

What the hell was the matter with her? Not only was he very likely The One, but even if she was wrong about that particular life-altering detail, he was, hands down, the hottest, most desirable, most intriguing man she'd ever met. He looked good, he smelled good, he tasted good, and he wanted her, maybe even more than she wanted him. Most women would run like crazy into the arms of a man like Gunnar Wolfe. But not her. Not now.

She pulled up short, pausing her third run of the day, and pushed the sweat up and away from her forehead. Reaching into the pocket of her Gore-Tex hoodie for a tissue, her hand found something else instead. She sighed as her fingers closed around the cool, compact canister. Mace. Her new, won't-leave-home-without-it running buddy. And, she realized, the clearest possible sign she'd changed, and not for the better.

She clutched the canister tighter, the word *change* spinning round and round in her brain like an actual mace, wounding and maiming from within. Dark waves of emotion washed over her—weeks of panic and helplessness ignored and left to fester—leaving a thick, inky residue in its wake. Though she'd denied him access so many times before, Brandon Fontanne's face pushed through her mind like a battering ram, hateful and ugly and entitled. Katy nearly vomited, hearing his voice like he once again lay over her, like he'd come again to take her body for himself. Her arms and legs burned anew, a skin and muscle memory of torture and bondage, and all she wanted to do was run.

Before she even decided where she was going, her feet took off. Her legs pumped hard, steering her out of the woods and into town. She registered nothing but the few feet in front of her toes, enjoying the rush of each well-earned breath and falling into the rhythm of her own steps. And then, just as quickly, the rhythm stopped.

She looked up, then bit her lip, uncertain whether to laugh or cry. Across the street, the women's crisis center building beckoned, its tall, rounded windows gazing at her like the eyes of an understanding friend. Apparently it was time to talk to someone and, apparently, that someone was Birch Callahan.

Katy started across the street, then pulled her feet back to the curb. This was a mistake. Birch was a friend, yes, but she was also family. Niall's wife, for all intents and purposes. And everyone knew that husbands and wives talked, even when they weren't supposed to. That was the last thing she needed, to be the subject of cozy pillow talk between her confidante and her overprotective Highlander of a cousin. She'd be hog-tied and carted home to her parents' house before she could say boo, and it would be completely her own fault.

No, that wouldn't do.

She shoved her hands in her pockets, ready to unleash a fresh round of determination, when her fingers came up against that Mace yet again. The tears came hard this time, like she'd used the can on herself by accident. She never used to carry props. No need, what with her father's painstaking self-defense training. She used to be enough, all on her own. She used to call her own shots, seize the moment—romantic or otherwise—and she never worried about who might be out there, waiting to harm her.

"You need some help, sweetie?"

Katy stiffened, skin bristling at the thought of being noticed, of being seen in such a state. She swatted at her damp cheeks, knowing she was only making the redness worse, then turned to face the owner of the voice.

A pair of fierce hazel eyes stared back at her, their olive tones intensified by a knit hat of the same color. Though her hair shone like sterling silver, had she tucked it all under the hat, Katy would have easily believed her much younger. They stared at each other for several long seconds, Katy's lips growing dry and unwieldy as the hazel eyes pressed harder for an answer.

Finally, the woman stepped closer. "What's wrong? Did something happen to you?"

Katy's chest started to ache, like someone had actually reached inside and yanked her heart right out. This was not good. Not at all. Literally anyone could glance out a window right now and see the town's newest paramedic losing it on the sidewalk.

"I'm good," she managed and then found what she knew to be the least believable smile of her entire life. "Just pushed myself a little too far on my run. My feet got away from me."

The woman nodded, brows high, exactly the way every mother on the planet nodded at a child's tall tales. "Did you now?" she said and then leaned her head forward like she had a secret. "If running makes you cry, maybe it's not the thing for you."

A chuckle bubbled up, its lightness such a welcome surprise. "I actually love running," Katy said. "Sometimes my thoughts get away from me, though."

The woman nodded and gave a chuckle of her own. "That happens to me even when I'm not running."

Katy felt her smile bloom, and her breathing came a little easier. Maybe the storm had passed for now. "Thanks for checking on me," she told the woman. "I don't want to keep you."

"Can't keep someone with no plans whatsoever."

"You must have been on your way to something."

"Not really. I just got to town, was doing a little exploring." The woman peered at her closely. "Could you point me to the nearest coffee shop? If I don't get a dose of caffeine every few hours, I'm a bit of a bear."

Katy grinned, not sure why she suddenly felt so relaxed but grateful just the same. "The Drunken Moose is just up the block. Definitely the best coffee in town. Amazing cinnamon buns, too."

The woman's rosy cheeks seemed to brighten. "Now I know why we ran into each other. I might have torn up the town if I went without my mid-morning latte. Care to join me?"

Katy's hackles rose a little, pushing her peace just out of reach. It was probably best for everyone if she spent the day alone. "Thanks, but I've already had all the coffee I need for now."

The woman nodded. "I'm sorry," she said. "Leave it to me to assume everyone else's day is as wide open as mine."

"Oh, my day's open," Katy blurted, then immediately bit down on her lip before she did any more damage. Smooth move, dummy. "I mean, I don't have to work or anything. I should probably get a shower, run some errands, that kind of thing."

The woman stared at her, long and hard. Her eyes reminded Katy of barcode scanners, able to pull up every one of her pertinent details in the quickest flash. The thought made her shudder, and she zipped her hoodie all the way to her chin.

"What's your name, dear?" the woman said as she linked her arm through Katy's and started walking.

"Um . . . Katy."

"You can call me Mayme," she said and set their pace

as they moved up the sidewalk. "I don't need coffee this very minute. Let's walk a bit."

Katy blinked, over and over, as she walked. What just happened? How was she suddenly strolling arm in arm with a total stranger?

"You know this town well?" Mayme asked.

"Pretty well. I grew up just down the road, a place called Pine Creek."

"Lucky you."

Katy sighed. Whether she felt it or not at the moment, her blessings column was still way longer than that of her curses. "I am lucky for sure."

Mayme patted her arm. "How refreshing; a young person who understands gratitude."

"What can I say? I was raised well."

"That much I can tell."

Katy couldn't keep her head from shaking. Why wasn't she taking control of this situation? Why couldn't she manage a polite exit? The woman was nice, sure, but she had plenty of nice people in her life.

"I can also tell that something's upsetting you."

Katy's feet halted, tugging Mayme's arm and making her stop, too. "I think I need to go," she said. That's it. No more chatting with strangers.

Mayme pulled on their clasped arms and set them in motion again. "Talking helps. Denial hurts."

"I'm not denying anything."

Mayme gave a purposeful side-eye. "Lying does even more damage than denial."

Katy chewed her lip. This was crazy. "Do you always talk to people you don't know this way?"

"I don't always do anything." The woman tightened her grip on Katy's arm. "I do whatever the situation requires."

"So, I'm a situation?"

"I think you're in a situation."

Katy frowned. "That's one way to put it."

Their feet stopped again, this time at Mayme's insistence. She turned and faced Katy, eyes bright and knowing. "I cannot force you to do anything, Katy, but I do feel compelled to speak when I see a potential problem. Whatever's wreaking havoc within must come out. If you allow it to stay hidden, it will snuff out your gorgeous light and create roadblocks in your life."

Katy's blinking began again, this time battling a fresh wave of tears. Who was this woman? And how did she know so much?

Mayme squeezed her hand. "It doesn't have to be me, dear. Just choose someone and set your pain free."

Something snapped in Katy's chest, loud enough, it seemed, for her to expect another question of concern. But the woman just studied her and waited, a peaceful smile on her face, as a strange, swirling pressure swelled under Katy's ribs. For a second, fear washed over her, like Mayme's warning had triggered action, like her light was already about to be snuffed. She pushed the panic back with a wave of deep breaths and looked right into Mayme's eyes.

"Okay," she said. "Okay, okay, okay."

"Good choice." Mayme patted her arm and then extricated herself and stepped away. "Now I need that coffee."

Katy's mouth fell open. This had to be the strangest

conversation of her life, and that was coming from the daughter of an ancient Highlander.

"Go find that someone, Katy. Don't wait. Don't give the pain any more of your time."

There were no words. She could only nod, almost smile, barely wave.

Grinning broadly, Mayme pressed her palms together in front of her chest and bowed her head before turning and walking jauntily up the street. Katy watched her, about as shocked as she'd ever been. And here she'd spent her life believing she was an expert when it came to magic.

Jane was the obvious choice. That's what best friends were for, right? Telling secrets, getting support, making each other feel normal? Katy pushed words around in her head, trying to come up with the right combination, as she pulled her phone from her hoodie pocket. Instead of figuring out what to say, though, all she could imagine was Jane's horrified face, and then her furious face, and then her I'll-be-on-a-plane-in-ten-minutes face.

Anxiety coated Katy's skin. Nope, that just would not do. She couldn't deal with Jane and Gunnar at the same time, in the same town. No freakin' way.

Maybe it didn't have to be right now, she told herself. Maybe she should go home and think on it. Her feet took charge like they approved of the idea, and it took her a few seconds to realize they weren't leading her back to the campground. She looked up, and there they were again, the compassionate window-eyes of the crisis center.

Okay, that was it, she decided. First instincts were the good ones, that's what everyone said. And though she would never have believed it possible, in the fifteen or so minutes since leaving Mayme, getting advice felt urgent, not optional. She needed to get a hold of whatever terror still rattled around in her body and fix the problem once and for all.

Before she knew it, she was heading toward the building. Her mind rushed to coach her, to soothe her, to remind her Birch was both family and friend, a sounding board as safe as her own mother. She halted. Her mother. The word swelled across her thoughts, a stabbing pain in its wake. What would her mother say if she found out Birch Callahan knew this first? Not even Jane, her dearest friend in all the world, but Birch. No again, she told herself. The list of choices had narrowed to one.

Sighing deeply, she looked around her for a somewhat private place. No telling how many more wandering visitors like Mayme might cross her path if she stayed on the main drag. Spotting the park a few blocks down, she headed for a sunny bench and tugged her phone out of the zippered pocket of her hoodie.

It took her six more deep breaths to dial. The coaching voice returned as the line rang, and it struck her that its wisdom suddenly ruled the day, like her gut made the decision for her and swept all the nervous, undermining, bargaining whispers out of reach.

"Katy? Oh my gosh, Katy! You okay?"

She smiled. Man, she'd missed that voice, its everpresent edge both touching and intimidating. "Yeah. Yes. I'm good. I'm sorry I've been so out of touch, but I'm good."

Jane's sigh was a tornado in her ear. "Where have you been? What in the ever-loving world is going on? I've been calling you for weeks. Literally weeks."

Katy looked down, tugged at the zipper of her hoodie. "I know. I'm really sorry. This new job is really intense. I've wanted to talk to you a million times, but with the time difference and the weird hours and—"

"I'm not buying it."

Katy took a deep breath and stared up at the sky. She could fudge this. She could just hit the highlights with Jane and save the tough stuff for some other time. Anxiety settled over her at the thought, a feeling so foreign and heavy it stole her breath. Now or never, MacBain, she told herself. Running away wouldn't do a damn thing.

"Well?" Jane's tone managed to get even sharper. Maybe new benefits came with her membership in the mothers' union.

With a quick thought to the lovely conversation beyond this one—cooing and fussing over the brand-new baby princess her friend had ushered into the world—Katy steeled herself and pressed on. "Okay, okay. I've been battling some stuff, stuff I should have talked about sooner." A tiny flicker of warmth sparked deep within, hungry for light and air.

"Okay, good. That's a start. Let's get to it."

Katy sat back, surprised but not surprised that relief flooded her chest, made her feel warm and safe. Still, her mouth went dry as she tried to speak, not ready to let the words tumble out. "I'm still settling in, I guess."

"Do you like the job?"

"Oh, yes. I love it." Her smile felt genuine for the first time all day.

"That's fantastic. You deserve that." Jane's voice lowered, like she'd stumbled onto some juicy gossip. "And how's life in a station full of firefighters? I'm guessing the view is amazing. Anyone in particular catch your fancy?"

A tiny flutter of panic made Katy's chest tingle. "Um . . . no. I haven't been paying that much attention," she murmured, giving herself a pass on the fib. It just wasn't the time for that kind of girl talk.

Jane sighed again, this time more like a straight-line wind, intense but not deadly. "Katherine MacBain, just how long are you going to make me fish for answers?"

Katy's cheeks flamed, and she took a second to feel grateful Jane couldn't actually see her. "Sorry. I should know better."

"Yes, you should. We're more like sisters than friends. There should be no clamming up with sisters."

"Fine," Katy blurted. "You're right. Something happened."

Jane gave a little gasp but said nothing.

Taking what felt like her millionth deep breath of the conversation, Katy fought to ignore the trembling of skin and bone and cells and made herself sit up taller. "There was a man at my wilderness rescue course." She stared down at the lush grass, knowing the truth had to bubble up from the depths. "He, um . . . put something in my drink. I don't remember what happened after that, but I woke up tied to a motel bed the next morning."

A second gasp echoed, this one sharp and sonorous. "Oh, honey," she said, and Katy could almost hear the tears sliding down her friend's cheeks. "He raped you?" Jane asked after a moment.

Katy nodded and fought to find her voice. "Yes," she finally whispered. "Yes, he did."

Something close to a growl rattled through the line. "Did the authorities find him?"

She pursed her lips and looked to the ground again. The fledgling lightness inside her disappeared. Now they'd reached the crux of it.

"Katy? Is he still out there? Is he bothering you? Is that what you've been struggling with?"

Katy swallowed hard, guilt like a cement block in her gut. "No," she murmured. "He's not bothering me."

"Well, good. So they got him?"

Her own tears started, tumbling out like they had to make up for lost time. "I didn't report it, Jane. You're the only person I've even told."

Silence echoed, though Katy knew that just meant big wheels were turning in Jane's head. "I'll talk to Mark immediately," she said finally. "We can help you. I mean, I have several branches of the armed forces at my disposal these days. He can't hide for long."

Katy smiled in spite of herself. Leave it to Jane to call in the troops. "It doesn't matter now."

"Of course it matters. You have the right to seek justice."

Her body went cold. Oh, she'd sought justice all right, her own very unique brand. But how could she tell her friend, even her best friend, that part of the story? Just admitting the rape was bad enough. She just didn't have it in her to survive being a murderer in the eyes of the people she loved most. Pressing her lips together, she said nothing.

"Why didn't you tell someone when it happened?"

Katy shrugged. "I was stunned, I guess. And then embarrassed. It just seemed easier to leave the place, and the experience, behind me." She gulped fresh air and wished she'd packed a bottle of water. "And you know how the family would react. They would have tracked him down and killed him. Seriously. You and I both know that."

"I guess I see your point, since that's pretty much what I just offered to do," Jane said, her voice low and thoughtful. "So, let's focus on you instead. How about a counselor? You could talk to Birch."

Katy shook her head, the refusal for herself more than Jane. "I don't need counseling. I just need to make sure it never happens to me again."

"How? By never going out with friends? Or drinking again? Or never dating?"

"It's worked so far!"

"You can't live every day in fear, Katy. You need to talk to someone about this."

"I'm talking to you."

Jane sighed. "Sounds to me like your rapist is no longer the demon. You're fighting yourself instead." She paused for a beat. "What about your mom?"

"What about her?"

"Are you going to tell her?"

Katy sighed. She couldn't even let herself imagine that conversation, imagine a different cascade of emotions in her mother's eyes—shock, horror, rage—not to mention how instantly protective she'd get. And what about her dad? Pillow talk was a real problem. She couldn't ask, or expect, her mother to keep such a thing to herself. "I don't think so," she murmured.

Jane tsked-tsked like a little old lady. "Don't be silly, Katy. Your mother happens to be one of the most wonderful women on the planet. She loves you, and I say that with a new understanding of the power of a mother's love. She'll just want to help, I promise."

"Yeah, she'll want to help me right back into my old life in Pine Creek," Katy muttered. "She and Dad have been celebrating my independence as much as I have. I can't let them know I didn't keep myself safe." Her voice broke on that last word, and she pressed her hand to her mouth.

"It won't be like that. Please take it from another mother."

The width of Katy's smile made her cheeks hurt, and her eyes brimmed with the gratitude she couldn't properly express. Though the telling made her feel like a completely new person, she also knew she'd taken the sharing about as far as she could. What mattered most was her ability to move on, to find the strength to get back on her feet and never fall in the same trap again. Never hesitate or back down. That's what her father taught her, wasn't it?

"I'll find a way to tell her, I promise." Katy got to her feet and started walking toward home, unable to bear the emotion roaring its way through her body. Gratitude and guilt couldn't sit with each other for long, but all this truth-telling had left her a bit too worn out to choose a winner. Once she'd recharged, she'd call Jane again. They both deserved to giggle over the good stuff.

Chapter Fourteen

Gunnar allowed himself a small smile, more pleased with himself than he'd been in at least a week. This was a good idea, assigning Katy to fire inspection duty at the campground. If she saw through his ruse, or if she thought it suspicious that he gave himself the same duty, there were no hints to be found in those haunting gray eyes.

The day's heat intensified on his shoulders, and he glanced at his watch. Lunchtime. Perfect. They'd been mostly working in silence all morning, moving from campsite to campsite and ensuring each fire pit was properly maintained, showed no residue of inappropriate burning, and had all the necessary safety equipment nearby. But now, with the sun high and his stomach growling, it was finally time to try to get past some of this blasted awkwardness pulsing between them.

"Let's take a break," he said.

Katy glanced up at him, her long legs bent in a low squat near the edge of the fire pit. "I'm fine, but you go ahead if you want."

"It's lunchtime."

"Didn't pack one."

Gunnar let his grin widen. Score another point for him. "I brought enough for both of us."

She shook her head and peered down into the campfire ash like diamonds might lie within. "You go ahead. I'm really not hungry."

"Fine, don't eat, but you can sit and rest a few minutes. Chief's orders."

With a sigh big enough to shake the leaves on the trees, Katy pushed to a stand and walked toward a nearby picnic table. "Aye, aye, sir," she said as she plopped down on the bench seat.

Gunnar tried to catch her eye, craving just one hit of that impish gleam, but she looked away and cast her gaze into the woods. He watched her for a moment more, enjoying the dance of sunlight across her hair. His fingers twitched, aching to touch the fiery strands. He clenched them into fists and headed to the tree near the lane shading his gear bag.

He opened the bag, fishing inside as he walked. When he reached the table, he popped the tab of an energy drink and held it toward her. "You're dehydrated."

She scrunched up her nose. "Thanks, but I don't like those. I'll guzzle down some water as soon as I get home."

He sat down across from her, then set the opened can between them on the table. "But I want you to drink this one."

"No, I'm good." Her smile forced, she pushed the can toward him and restated her refusal by slipping her hands under the table to her lap. "You probably need it more than I do."

He pushed it back, not stopping until it was almost touching her chest.

Her smile vanished. And almost as if a switch clicked in her head, she went as still as a stone. Her complexion paled, and her breathing went shallow. Seconds stretched to minutes as she silently stared into his eyes as though hoping to find the answers to all her unspoken questions. Gunnar knew that look, having seen it every day in the mirror from the age of eight until shortly after turning seventeen, when he'd taken a job on a fishing boat that hadn't had mirrors. He'd jumped ship in Oslo, called his aunt to say he was fine and would keep in touch, and set off to search the world for those answers.

Hell, he was still searching. "Drink it, Katy."

She flinched and broke eye contact by simply looking down at the can. "I don't want . . . I can't."

He already knew that. What he didn't know was why. "Why can't you?" he quietly asked.

The woods fell silent again. More seconds stretched to minutes before he saw her entire torso expand on a deep breath and deflate on a violent shudder. "Because—" More seconds passed. "Because the last time I drank something someone gave me," she said, still looking down, "I apparently spent the rest of the night being ra— being sexually assaulted."

Well, fuck. "Explain 'apparently,'" he gently commanded, even as he braced himself for the answer.

"I was . . . I woke up in a motel room the next morning,"

she said in a barely audible whisper, "naked, tied spread-eagle on the bed, every cell in my body screaming in pain, and . . . and not knowing why."

"Who found you?"

"It took me most of the day," she softly continued, her arms moving ever so slightly, as if she were rubbing her wrists under the table, "before I was able to free myself."

"Tell me his name."

"There's no reason for you to know his name, because he's already . . . I killed him."

It took every bit of willpower he possessed, and some he didn't know he had, not to roar. "Would you mind at least telling me where the bastard's body is buried?"

He nearly lost the battle when she looked up—not at him, merely toward him—and Gunnar saw tears threatening to spill from her utterly emotionless eyes.

"I believe it's still buried under several tons of snow on some mountain in the Swiss Alps."

Of course it was, because *I buried it in Idaho* would have made too much sense.

She stood, the movement finally freeing her tears to form two damp tracks in the dust on her cheeks. "This conversation is over," she said, striding toward the trees.

"Katy."

She stopped and looked directly at him, those two dusty tracks now muddy rivers. "In fact, we never had it. And if you ever try to bring it up again, I won't . . . I'll probably kill you, too."

He believed her, Gunnar decided as he watched her quietly walk away. Not the killing him part; but the bastard who'd raped her was indeed dead. Gunnar believed Katy believed she was somehow responsible. He closed his eyes and dropped his head onto the table with a growl, wishing she hadn't beaten him to it. And then he began another battle with himself, this one to replace the image of her being drugged and bound and brutalized with images from this past month of a vibrant, flirtatious enchantress captivating him with killer smiles and life-saving kisses.

Hell, he wouldn't have disappeared for two weeks; he'd probably still be running.

And she'd been dealing with the consequences. Alone. Thousands of miles from home. Telling strangers in some clinic or emergency room what had happened, then hiding in Idaho while she healed—also alone. Because if Katy had told anyone in her family, she sure as hell wouldn't be in Spellbound Falls now; she'd still be locked in her childhood bedroom in Pine Creek, her parents probably too shaken to let her even walk to the store by herself.

He wouldn't blame them, because even though he couldn't begin to imagine the hell Katy had gone through—and still was and likely would be forever—he wanted to hunt down the bastard and kill him himself. Or kill him again if he truly was dead, even if he had to climb a god-damn mountain to do it.

Gunnar sat up taller. That's why Katy hadn't told her family; not because she was afraid they wouldn't have let her out of their sight for the next hundred years, but because she knew they would have gone after the bastard.

But for reasons he couldn't fathom, she'd told him, and unwittingly provided enough pieces of the puzzle to put a name to her rapist. Because the odds of one of the men at the school celebration that night also recently dying had to be a billion to one.

Peering through the trees and glimpsing her sunfire hair at least three campsites down the lane, Gunnar pulled out his phone and called the best damn researcher no amount of money could buy. "I need you to find out if any mountain climbers have died in the Swiss Alps within the last six weeks," he said as soon as the line was picked up. "I want his name, how he died, and exactly when."

"Brandon Fontanne, age forty-six, and he suddenly keeled over dead two hundred meters from the summit of the Matterhorn exactly two days ago."

"You can't possibly know that off the top of your head."

"Sure I can, if I've been seeing the guy's face plastered on every cable news channel at least once an hour for the last two days. And thank you for asking," she drawled. "I'm feeling quite fine today. And yourself? I see nobody's killed you in the last month."

Gunnar dropped his chin to his chest. "I'm sorry. I've been . . . preoccupied."

"If that Scottish girl you're chasing is what's keeping you too busy to call and see how your dear old aunt is doing, then I forgive you—assuming she's as sweet as she is pretty."

Gunnar muttered a curse under his breath. "I am firing Hanson today. I'm not bluffing this time, May. I pay that man to keep his mouth shut."

"You fire your tech guru and you're going to be looking for a new researcher, too."

Gunnar couldn't quite stifle a grin. "Please tell me he at least got you for more than a couple of apple pies and some cookies this time."

"Do you know what it costs to overnight pies and cookies to Toronto? And when he finally got around to calling me two weeks ago, the little weasel said that because you were working on something personal, he felt his info was worth a vacation in Reykjavik in my newly remodeled house for an entire month."

Gunnar openly chuckled. "That should teach you to do business with a computer hacker. And didn't I warn you about posting pictures of your home on Facebook?"

"What's the point of getting a master chef's kitchen if I can't show it off to my friends?"

"Which tells me you friended someone you knew is a cybercriminal."

"Whom you pay to commit those crimes."

Well, she had him there. "So, what's the problem? You've been sending Hanson pies for over two years now, and you've got three empty bedrooms and no one to eat your cooking. Offer to let the guy stay for a couple of weeks and feed him until he bursts."

"Gunny," she whisper-growled. "I can't let a virtual stranger into my home. For all we know the man moonlights as a paid assassin. And if he doesn't kill me in my sleep, I'll die of mortification when the neighbors start gossiping."

"Hanson's just a kid, Aunt May, no more than twenty-one or -two years old. The neighbors will think you're taking in strays again instead of having a flaming affair with a foreigner."

"He's just a kid?" she said in surprise. "On the phone,

he sounds old. All this time, I've pictured him as a middle-aged, potbellied nerd with thick glasses and thinning hair who's addicted to sweets. Oh, that poor dear is just a starving child. Now I feel bad for running off."

His spidey-senses tingled. "Running off? Where are you?"

She chuckled. "Oh, just a little R & R. I'll be back home before Hanson hits town."

"Be careful," Gunnar warned. "You start mothering him and you're going to find yourself with a permanent guest. And as you well know, I pay that poor dear enough to hire a personal cook. So, are they saying what made the bastard suddenly keel over dead two hundred meters from the summit?"

May paused, like she'd expected him to say something else. "Um, they won't know until they dig his body out of the avalanche it caused when he fell and then do an autopsy. But you go ahead and keep right on cussing like that," she snapped. "I'm sure it will really impress Miss MacBain. So," she rambled on when he snorted, "if you're in some town in Maine that I needed a magnifying glass to find on the map, why are you asking about a dead mountain climb— Wait a minute," she muttered, her tone growing soft and distracted.

Gunnar sighed. She must have pulled out her tablet.

"Here it is," she said after a few moments. "I assumed Fontanne had been highly respected in the climbing world to be making international news two days running, and I see he's been a guest instructor at the mountain rescue school your Scottish lady attended." She gave a little gasp. "In fact, he gave a clinic on technical climbing at the session Miss—"

Aunt May fell silent again, and then a heavy sigh came over the line. "Please don't tell me you've spent all this time and energy pursuing the woman only to learn she's emotionally unavailable. Gunnar Wolfe," she rushed on in her listen-up-buster voice, "you better not be entertaining the notion you can step in and heal her wounds." An even longer pause this time. "Oh, sweetie," she said gently. "Hearts shatter into too many pieces when we're abandoned or betrayed, and no one—not an eight-year-old boy and not even the amazing man he became—can ever make that heart whole again."

Gunnar in turn fell silent as memories he'd thought long buried tightened his chest.

"You are such a hard man to pray for," May whispered. "Half the time I pray you'll find a woman who deserves you, and half the time I catch myself praying you don't."

"This isn't exactly a case of heartbreak, Auntie," he returned just as softly. "In fact, I'm pretty sure Katy hated Fontanne's guts."

Another deep sigh, and then, "Is she as sweet as she is pretty?"

"You tell me," he said dryly. "You've had her name an entire two weeks now. Hell, you probably know more about Katherine MacBain than I do."

"Touché," she said and gave an overly exuberant chuckle that made him a little nervous. "She didn't go to college," May continued.

"Neither did I."

A snort came over the line. "There isn't a college course you couldn't teach. So," she rushed on, "if you've spent tens of thousands of dollars flying all over creation, have called in probably another hundred thousand in favors, and are pretending to be a fireman, I'm guessing if this girl's not sweeter than Mother Teresa, then she must be hell on wheels in bed."

Gunnar laid his head on the table again. "Right after I fire Hanson," he muttered into the phone, "I'm taking your name off all my bank accounts and getting my fuel bills sent to my new bookkeeper."

Another snort. "As if that would get rid of me."

"Also, I'm a fire chief now. And Katy—" He closed his eyes. "You'd love her, Auntie."

"I already do," May whispered. "Because you do," she added a beat later.

He shot upright. "I never said that."

"You didn't have to. And you know what, Gunny?"

"What?" he barely managed to get out as he thumped his head back down on the table.

"I also love you." She gave a small laugh when his only response was silence—because hell, it's damn hard to talk with a heart lodged in your throat. "And you know what else?"

He did manage to grunt this time.

"I got my passport renewed last week, and I've got a bad case of travel-itis," she said, her laughter abruptly ending when the line suddenly went dead.

Gunnar opened his hand and let the phone drop to the table with another groan, only to bolt upright with a curse when her words finally sank in.

Son of a bitch, she was coming here!

To Maine.

To see for herself if Katherine MacBain deserved him. Hell. If he couldn't find a decent house to rent, he'd have to buy one, because he couldn't have May traipsing to the bathhouse every time she needed to— No, wait. If he got them a house, she'd stay a month, but she'd hightail it home within a week if he simply bought another sleeping bag.

Gunnar stood and slipped his phone in his pocket with a sigh of defeat. He might be an ass, but he drew the line when it came to making the closest thing he'd ever had to a mother sleep in a wooden tent.

Chapter Fifteen

"So, tell me again what's so all-fired important out here?" Katy gave her brother her twenty-fifth scowl of the morning.

"It's hard to describe," he said and looked out over the Bottomless Sea like he was searching for clues to a treasure hunt.

"When you asked me to come for the day, you might have mentioned we'd be out in the boat, Robbie. I'd have packed a hat." Libby pushed flailing strands of hair out of her face and shielded her eyes with her hand. "It's a little blustery."

"Sorry. This came on sort of suddenly."

"What came on? And what can we do about it?" The farther out they got, the more Katy's annoyance grew. She didn't get that many days off, and while she loved the surprise of time with her mother, it would have been nice to have some say in how they spent it.

"You'll see soon enough." Robbie slowed the boat and steered them toward the island off the starboard side of the boat.

"We're going to the island?" Katy said. "What in the world, Robbie?"

"On the plus side, I guess we'll know what he's planning soon enough." Ever the peacemaker, Libby pushed her hair out of her face yet again and smiled at her daughter.

"Yeah, Katy. You'll know soon enough." Robbie flashed her a secretive grin. "Can you tie us up?" He tipped his head toward the approaching dock.

Eyes rolling, Katy hurried to the bow and grabbed the dock line. Poised and ready, she waited until they got a foot or two away and then jumped to the dock platform. Quick as lightning, she secured the line, then hurried to the stern, caught the second line as Robbie threw it her way, and wrapped it around the cleat.

"Nice job," her mother called.

The sight of her pride over such a small thing softened Katy's mood. It was really nice to have her mom there, and no matter what Robbie had in mind for them, she couldn't deny that she really needed to soak up some maternal comfort. Just being around her mom always made her feel better.

"Yeah, seems like you've still got it," Robbie said, face shining like he'd just cured cancer or something.

"Um . . . of course I've still got it, brother. My new job keeps me kinda active, in case you hadn't noticed."

"Does it now?" he said with a smirk, then jumped to the dock and held his hand out for Libby to do the same. "Happy to know you can handle yourself, little sister."

Katy studied him and readied her twenty-sixth scowl. She knew that tone; he was up to something, and not a surprise-birthday-party sort of something. Her brother was winding up for a curveball, his favorite pitch. But before she could figure anything else out, he was scurrying behind her, untying one rope and then the other. Her mouth fell open as he hopped back on the boat.

"Robbie! What are you doing?" Libby's voice held a tone Katy hadn't heard in years, not since the days of full-on sibling squabbles.

"Sorry, Mom. This needs to happen. I'm done watching the two of you dance around whatever's going on." He fired up the boat and slowly backed away from the dock. "Here," he called and tossed an insulated bag at Katy's feet. "I packed you some lunch. Have fun."

Katy glanced at her mom and saw the same slack-jawed surprise she felt on her own face. A warm blush followed, reminding her that, unlike her mother, she knew exactly what Robbie was talking about. "I am so going to kill him."

"You're going to have to get in line," Libby said, also glaring at their only means of leaving the island racing away.

After a few moments, the two women looked back at each other, and Katy instantly smiled when she saw her mother's eyes narrow. "Why would Robbie go to all this trouble to maroon us out here together?" Libby asked, gesturing in the general direction of the campsite while keeping her eyes locked on Katy.

"How should I—" Katy snapped her mouth shut when those big brown eyes narrowed even more, then hung her head on a sigh. "Because he loves me," she whispered. She looked up. "And because he loves you. He doesn't want there to ever be any secrets between us."

Libby's face softened, a mixture of anxiety and concern. "What secrets, honey? What is he worried about?"

Katy hung her head, picked up the insulated bag, and walked toward the shore. "Maybe we should have some lunch," she said.

After she'd laid out every single item Robbie had packed in the bag—ham sandwiches, homemade pickles, thick slices of cheese, and a tin of snickerdoodles—then doled out bottles of water, paper plates, and napkins, Katy finally felt ready to look her mother in the eye. As soon as her pupils landed on the shimmering wall of love looking back at her, the words came and the whole story tumbled from her lips.

Within minutes, her mother knew it all—the real adventure, the man who took advantage, the sordid next morning, complete with her abuser's brand, and the running and hiding she'd done, particularly from herself. Next, she moved on to what she knew her brother worried about, the reason he'd taken matters into his own hands: her inherited gift. And finally, when she'd purged her body of every secret but the worst one, she pulled that one out like a rotten tooth and laid it at her mother's feet.

With slow tears and soothing hands, her mother listened. She pursed her lips, wiped her eyes, and squeezed hands tight, both her own and those of her daughter.

When the worst of the story came, she reached out and pressed her hand to the side of Katy's face.

"Oh, my beautiful girl. I'm devastated to know how much you've suffered. And I'm so awed by your strength."

Katy winced. "That wasn't strength."

"Oh, but it was, dear girl. Strength on top of strength."

"And yet, in the end, I'm still sort of a murderer."

Libby's head shook in slow, purposeful arcs. "Oh, honey. I don't think you can 'sort of' be a murderer any more than you can 'sort of' be pregnant. Either you are, or you aren't."

"Then I guess I am."

Her mother's eyes grew steely, and she straightened her spine like she meant to do battle. She reached out, gripped her daughter's arm, and stretched it between them. The flesh, though healed beneath the bandage, seemed to throb with new anger. Katy winced at the memory of the brand, a V turned upside down—Fontanne's version of a mountain, no doubt—with a tiny letter B at the top, like a flag planted by a victorious climber.

"So you're keeping that mark to remind yourself that you're a murderer?"

"Yes. No." She stood, looked out over Bottomless, and hugged herself. "I don't know," she whispered.

"If you keep it, will the man be less dead?"

"No."

"And if you let me remove it, will you be less of a murderer?"

Katy turned to face her mother. "It's not that I withheld the information from him that bothers me as much as . . . as why. I've heard Papa tell the boys more than once when they spoke of their tours in Afghanistan and Iraq that the intent in a man's heart when he kills another man—or even an animal—is what's important. That if he's killing in anger, or hate, or for revenge, then he's no better than a murderer."

"And if he's defending himself or protecting someone or being a soldier doing his duty?" Libby asked softly. "What is he then?"

Katy smiled sadly. "A hero."

"And did you keep the knowledge of Brandon Fontanne's aneurysm to yourself because you were angry at him and hated him and wanted revenge for what he did to you? Or," Libby firmly rushed on before Katy could answer, "did you see it as a way to stop him from drugging and raping more women?"

"I knew who he was and where he could be found," Katy said softly. "I could have gone to the hospital that day and had evidence collected and report it to the police."

"And you didn't . . . because?"

Katy lifted her arm to show the mark. "It was obvious to me, even in the frame of mind I was in at the time, that this wasn't an isolated crime of opportunity. And I also knew Fontanne would have flown directly to a country that didn't have extradition and that he was probably sitting in some bar looking for his next victim before I was even able to untie those ropes. So what would reporting it to the police have accomplished besides leaving me with a kit full of evidence, an arrest warrant that couldn't be carried out, and an angry and deeply wounded . . ." She dropped her head on a shuddering sigh. "I wasn't about to let that bastard hurt my family, too."

"Okay. It's done. Over. History. Your demon is dead. And you're letting me make that arm baby-soft smooth again, because you didn't give the bastard that aneurysm. And," she rushed on when Katy tried to speak, "we are never, ever telling your father or Robbie or any male in any of the clans. And Winter. Oh, God, we can't ever tell Winter."

"I have no intention of ever telling anyone, but why not Winter?"

Libby screwed up her face. "Are you kidding me? The woman's a wizard. She'd try to find a way to resurrect Fontanne just to be able to kill him herself."

Katy very gently broke free of her mother's grasp and stepped back. "I, ah . . . I sort of already told Gunnar," she confessed.

Libby went perfectly still except to blink at her. "Why would you have told your boss?"

"Because I think he's . . ." Katy gave a tentative smile. "I think he might be The One."

Her mother did not smile back. "You haven't even known the man a month, Katherine," Libby whispered. "And less than two months ago you . . . you were raped."

"But I don't remember being raped," Katy whispered back.

"But your body does. Have you been with Gunnar . . . romantically?"

No longer able to look at the concern in her mother's eyes, Katy dropped her gaze to the ground. "We haven't made love yet," she said softly. "I wanted to, but I couldn't."

"It wasn't the right time."

Katy looked up at her mom once again. "What if it's never the right time again?"

Her mother almost smiled, eyebrows high. "Do you actually believe that?"

A sharp poke shook Katy's insides, like a crack in her soul. She almost smiled herself. "How do you happen to know everything?"

"Isn't that a mother's job?"

"I guess I forgot I'm a Highlander." She grinned crookedly. "And an equestrian. Whether we fall, or someone knocks us down, we get back on our feet or in the saddle and try again. We don't give up or give in; we get stronger. Someone like Brandon Fontanne doesn't get to take that away."

Her mother nodded. "Exactly. And I'm guessing someone like Gunnar Wolfe knows better than to question that strength. If he's The One, that is." Libby's eyebrows arched in challenge.

Katy chuckled. "I'm pretty sure I've made that clear. And besides, Gunnar's one of us."

The eyebrows fell. "What?"

"He's from Atlantis. He's one of Nicholas' warriors."

"Oh, but that's no good. You need a mortal, Katy, to keep you grounded. Michael understands the magic but doesn't command it. He's my anchor. Without him to hold on to, I could get swept away."

Katy studied her, heart sinking. She'd always known her father supported her mother, and her mother's magic, but she'd never quite understood his role. "It always has to be that way?"

Libby nodded. "I don't know how someone like us survives the magic otherwise."

Katy sighed, suddenly overwhelmed. "There's just so much I don't understand yet. How do you decide if you're supposed to intervene or not? When is it my place to help? Five years ago, I started . . . feeling people's pain. Not as pain itself, but . . . Oh, I can't describe it. I didn't see colors, I felt them. That's why I went to paramedic school, so I could understand. But ever since I healed the cat, I can . . . I feel people."

"You and I," Libby said, leaning into her, "are not in the business of deciding who lives and who dies. Our job is . . ." She squeezed Katy's hands. "We're not healing them, Katy—we're helping them heal themselves."

"But can they all do that? Aren't we supposed to ease the way if we can?"

"It's not our decision to make. If it's a person's day to die, all your training and all that fancy equipment in your ambulance, and even your beautiful magic, won't be able to save them. But if it's not their time, then you are God's answer to their prayers." She leaned into her daughter's shoulder. "I believe you'll find that the true value of your gift will be being able to tell if you're there to help that person live or offer them comfort in their final moments."

"But how will I know?" Katy whispered. "What if I'm wrong and give up too soon?"

Libby patted her knee and stood, then smiled down at her. "You'll know. Even without your unique gift, paramedics learn to read the subtle signs a person gives off." Her smile turned sad. "I imagine, for you, that sign will be finding yourself inexplicably angry at your patient."

"Angry?"

"Even as your mind races through the steps you need to take, your heart will sense they're already moving on. I spent six years as a full-time surgeon, but it wasn't until

I discovered I could heal people without a scalpel that I learned having someone die on my table or in my arms is not defeat but merely the next natural step on their personal journey." She softly snorted. "Not that that stops me from getting angry at what I perceive as them giving up or running away or . . ." She went back to smiling sadly. "Or running to something I can't see."

She reached down and pulled Katy to her feet, then wrapped her arms around her in a hug. "I know it's scary and confusing and seems more like a curse than a blessing right now." She leaned back enough to flash a crooked smile. "But once you truly understand that you can't mess it up because you're not the one calling the shots, you'll have fully mastered the magic. That's when the healing begins."

"Have you seen Katy?" Gunnar asked Robert MacBain as the man tied the bowline of a sleek-looking runabout to the dock. "I checked at her campsite and her truck's here," he continued as he scanned the beach and then the front of the office store, only to still when MacBain straightened and looked at him with narrow-eyed . . . interest. "Did she go for a walk with her mother?"

"Nay. Katy and Mum are enjoying some mother-daughter time on one of the islands."

Gunnar used the excuse of looking toward the array of small islands scattered along the eastern shoreline to break eye contact. "When will they be back?"

MacBain said nothing, so much nothing that Gunnar had to glance back at him. The giant man's posture said it all, his wide back more dismissive than any words could have been. Well, shit. He should have freaking asked for information, not demanded it. Because he was pretty sure his usual practice of "forgiveness over permission" wasn't really the way to go with this particular man.

He just knew he couldn't possibly have much time before Aunt May arrived, and if he wanted that visit to go well, he better figure out exactly what she was coming to Spellbound Falls to observe. If it was just him, single guy with an interesting new job, that was one thing. But if he and Katy were really going to be GUNNAR AND KATY, package deal, well, that was something completely different.

The silence continued, and Gunnar decided some serious backtracking was in order. "I . . . um, well . . . I'm sorry if that sounded demanding. I've been working hard to whip the fire department into shape, and I guess I forget sometimes I don't need to talk to everyone like I'm the boss."

MacBain glanced at him, no emotion in his expression, and then went back to tending the boat. Clearly, the new boss had been decided. Gunnar took a step closer and lowered his head. "I'm more than your sister's supervisor, or at least I'd like to be."

That got the man's attention. "Pretty sure she gets to make that call," he said, eyes narrow and skeptical.

"Oh . . . oh, yeah. Of course." Gunnar felt the blood drain out of his face. Shit. Had he sounded like he was asking MacBain to hand her over? "I wasn't being a jerk. I was just trying to be real, you know? Let you know where things stand."

MacBain turned, faced him full on. "And where do they stand?"

Gunnar actually gulped, something he hadn't done in the presence of another guy since he was like fourteen. Damn, these Highlanders were intimidating. His determination wavered, made him wonder, for just a second, if he really wanted to be involved with a girl from this particular family. Of course, as soon as his mind wandered anywhere near thoughts of Katy, the question became a moot point. There was no other for him.

"We're still figuring that out," he managed. "But it's not just me pursuing her. I know she's interested. It's just, well . . . complicated."

MacBain snorted. "Welcome to the world of a Scottish woman."

Gunnar chuckled. "You can say that again. I'm seriously unprepared for this."

"Then why do it?"

Gunnar shrugged. "Is there another choice?"

The man's face broke into a grin. "Look at you, knowing the right answer already. There might be hope for you and my sister."

"Maybe you could tell her that."

MacBain's grin slipped away. "Katy doesn't like to be told much of anything. Though, if she's fighting you that hard, maybe you need to back off."

"I'm actually looking forward to her getting back to fighting me. That's kind of our thing. I mean, not fighting, just, you know . . . spirited discussions."

"Got it." MacBain nodded. "So, you're saying she's changed? Did something happen?"

"Not with us. Not really. She's just dealing with some stuff."

"What kind of stuff?" MacBain's eyes looked more

wary than curious, almost like he already knew the answer.

"That's for Katy to tell you." Gunnar lifted his hands, palms out in the "no offense" position. "Not trying to start anything, but you know your sister better than I do. She's not going to like us discussing her business."

MacBain's gaze grew steely. "Then why ask me about her?"

"I just couldn't find her, was a little worried, honestly. It's good to know she's with her mom."

"Yeah, they needed to talk."

"If you see her, could you tell her I was looking for her?"

MacBain studied him long and hard, then nodded.

"Could you ask her to call me?"

"That'll be up to her."

"Right. Scottish woman. Got it." Gunnar sighed, though the sound made him cringe. When had he become the hand-wringing girl in this situation? Katy's voice immediately darted into his head to scold him, reminding him that girls were capable of a lot more than wringing their hands, and that if he continued to be such an uninformed jackass, he could just walk himself in the other direction. Forever.

"Chin up, man. Katy's smart, and she's really good at figuring out the right thing, even if it takes her a while." MacBain looked almost sorry for him.

Gunnar shrugged and looked out over the water. "Thanks. That would be great if we actually had a while."

"What's that supposed to mean?"

Hearing the new alarm in MacBain's voice, Gunnar turned back. "Nothing for you to worry about. This particular ticking clock, and all the meddling that goes with it, is mine and mine alone."

MacBain frowned, clearly not satisfied, but Gunnar decided he'd said all he felt ready to say. With a small wave, he headed back down the dock. It suddenly felt like a storm was coming and all of the stores were sold out of candles and batteries. He'd just have to wing it, an approach that used to be his strong suit but now made him feel like he'd left the house in two left boots. Women! That was all.

Chapter Sixteen

"Attention Spellbound Falls Fire & Rescue. Spellbound Ambulance One is asked to respond to 505 Spooner Street for a nineteen-year-old male, breathing but not responsive, possible overdose. Copy Spellbound Ambulance One: 505 Spooner Street, nineteen-year-old male, possible overdose. Piscataquis out, thirteen-forty-one."

"Got it, boss," Gretchen called as soon as the tones faded.

"I'm in," Katy said and hurried to follow her out the door.

With a quick nod at Gunnar, Paul grabbed his gear bag and jumped in the back of the ambulance. More than enough personnel to cover it, Gunnar thought, but he'd barely had more than two words with Katy all week. He needed to let her work, of course, but maybe if he followed the bus, he could come up with a reason for her to ride back to the station in his truck after the call. And if he was being honest, as acting chief, it wouldn't hurt to assess her in action, to make sure her work wasn't suffering as she worked through her challenges.

He pulled up moments after the ambulance and saw the team gathered on the small front porch. He watched as Paul knocked, waited, then reached for the doorknob just as the door swung open. From where he sat, Gunnar could see the top of a blonde head, but nothing more. Not wanting to miss any aspect of the call, he jumped out of his truck and ran to the door, slipping inside right behind Gretchen.

"What happened?" Katy asked the blonde, a very petite teenager with giant brown eyes.

"I couldn't wake him up," the girl said and pointed to a lanky, dark-haired guy stretched across the living room floor.

"Did he fall?" Gretchen asked, squatting down beside him.

The girl shook her head. "No, he laid down there after he took the pills."

Katy peered at the girl. "What pills?"

She shrugged. "I don't know. He said he met up with Stinky Joe before he came over. He didn't offer to share."

"Wow, swell guy," Katy muttered and dropped to her knees on his other side.

"How long ago did he take them?" Gunnar asked. Everyone in the room jumped at the sound of his voice.

"Hey, Chief," Paul said. "Didn't know you were here."

Though Katy didn't look up at him, her scowl made the room feel about thirty degrees chillier. Nice move, Wolfe. Didn't look like he'd be easing the awkwardness anytime soon. "Thought I might lend a hand for once," he murmured and tried to set them all at ease with a smile. "Carry on."

"Vitals are good." Gretchen put her stethoscope back in her kit. "What's his name?" she asked the girl.

"Dylan."

"Hey, Dylan," Katy leaned down and called in his ear. "Wake up, bud."

No response.

"C'mon, dude," Katy said, giving his cheeks a light slap. Pulling out her small flashlight, she checked his eyes. "Pupils round and reactive."

Gunnar nodded to himself. She seemed in complete control, even more confident than she'd been in the past. Maybe he should have just stayed back. Last thing he needed was to look like he was following her around.

"I'm going for the sternum rub," Katy announced.

"Whoa," Paul said, digging through his kit. "Let me—"

Before he could finish, Katy made a fist and rubbed her knuckles along the center of Dylan's chest. Gunnar winced. It was an effective technique, but really uncomfortable for the patient. No one woke up happy from a sternum rub.

"Owwwwhat the fuuu . . ." Dylan squirmed beneath her fist, trying to get free.

"Easy, Katy," Gretchen warned. "I think you got him."

"Did I, Dylan? You with us?" She gave his chest one more quick rub, though judging by Dylan's writhing response, she didn't use a lighter touch.

"Dammit!" he screamed, now awake and furious.

Katy pursed her lips and arched her brows, clearly holding back some sharp comment. "Welcome back," she murmured and reached for his wrist. She glanced up while she counted, held Gunnar's gaze for the briefest of moments, then looked away without changing her expression.

At least four different comments formed on his tongue, none of them right for the situation. Move it along, Wolfe. Nothing to see here. Back in chief mode, he stepped closer and watched his paramedics work. Fortunately, by this point, Dylan looked more angry than high, which probably pleased his team far more than the kid.

"What did you take?" Gunnar asked him.

"I didn't take anything," Dylan mumbled.

Gretchen scowled. "That's not what your friend says."

Glaring up at the blonde girl, he huffed, long and hard. "Nice, Carly."

"I thought something was wrong with you, Dylan. You're welcome."

Dylan scoffed and shook his head, and Gunnar noticed an odd expression come over Katy's face; her eyes widened like she was shocked, while her mouth turned down in disgust. Deciding a little alpha-dogging might turn the young man around, Gunnar squatted down and looked him in the eye. "Rule number two—never, ever lie to a paramedic."

"What's rule number one?"

"Never put anything in your body that you bought off a guy named Stinky Joe."

Dylan glanced at Gretchen, who probably seemed like the most sympathetic thus far, eyes round like he was pleading his case. "I thought I was buying Percocet."

"You stupid shit," Gretchen rasped. "How many did you take?"

"Two. I only took two."

"You got any more?" Katy asked.

"I want to file assault charges against her," he said, glaring at Katy.

"I'll get right on that," Paul drawled, "just as soon as I finish filling out paperwork on your illicit drug purchase."

Dylan swallowed hard, then bit his lip and closed his eyes, clearly wishing to be anywhere else.

Katy nudged him. "Once again, you got any more pills?"

"In my pocket."

Gunnar reached in the kid's pants pocket and pulled out three more tablets, definitely not Percocet. He sighed and shook his head. "How old are you?"

"Nineteen."

"Wow," Katy said. "Talk about arrested development. You have any health problems, Dylan?"

"No."

"So, you've decided to destroy a perfectly healthy body with whatever crap you can find on the street?"

"My body, my choice," he said with a smirk.

"Knock it off, dumbass," Gretchen growled, just as Katy leaned forward, fist clenched.

"You want another chest treatment?"

Dylan stiffened. "You can't do that." He peered up at Gunnar. "Can she?"

Gunnar exhaled, nice and loud for effect. He sure as hell hoped he hadn't been this clueless at nineteen. "She can, but she won't, because she's a professional, and because her main priority is seeing to your health, even though you don't seem interested in preserving that for yourself." He glanced at Katy at he spoke, thinking they might at least share a grin over the kid's stupidity, but she glared at him instead.

"Yeah, well, I didn't call you, remember?" the kid snapped.

"You're a jerk, Dylan," Carly called out from the doorway. "Next time, take your drugs at your own house."

"Thatta girl, Carly. You tell him," Gretchen said as she stood and headed for the door. "I'll get the gurney, Chief."

"Yeah, load him up," Gunnar said, stepping back to make room.

"Load me up? What the hell? I'm fine."

"Oh, for cripes' sake," Katy hissed. She bent down, close to Dylan's face. "You don't even know what you took. Don't you think you should go the hospital and see if there's a problem?"

The kid drew back, clearly not sure what to make of Katy. "Wouldn't I feel sick if there was a problem?"

"Not necessarily," Jake said as he helped Gretchen get the gurney through the door. "Better safe than sorry, kid."

"Fine," Dylan huffed and gave an exaggerated eye roll.

"I need some air," Katy said and pushed to a stand.

"We're not finished here, MacBain." Gunnar placed a careful hand on her arm. "Your participation is a requirement, not a suggestion."

"Paul and Gretchen can handle it," she said and shrugged away from his touch. "And didn't I hear you say something about wanting to lend a hand?"

He pulled back like she'd bit him. For a second, he wondered if this call would have gone better if he hadn't tagged along, but the frustration in her eyes told him otherwise. Katy had things to figure out, a good many of them, and as impossible as it felt for him to do so, if he wanted to keep life and limb safe, he best suck it up and get out of her way.

After the call, Katy found Gunnar by the fire pit, staring into the empty hood like a huge blaze crackled within. He looked a little sad, and somehow young, and for a split second she caught a glimpse of the boy he'd once been. Her heart squeezed, since she had no beef with that boy, and she felt pretty sure she'd triggered whatever sadness he struggled with. She slowed her steps, no longer quite sure what she wanted to say. A twig snapped beneath her boot, making them both startle.

"You need something?" Gunnar squinted up at her.

"Probably."

"Do I need to make my question more specific?"

Katy shook her head. "I need to speak to you . . . officially. Do you want to go to your office?"

Gunnar looked over one shoulder and then the other. "This seems pretty private at the moment."

She nodded. "Fair enough. I'll be quick."

As soon as she said that, though, the words turned to glue in her throat. Why had her life suddenly become this messy quagmire, a big, fat swamp of confusion between what she wanted and what she could actually handle? As if Gunnar's face might hold the answer to that question, her eyes sought his, and she immediately wished they hadn't. As the human embodiment of her quagmire, he was probably the very last person she needed to see right now.

Except that he was her boss. And she needed to quit her job. Which made him an impossible necessity.

"Is this what you call quick?"

His voice felt like a slap, but maybe one she needed. "Sorry. Lost my train of thought."

"You were going to tell me something official."

"Yes, I was." She walked closer, sat down on a stump opposite his. "Consider this my resignation."

He didn't so much as blink, which both shocked and infuriated her. And then he didn't speak for at least a minute, which took her from infuriated to incensed. Was that how he was going to play it, like he saw her coming all along?

She gave him her best glare. "Is silence what you call a response?"

Finally, he blinked. His mouth pressed itself into a thin, sad line. "A resignation isn't really a conversation. What do you need from me?"

"Acknowledgment would be helpful. Not to mention polite."

"Oh, are we being polite?"

"Are we not?"

Gunnar sighed, longer than she'd ever heard a person sigh. "Fine, MacBain. Resignation acknowledged."

Oh, no he didn't. No questions? No fight? Was she that irrelevant to the station and its operation? "Seriously?" she managed through her fury.

He blinked again, the motion slow, pained. "I think you're making a mistake, but I accept that it's yours to make. What else are you looking for from me?"

"You're not even going to ask why?"

"Isn't that for you to tell me? It's a standard part of a

resignation, as I understand it, but given our history, I'm not going to push."

Katy sat up straight, her arms folding themselves across her chest like a shield. "I'm not quitting this job because of our history."

Gunnar's mouth twitched, the motion quick and slight, and he gave her a slow nod. "My mistake."

"I mean, I'm resigning because of you, but not in the personal sense."

He raised an eyebrow but said nothing.

Katy jumped to her feet, body craving both fight and flight. "Okay, fine. Have it your way. You sit there like a bump on a stump, and I'll say what needs to be said." She paused, waited to see if he might answer the challenge in her words, then decided not to give him the chance. "I'm not staying on a squad with a chief who doesn't trust and support his crew."

Gunnar cocked his head and studied her. "That's simply not true."

"It is from where I stand."

"And how, exactly, did I not support you?"

"You've already forgotten today's call?"

"No. In fact, I remember it very clearly, which is why I'm confused."

"You hovered over me like I couldn't be trusted to make the right decision, and you acted like I was an embarrassment."

He pressed his fingers to his forehead. "You were very aggressive with the kid."

"He was an idiot."

"He was a patient. You lost your objectivity."

"I'm allowed to have opinions. I can have strong

feelings about a patient's choices without compromising his health."

Gunnar eyed her pointedly. "They taught you that in your paramedic training?"

"They don't cover common sense in paramedic training. I would expect the chief to know that."

His eyes narrowed, and every trace of the young boy she'd seen earlier disappeared. "You grew up pretty much getting your own way, didn't you?"

"Excuse me?"

"Spoiled. That's your problem—well, one of them— you're spoiled." His face slipped into a deep scowl and he shook his head in disgust. "I shouldn't have come looking for you in the first place."

Katy's mouth dropped open, and molten lava-level heat rushed through her body. Spoiled? Spoiled? Oh, that was rich. A wave of regret enveloped her, a wish that she'd never let him get close to her and, even more, that she hadn't confided in him, hadn't told him the secret she might never tell anyone again. And what did he mean about coming to look for her? She'd come to find him. She'd been the one to grab this particular bull by the horns.

Uncrossing her arms, she took a step away from the fire circle. "Clearly, you have no idea who I am or what's going on here. Thanks for giving me even more reason to leave this job."

The sadness filled his face again, like he struggled with his own version of regret. His lips parted, ready to say something, but then he pursed them and squinted up at her. After a few moments, he raised his right hand and gave her a quick, sharp salute. "Best of luck to you, MacBain. I hope you find what you need."

Katy's knees wobbled a little, made her wonder if she was really ready to walk. With one last look at Gunnar Wolfe, one last sweep of all she'd thought she wanted, she nodded and turned away. The relief she expected didn't come, but she shrugged that worry off as well. Sometimes logic had to trump heart and gut, and right now, logic told her this was the only way.

Chapter Seventeen

Gunnar sat on his cabin steps staring out across Bottom-less, hoping the moonlight dancing off the gentle swells of the incoming tide would settle his mood. In addition to feeling completely gobsmacked by the day's unwanted drama, he once again struggled with his lack of patience. Although he could usually prod talent along to get what he wanted, apparently even gently nudging true genius was impossible; a lesson driven home the first time he'd interrupted Hanson's train of thought about a month into their new business relationship two years ago, when he'd called to ask for information he'd requested two days prior and instead had gotten a twenty-minute tirade explaining exactly what he could do with his request.

But he'd asked Hanson for every last speck of dirt on Brandon Fontanne five freaking days ago. And having seen the kid break into a first-world government system in a matter of hours, how damn hard could it be to get inside a perverted, overhyped, sponsor-whoring mountain climber's personal computer?

Of course, after today's fiasco with Katy, including nearly blowing his cover and reason for coming to Spellbound Falls in the first place, he wasn't sure why it mattered anymore, but he just couldn't let the search go. Even if she never spoke to him again, he could seek some sort of justice on her behalf. His gut, which originally pushed him to find her, clearly still had its own agenda. Now he just needed to figure out what that was.

Gunnar stilled at the sound of the very ringtone he'd been waiting five days to hear. He stood and walked to his truck, got in, and calmly pulled his phone out of his pocket.

"Brandon Fontanne," Hanson began without preamble, his tone making the fine hairs on Gunnar's neck raise, "is—was—on a personal mission . . . sort of a sordid competition with himself . . . to rack up as many . . ."

"As many what?" Gunnar growled when Hanson fell silent.

"Jesus, Wolfe, give me a minute. I just spent the last two days puking my guts out."

From Hanson's tone, he guessed it wasn't from food poisoning. Gunnar inhaled deeply, held it to the count of eight, then slowly exhaled, trying to head off the rage he already felt building inside him. He almost didn't need to hear anything else, as "sordid competition" and "rack up" pretty much said it all.

"Rape scenarios," the kid whispered.

Gunnar stopped breathing altogether. Rage flashed blue-white, a lightning strike behind his eyes.

"Sometimes he used drugs to handle his victims, other times brute force. It seems to depend on the type of person chosen."

"Type?"

"He selected some random characteristic, like age or ethnicity or profession," Hanson whispered.

Gunnar groaned. "So, he—" He had to clear his throat. "Was he trying to see how many people he could rape in—what? A year?"

"He wasn't going for numbers," Hanson continued gutturally, "but . . . uniqueness."

"Come again?"

A deep, steadying breath came over the line. "The agenda changed every time. Like I said, sometimes it was a particular ethnicity or specific age, or it took place on a specific day—stuff like that. Other times, he went for the most bizarre location or . . . circumstance. The victims could be male or female or even transgender," Hanson rushed on thickly. "But it seems he never duplicated a scenario."

"What was the agenda a couple of months ago?" Gunnar whispered to keep from roaring.

"Professions, starting with blue collar and working his way up."

Gunnar said nothing when Hanson fell silent, because hell, he could barely breathe, much less talk. How high up the scale could a paramedic be?

"How long had this bastard been doing this?"

"Looks like he started six years ago, and based on his vlog posts, his numbers are at least in the mid double digits."

"He actually recorded the details?"

"Well, yes, but on a strongly encrypted website on the Dark Net. I was able to hack into Fontanne's laptop and cell phone within a couple of hours after you called, but while I was looking around in them, I saw signs he had a second unlisted and untraceable cell phone. So I spent two days finding it and then getting in, and that's where I came across a link to the vlog website. But whoever runs the site apparently voided Fontanne's link within hours of his death making the news, and it took me a whole day to find another way in."

"I can't believe the jackass would post something like that—" Gunnar suddenly stiffened. "Did he post pictures of his victims?"

There were several seconds of silence. "Ah, not anything identifiable, like no faces or even distinctive tattoos or birthmarks. I did see . . . there were photos of victims tied to beds and tables and . . . other places." Another breath. "But most of the photos were of arms. It's always the underside of a right forearm that has a small, freshly made . . . brand."

Gunnar stopped breathing again. It wasn't enough to just rape them? The fucking bastard branded his victims? On their forearms, where the victims would see it every day for the rest of their lives, he realized. "Holy hell," he said, fighting to get back on firmer ground. "Do you know if it's done the same way on people as it is on cattle?"

"I checked into it, and human body-branding is done fairly much the same way, and it's actually starting to gain popularity as the new tattoo. He apparently branded his victim, snapped a photo, then immediately posted it to the site."

"Did your research on body-branding show what it involves? The bastard would need something portable that would heat up easily and fairly fast."

"All it takes is for the symbol to be carved into a small piece of metal. It could even be a piece of jewelry, like a ring. He'd only have to heat it up with a cigarette lighter."

Gunnar closed his eyes on a silent curse, finding he was damn close to puking out his own guts. He'd dealt with any number of arrogant criminals, crazed terrorists, power-hungry idiots, and assholes in general, but none as sick as this bastard. No wonder Katy reacted so strongly to him managing the situation—meaning her—on the paramedic call. And then, to her way of thinking, he'd judged her, which had to have felt like a betrayal.

He sighed, overcome by the need to make things right on some level. "Can you do something to shut down, or better yet get rid of, that vlog site?"

"I'm already on it."

"Can you find out who any of the victims are?"

"I tried, but no. For as arrogantly boastful as this guy seemed, he was very careful about posting anything that could identify him or his victims."

Gunnar silently sighed, not sure what he would have done with that information anyway. At least those poor people had their privacy. And a guy like Hanson standing guard. "Good work, man," he said, ending the call.

He gently set his phone on the truck's console, scrubbed his face for a good five minutes trying to erase the images roaring through his mind, then closed his eyes and dropped his head to the steering wheel. Christ, what kind of sick, unconscionable freak made a sport of targeting specific people to rape? And think about all of those victims, right now walking around with the mark of their rapist on their forearms. Talk about scarred for life; could a brand be surgically removed? Chemically peeled? Or would it require a series of skin grafts? Then again, maybe it could be disguised with a tattoo, or the symbol could at least be altered with more branding.

Gunnar sat up and gave his face another good scrubbing, then stared out the windshield at Bottomless and thought about Katy's belief that she was somehow responsible for Fontanne's death. The bastard had been lugged off the mountain three days ago, the subsequent autopsy revealing an aneurysm had ruptured in his perverted brain, thus making him suddenly keel over dead two hundred meters from the summit.

And Katy was—had been—a paramedic. But to the best of his knowledge, she didn't have X-ray vision, so there was no way she could have known Fontanne had been on the fast track to hell.

She had, however, told Shiloh that she could see—in her mind—what was wrong with people, much like he could see angels. Which, in Gunnar's book of how the world worked, was about as likely as him being a mythical warrior from Atlantis who traveled through time killing demons—whatever the hell those were—with a sword.

Even though he'd seen a lot of strange things that defied science during his real-world travels, Gunnar couldn't decide if he was having the mother of all dreams or if he needed to be locked up for his own protection. Because, since arriving in Spellbound Falls, he'd been taking almost daily swims in an inland sea that shouldn't exist, waking up some mornings to the sound of a dead cat loudly purring on his chest, and falling under the spell of a beautiful, definitely real angel/enchantress. Oh, and he'd taken an eagle's word for it that hiking down to the fjord—which also hadn't existed five years ago— would net them a ride back to Inglenook in a boat.

Realizing he was in danger of self-destructing if he stalled any longer, Gunnar forced himself to get out of the truck. He went in his cabin and put on his swim trunks, headed down the stairs and across what was left of the beach, then walked into the water up to his waist. He dove into an oncoming swell and surfaced several yards from shore, then started swimming with every intention of not returning until he'd purged at least enough rage to be able to control his reaction the next time he saw that square, two-inch, flesh-colored bandage on the inside of Katy's right forearm. If she ever let him near her again, that was.

Chapter Eighteen

The morning after her resignation was not nearly as satisfying as Katy expected. With nowhere to go, nowhere she was needed, she stood in the doorway of her cabin and stared out at the woods, wondering what she'd been thinking. She'd stood up for herself, sure, but at what cost? So much for logic if it took away what she cared about most.

With a deep breath, she pushed herself out of bed. Maybe, with nothing but free time on her hands, she should spend the day with the people, and animals, she loved. Okay, she told herself, making a list in her head. After she got dressed, she'd hit the coffee shop, grab some coffee and donuts to take to see her parents, then swing by and take Quantum for a ride on the way back. By the end of a day like that, she might just start to see the big picture.

Just as she was about to head out, she heard the sound of truck tires on gravel. Katy peeked out the window, and the sight made her head buzz. What was he doing? There was no room for Gunnar Wolfe in this day. What nerve to just show up, especially after the way he'd acted the day before. A small voice whispered something about the way she'd acted, too, but she pushed it away and stepped back from the window.

"Katy?" he called as he knocked.

She froze, considered pretending she wasn't there, then remembered her pickup sitting out front. But she could be out for a walk, couldn't she? Or maybe someone came and picked her up, a guy even. She could have a date, a morning date, couldn't she? Who was Gunnar Wolfe to decide she wasn't allowed to date anyone else?

A second knock stilled her thoughts and made her smile. They hadn't even spoken, and she was already picking an imaginary fight. At this point, he probably wouldn't care in the slightest if she had a date. She felt pretty sure she'd sealed their future fate, or lack thereof, yesterday. But then, why was he standing outside her front door?

"Katy, it's Gunnar," he said, voice quieter but somehow more intense. "Please let me in."

A curious tingle started at the back of her neck. Maybe she could spare a few minutes in her wide-open day. With a deep breath and a big flourish, she swung the door open.

Gunnar's eyes went wide, as if he hadn't really expected her to answer. "Oh, hey. You're here."

"Yep. Though just about to head out."

He nodded. "Understood. I won't keep you long."

Katy smiled without meaning to, realizing in a hot rush that she'd missed his face. Apparently, she'd gotten quite used to starting her day with those penetrating blue eyes and that cocky smile. She stared down at the floor until the heat passed. Last thing she needed was for him to feel like more than an interruption.

She stepped back to let him enter, then folded her arms and waited for some explanation.

"Sorry to intrude," he said, "but I need your help."

"Is something wrong?" Sharp prickles of concern now crawled up Katy's back.

"No. No. Nothing's wrong."

"Then why me?"

Gunnar flashed a sheepish smile, then glanced around the room. His gaze landed on her sloppily made bed, the turquoise comforter crooked and lumpy. "Nice place. Looks lived-in."

Her frown actually stung, it landed so hard. She opened her mouth, ready for some verbal pouncing, when he held up his hands, palms out in clear surrender. "That wasn't a criticism," he said. "I'm always suspicious of people who are too neat. A home should look like people want to be there."

"Great. I passed your test. Now, what do you need?"

"I was wondering if you'll be going back to real estate now that you've left the department."

She peered at him, hard. "You came out here to discuss my career plans?"

"No. I mean, perhaps indirectly. I happen to need a real estate agent, and since I'm new to Spellbound Falls, you're the only one I know."

"Is there something wrong with your cabin?"

"Other than being small and full of mosquitos, you mean?"

"Here in Maine, we call that charm." Katy grinned, unable to resist reminding him he was an outsider.

The blue eyes twinkled. "Oh, I'm well acquainted with the charm of the place. I'm just not sure my Aunt May will share that view."

"You have an Aunt May?"

"I most certainly do. And she means to come visit very shortly."

Katy felt a little like the top of her head might lift off. This couldn't be, not if Gunnar was a warrior from Atlantis. Not if he was ages old. Unless Aunt May was from Atlantis, too . . .

Needing to center herself, she walked over to her table, pulled out a chair, and gestured for Gunnar to take the other. "Let me get my notepad," she said as she dug through a kitchen drawer.

"You'll help me?" He sounded like a kid who'd just been given ice-cream money.

"I'll listen. Do some looking. No promises."

He dropped into the straight-backed chair. "None expected."

Pen and pad in hand, Katy sat down opposite him and fixed her eyes on his. Something flickered deep inside, equal parts hope and intrigue and desire. How was this man constantly able to surprise her? "So, you need a house for Aunt May?"

"Well, I need a house for me, so I'll have a comfortable place for her to stay."

"Any specific location?"

"I was thinking I'd like something on Bottomless."

Wow. Nice choice. "That's going to be pricey."

"I figured. But something about it reminds of me home, of Iceland, which should make Aunt May feel right at home."

Iceland? Really? "You looking to rent or buy?"

"Maybe rent with the option to buy?"

Katy grinned again. "Commitment issues?" she said before she'd even realized her intention to speak. Why did this man make her want to flirt like crazy, even when she was mad at him?

Gunnar chuckled. "I'm working on it."

Hmm . . . was he now? She took a minute to jot down the details, a break from his rugged face her ulterior motive. His smile was still impossible to resist.

"Tell me about Aunt May," she said after a few moments.

"She's hard to describe. I think you're better off just meeting her."

Her heart thrummed faster than seemed healthy. "I'll be meeting her?"

He shrugged. "I think that's part of the plan."

Huh? Katy gulped. "Whose plan?"

"Well, Aunt May's mostly, but I guess mine, too."

"Why would that be her plan?" Katy's voice sounded like it had in high school, squeaking exactly like it had when Ryan Forrester asked her to prom.

"I told her about you. Before. When it seemed like there was something to tell."

"You talked to your aunt about me?"

He leveled a look on her, full of oh-please-you-know-what-I'm-talking-about energy. His eyes rolled gently, clearly calling her crazy. Katy's smile begged to come back, but she held it at bay. Man, talk about an unexpected turn of events.

"What did you tell her?"

"Apparently, more than I've ever told her about a woman before. Hence the visit."

Suddenly grateful she was already sitting down, Katy shook her head and looked back at her notepad. "You two sound close," she said.

"Well, she raised me when my father couldn't do the job. And she protected me, pulled me free of his toxic, alcoholic cloud."

Katy's heart wobbled. The little boy softness took over his features again, and a gust of gratitude blew through her, made her want to know this woman and to be a woman like her, someone who made space in her life for a child in need.

"She sounds wonderful."

"She is. She's also a handful, but I guess I consider that part of the wonderful at this point."

Her own mother's worried face flashed in Katy's mind, bringing her back to their conversation on the island and the way she'd looked when Katy told her Gunnar was one of Nicholas' warriors. There was no reason for that worry now. With the troubled childhood he'd described, Gunnar had to be mortal, had to be an ordinary human. Well, maybe not quite ordinary, with abs like his, but . . .

She grinned, heart light and relieved as it dashed out of the shadow of yesterday's conversation. She'd been wrong, about a lot of things. And now, magically, they were righting themselves before her eyes.

"Care to share the joke?" Gunnar asked.

Katy gasped and glanced up at him, blushing to think that she'd been so caught up in thoughts of him that she'd forgotten he was in the room. "I'll see what I can find on Bottomless," she said. "How soon do you need something?"

"I think it's safe to say immediately."

She laughed. "And when will your whirling dervish of an aunt arrive?"

"A day or so after immediately?" he said with a wink.

Oh, good gracious. This man should not be allowed to wink. Katy smiled at him, hoping she didn't look like a lovestruck idiot. "I'll get to work, then," she managed.

"Not a problem, considering I don't have anything else to do these days."

Gunnar dropped his head and peered up at her contritely. "Yeah, about that."

She watched him, eyebrows raised. Now what?

"I was hoping, if I offered a decent-enough apology, you might consider taking back your resignation."

The room brightened, like the sun had been waiting for a good reason to shine. Katy reached across the table and touched his hand. The heat of his skin set hers to tingling, but she tried not to think about that. "I don't think you're the one who needs to apologize."

"I did undermine your authority," he said. "And I didn't trust that you had it together."

"Well, to be honest, I'm not sure I did. I brought my baggage to the job, and that's never okay. You did what a good chief should. You kept my feet on the ground, even if that wasn't what I wanted."

"So, resignation rescinded?"

"Yes, most definitely rescinded."

Gunnar's smile lit up the room where the sun couldn't reach. Katy leaned into its warmth and let the magnitude of her thoughts sink in. This man kept her feet on the ground. He was an anchor. He was her anchor, just like her father was for her mother.

Joy flooded her body. From now on, her gut got top billing, no matter how brilliantly logic played devil's advocate. Ah, how she loved magic.

Chapter Nineteen

———

Katy closed the door on the stunning lake home and decided that, despite not really being a bona fide agent anymore, this might be her proudest real estate moment. Not only had she found the perfect house for Gunnar in record time, the price fell below his budget and offered one of the prettiest water views she'd seen anywhere on Bottomless. Plus, it was vacant and waiting for him to move in. If this place didn't make him happy, the man simply could not be pleased.

Now all she needed to do was show him the house and then show him where to sign. She glanced at her watch; three hours until sunset. He needed to see this place in daylight to properly appreciate it, and since she was due back at the station tomorrow, this afternoon offered their only shot. The thought of being back at the station made her smile since, only a day ago, she thought she'd worked her last paramedic shift ever. What a difference a few days, and one seriously important conversation, could make in a person's life.

Pulling out her phone, she texted Gunnar the address and asked him to meet her. He texted back asking if she could give him two hours and, though it bummed her out to have to wait longer for him to see it, she realized that would give her a good window to go see Quantum and to check on Shiloh. He'd been on her mind lately, like something about his life needed her attention. Plus, she really wanted to see what he'd done with his chickens.

As she pulled up to the stables at Inglenook, those very chickens seemed to form a welcoming party, swarming into the yard when she turned off her truck. Shiloh had certainly not exaggerated when sharing his poultry plan—chickens of every imaginable shape and color bobbed happily at the ground: red, brown, black, white, speckled, puffy, and plumed. The kid's vision made her smile, and she couldn't imagine a better, more inspiring and imaginative place in the world for him to grow up.

She slipped out of the pickup and immediately heard her name ring out.

"Katy! Hey, my friend Katy!" Shiloh rushed her way, his body moving not unlike those of his chickens.

"Hey there," she said and held out her arms for a big hug. "How are you doing?"

"I'm very good. Excellent." He stepped back and beamed up at her. "My chickens are laying all kinds of eggs, and Mrs. Oceanus is very happy about our business deal."

"I knew you could do it," Katy told him. "You're an amazing kid."

Shiloh's face tightened a little, wavering between nervous and perturbed. "I'm not really doing a lot of kid stuff anymore. I have a lot of jobs around here now."

"Oh, do you now? What kind of jobs?"

His small chest seemed to puff up two sizes. "I take care of the chickens all by myself, and I help out in the stables, and I keep track of how many eggs each chicken lays for Mrs. Oceanus. I even help Mom with the kid activities sometimes."

A worried twinge poked Katy in the ribs. He'd settled in just fine, made a real place for himself, but she felt suddenly concerned about him growing up too fast. Though he sounded a lot like the kid she'd met on the plane, there was a disconnected air about him, as if facts and figures had taken the place of laughter and whimsy in his life. Thinking back to that conversation on the plane, she wondered if he'd simply found a new way to avoid facing his fears.

Spotting a log bench near the stables, Katy flashed him a smile and tipped her head in the bench's direction. "Let's go sit for a minute."

"Okay, but just for a minute. I have a bunch of things to do this morning."

"So, what do you do in your free time?" she asked when they'd planted themselves side by side on the cool, planed wood.

He peered up at her. "I don't really like free time."

"What? All kids like free time. When do you play games and run and swim? And Inglenook has to be a great place for bike riding."

Shiloh shook his head. "I don't have a bike."

Katy grinned. Finally, something she could take care of. "Oh, that's an easy fix. I'm sure my cousins have extras. I can bring you one."

His head shook harder. "I don't know how to ride," he said quietly.

"Oh. Well, that's an easy fix, too. I can teach you."

Eyes narrow, Shiloh peered up at her. "I thought you were my friend."

Katy's pulse did a double-take. What a strange reaction. "I am your friend, Shiloh. Friends have fun together and teach each other things."

"What if I don't want to learn them?"

"Is that because you're scared?"

He looked away, stared out into the trees. "Why does everyone always ask that? Can't I just not like things sometimes?"

The quiver in his voice stabbed Katy in the heart. Time to back off. "Sure, buddy," she said. "You get to decide what makes you happy. Friends also care about that." She smiled down at him and waited.

After a few long moments, he nodded up at her. One side of his mouth allowed a half-smile. "Thanks, Katy," he whispered.

"Of course." She glanced at her watch. "Hey, I've still got some time. Want to go for a trail ride?"

Shiloh shook his head yet again. "That didn't go so well last time."

Katy chuckled. "Yeah, I guess you're right. But we survived, huh? Even had ourselves an adventure."

"I don't think I like adventure."

She took a deep breath. The kid meant to put her

through her paces today. A memory flashed through her mind, and her spirits lifted. "We had some fun that day, didn't we? Remember we even saw that bald eagle?"

Shiloh's eyes widened. "Oh, yeah! That was really cool. I wish we could have spent more time with him. His name is Telos, right?"

"That's right. He's a very special eagle."

He scooted a little closer on the bench. "Special how?"

Wow, the kid was a bird lover for sure. She'd have to remember to lead with that in the future. "Well, I think he has powers, and he uses them to protect the forest and the people in it." She purposely avoided the "god" word, since it might complicate what was basically a simple idea.

"Is he like a superhero?"

Katy shrugged. "Sort of. Except superheroes are fictional, made up by writers and artists. Telos is definitely real."

Shiloh let out a long, slow sigh. "I wish I knew where to find him," he breathed.

"Well, that's the thing, you don't find him. He finds people in trouble and helps them."

The boy nodded and looked back out into the woods again. Katy watched his wheels turn for a moment, then decided he needed a distraction. "Do you remember me talking about my cousins who are about your age and live near here?"

"Yeah," he said without looking her way.

"How about if I arrange for them to come and meet you?"

Shiloh pursed his lips and squinted into the distance. Just as it seemed like his thoughts might have wandered off, he said, "I'll bet they'd like to see my chickens."

Katy laughed, big and loud. This kid was something else. "I'm sure they would. I predict you'll all be instant friends."

Decision made, he glanced up at her with bright eyes. "Maybe they'll even want to help me collect the eggs. Sometimes there are even blue ones!"

Her laughter continued as she reached over to ruffle his hair. "They've seen an egg or two in their day, my friend, but I have no doubt you three will find your own sort of excitement."

Chapter Twenty

When Katy walked into the station the next morning, it felt like she'd been gone years instead of days. So much had changed, tiny shifts she couldn't exactly define but that seemed to leave monumental waves in their wake. She glanced around her, taking in the shine and power of the equipment, the organization and purpose in their arrangement, and the health and strength of her team. And they were her team, she realized. Instead of waiting for them to choose her, she'd chosen them—and this life—with her return.

Of course, before they could do any of the important work together, she had to face the elephant-sized hurdle in the room—the fact that she'd quit on them, for reasons that, to them, must range from silly to nonexistent. Though she'd practiced in her bathroom mirror all morning, she knew she ran the risk of alienating them even more than when she'd first started, if her behavior the other day hadn't already done so.

Seeing Gretchen near one of the buses, refilling supplies in the kits, she decided to start there. While she would never characterize them as close, they had bonded here and there in a way she hadn't with any of the guys, so maybe that might buy her a little leeway.

"Morning," she called out, much more exuberantly than intended.

Gretchen raised her brows and gave her a wary side-eye. "Hey," she said.

"Need any help?"

"Nope. Just about done."

Katy nodded, hopes quickly deflating. Maybe she should just plunge in and apologize. Get it over with. "So . . . I feel like I need to—"

"Listen," Gretchen said, a halting hand in the air, "no offense, but I can't work the checklist and carry on a conversation."

"Oh, sure. Right. Sorry." Katy nodded as she backed away. "We'll talk later."

Gretchen's expression twisted into a smirk. "Jeez, MacBain. You had a day off yesterday. You couldn't have gotten your talking out of your system then?"

The station stilled around her. Day off? She stared at Gretchen until it got weird, then found the best smile she could manage. "That would have been smart, wouldn't it?" she fudged. "Moving along."

"'Preciate it. Chief wants everything shipshape by the time he gets back."

The "where did he go" question blossomed, but Katy made herself bite it back. She, better than anyone, already knew that answer. He had a lot to do, what with his new house and his total lack of furniture. Moving would be easy but getting ready for Aunt May would likely not. She didn't blame him for taking the day off.

On that subject, though, her mind tripped over itself again. Gretchen acted like she'd simply been enjoying scheduled PTO instead of lying in the bed she'd made when she'd stomped off the job. Maybe Gretchen had actually had PTO, or maybe she just hadn't taken part in the gossip.

Curious, Katy set off to see who else was at the station. She walked into the kitchen, mostly for information but also for coffee, and found Welles, Paul, and Ike clustered around the table. Apparently they weren't as worried about Gunnar's "shipshape" directive.

"Hey, guys," she said, grateful for the distraction of the coffeepot. She peeked at them as she poured, eager for clues.

"Yo." Welles gave her a small salute and a decent-sized smile.

She took a little breath and tended to cream and sugar.

"Morning," Ike grumbled, sounding like ordinary Ike.

Just as Katy took another breath, inching her way to relief, Paul looked up and caught her eye. "About time," he said. "I've been waiting for you."

Her nerves flared like a grease fire. There it was, the moment. She'd come to the kitchen to face it, and the fire wasn't going to put itself out, so that made it go-time. "Let me sit first," she told him.

Pursing his lips with almost comic annoyance, Paul watched and waited. "You situated, princess?"

Katy winced. She'd pissed him off. That made sense.

Only he and Gretchen had been there, and she'd bailed before transport and paperwork, which wasn't cool. And then she'd bailed on the department entirely, which was just cowardly and stupid. She picked up her coffee and held it in front of her like a tiny shield. "Go for it."

"I never got to ask if you were okay the other day."

She cocked her head and peered at him. "Excuse me?"

"That kid obviously pushed your buttons, and I could see you were losing it, but I want you to know I respect you for stepping back instead."

Katy nearly dropped her cup. "Wow. Thanks."

"You sound surprised."

"I guess I am."

Paul chuckled. "Don't blame you. We're not so good with the praise around here."

"You can say that again." Welles scanned the table, as if hoping he might be next in line for a compliment.

"Do something worth praising and you'll get yours, kid," Ike barked, though his eyes twinkled.

Katy took a huge gulp of her coffee, mostly to hide as much of her face as possible, and then had to fight to keep the scalding liquid in her mouth instead of spitting it all over the table. Smooth move, slick. But none of this made sense. They all acted like nothing had happened, or, even stranger, like the exact right thing had happened.

Then it hit her. No one knew. Though she quit on him, Gunnar said nothing to anyone. He'd protected her, and all she'd shared with him, even when she probably didn't deserve it. And then, the next day, he'd apologized. This was no ordinary man, ladies and gentlemen.

She glanced up and found three sets of eyes on her,

the accompanying expressions ranging from concerned to bemused to annoyed. "Guess I should get to work," she murmured with a sheepish smile.

"Everything okay in there, MacBain? That brain of yours seems like a busy place."

Katy stood and walked her cup to the sink, a new lift in her step. "Busier than you could ever imagine, Higgins. And since when do you care?" She turned back and treated him to her most intimidating glare.

He grinned and shrugged. "Just making conversation, like I do with everyone on the team."

She tried to hold her glare, but it wouldn't stay. The team. That sure had a nice ring to it. Before she could think of an appropriately quippy response, the tones sounded.

"Attention Spellbound Falls Fire & Rescue. Units Nine-eighty-seven and Spellbound Ambulance Two are asked to respond to Inglenook Resort for a group of missing kids, all believed to be nine to ten years old. Subjects were last seen in the woods near the stables and have not been heard from in a couple of hours. The children's parents are onsite and will assist with the search. Copy units nine-eighty-seven and Spellbound Ambulance Two: Inglenook Resort for three missing children, believed to be lost in the woods. Piscataquis out, twenty-two-fourteen."

Every bit of the previous moment's pleasure drained from Katy's body. She'd arranged a playdate for Shiloh and her cousins today. That had to be them.

With a ferocity she'd never felt before, Katy dashed to the bus, loaded her kit, and jumped into the cab. "Whoever's driving has exactly five seconds to get us rolling or I'm on my way," she called, just as Gretchen opened the driver's door.

"I'm on it, MacBain," she said and fired up the engine.

The ambulance's back doors slammed shut, and two quick smacks on the side of the bus set them in motion. Eyes fixed straight ahead, Katy started counting to keep her mind from wandering. The last thing she needed was to picture even one of those kids in any kind of trouble.

Chapter Twenty-One

As soon as Gunnar heard "Inglenook" come across on his radio, he turned the truck around and, tires squealing, raced in the other direction. As if he didn't have enough to deal with, having just discovered that his darling, and highly nosy, aunt had actually been hiding out in Spellbound Falls for days, doing a "different sort" of research, as she put it. He knew that gray head he'd glimpsed in the crowd on the night of the campfire looked familiar.

"Change of plans, Gunny?" Aunt May said.

He glanced over at her, saw the hint of a smile in her questioning face, and rolled his eyes. "I think it's more accurate to say one more change of plans, don't you agree?"

She let the smile loose. "I told you I was coming for a visit."

"Yes, but you didn't mention that you were already here at that point."

"I needed a little time to myself. Plus, I wanted to check out your new hometown for myself. What's the big deal?"

Gunnar sighed. "No big deal at all, apparently."

"And just as soon as I finished my research, I called you to come pick me up."

"Which nearly gave me a heart attack!"

"A strong, healthy guy like you? Never." She pursed her grinning lips and stared out the window, obviously pleased with herself.

"So, what deep dark secrets did you uncover about Spellbound Falls?"

Aunt May looked back at him, her brow arch promising intrigue. "All in good time, Gunny. All in good time." She tucked that trademark silver hair behind her ears and leaned back in her seat. "I assume we're going on that rescue call?"

"Can't get anything by you," he said with a smirk.

"Do you even have to respond on your days off?"

He shook his head and gripped the wheel tighter. "No, it's my choice, but this one sounds like I might want to be there."

Silence swelled, long enough to surprise him, and he looked over at his aunt once again. Her face questioned more aggressively this time, discerning hazel eyes in full squint and thin lips pooched. "What's different about this one?"

"I have a young friend who lives at Inglenook. And I have a feeling he's one of the missing kids."

"And?"

"That's not enough?"

"Of course it's enough, but it's not the whole story."

Gunnar sighed. He was clearly a little out of practice when it came to handling May. Nothing slipped past her. Not. One. Thing.

"Okay, Aunt Sherlock, you got me. Katy boards her horse at the Inglenook stables, and she's particularly close to the young boy I mentioned. Even worse, I have a feeling the other two missing kids are her cousins."

"Got it," she said. "You absolutely have to be there."

"Thanks for understanding." Gunnar almost missed the turn for Inglenook and skidded them where they needed to go at the last minute. "Sorry about that."

"No need for apologies. I'm enjoying seeing you in action."

Though his worry intensified with every mile, a small bit of amusement slipped between the cracks. Leave it to his aunt to turn this into an experience she could use for her own purposes. Maybe the crisis would even take the edge off her curiosity about Katy.

"So, how will I recognize her?"

Gunnar rolled his eyes. That had to be a new record for dashing his hopes. "Okay, time for some ground rules. I know it's not ideal, but I'm really going to need you to stay in the truck. My team needs to be able to do its job without interruption."

May gasped loudly, obviously for effect. "I'm not an idiot, Gunny. I would never endanger those children by distracting the searchers. I might be a busybody, but only in the right circumstances."

He nodded and peered into the distance. Flashes of rescue red and yellow glinting between the leaves told him he'd nearly reached the stable.

"You didn't answer me," Aunt May said.

"You don't need an answer. You're staying in the truck."

She rapped on the window. "Fortunately, this truck has these clever glass inserts in every direction. I feel like I'll be able to see a great deal from here."

That one made a laugh tumble right out. "Touché, Auntie. Touché."

He slowed the truck and scanned the road ahead. There was the bus, parked near the stables, and the big engine still on the road. He sure hoped the team had been able to make some progress with his checklists before the call came in. It would only cause delays if any equipment still awaited inspection back at the station. Swinging his truck in behind the engine, he shifted into park and turned to his aunt.

"There's water in the cooler behind the seat if you get thirsty, and I'm leaving the keys in the ignition in case you have to move the truck. Anything you need, help yourself. Hopefully they just made themselves a fort out of branches and leaves and we'll find them in no time."

"Fingers crossed. Go get 'em, Gunny," Aunt May said.

"Thanks for understanding." He opened the door and stepped out of the truck.

"Oh, one more thing . . ." His aunt held a petite finger in the air.

"Yes?"

"If I see Ms. MacBain, can I introduce myself?"

Exasperation washed over him. "Can't you just wait until this is over? I promise to introduce you properly," he said, then stopped to think. "Wait. I didn't tell you what she looks like."

A mysterious smile spread across her face. "I have excellent powers of deduction."

Bewildered, Gunnar opened his mouth to say more, but she fluttered her hands at him. "Go, go. You have a job to do."

Yes, he did. And now that thoughts of Katy were in his head, the need to see her overwhelmed him. She had to be worried and, knowing her, she'd been leading the charge in his absence.

He quickened his pace and hurried toward the stables. A crowd of people gathered on the lawn just beyond the building, and the sun glinted on the particular shade of mahogany he loved best. No matter what happened this day, it needed to happen with him by Katy's side.

Katy patted her vest and checked her gear one last time, as much a tactic to quiet the voice in her head as to make sure she was as prepared as possible. The voice had no intention of being quieted, however. *This is your fault. You were in such a hurry to get him out of his comfort zone, to find him friends and get him to do kid things. Now they're all missing. What if they went swimming by themselves? What if you made Shiloh feel like he had to prove himself in some way?*

Tears wobbled atop her lower lashes. Slowly, carefully, she inched a hand up to sweep them away. Pros didn't cry on rescue calls, even when they knew the person needing help. Instead of crying, she needed to be doing something, she needed to put all her skills and senses to use to bring this awful situation to a close.

She stood in the crowd of SFF&R personnel, police officers, and volunteers, trying to listen to Jake Sheppard's instructions, but her feet just wanted to get moving. She cast her gaze into the distance, scanning the trees for the best place to start looking, for an inviting forest path that might appeal to three adventure-seeking kids.

What were they looking for? What were they thinking?

Frustrated, Katy brought her attention back to Jake and, standing near him, she spotted Margo. The woman looked so terrified Katy's own knees almost buckled. Margo seemed to hang on Jake's every word, nodding and clutching a flashlight to her chest. In the woman's face, Katy glimpsed shades of the concern she'd seen in her own mother's expression throughout her life, especially that day, not so long ago, when she'd told her what had happened with Brandon Fontanne. A wave of indignation, sharp as a bundle of knives, lodged in her gut, stole her breath. From now on, she promised, she'd do whatever she could to make sure she never saw that kind of concern on a parent's face again.

"Everyone clear on that?" Jake's voice broke through the fog of Katy's thoughts.

She startled and glanced around her. Everyone nodded and prepared to head out. Great. She'd missed the instructions. She and her promise were off to a wonderful start.

With a huff of exasperation, she turned and spotted Gunnar working his way through the crowd. Relief swept through her, made her realize why she'd felt so unsteady. His presence was exactly what she needed. Together, they could find the kids, she just knew it.

"Gunnar," she called out.

He glanced up and caught her eye. He held his smile in check, she knew, but she felt it warm her nonetheless. In a few quick strides, he stood at her side. He reached out and squeezed her hand, then put on his business face. "Ready to move out?" he said.

Katy nodded, finally feeling like all of her systems were set to go. "Glad you're here."

Satisfaction warmed his features. "Couldn't be anywhere else. Any ideas about where they might have gone?"

She shook her head. "I've been wracking my brain, but no. I say we pick a horse trail and head out. I don't think I can see Shiloh venturing too far off the beaten path. He's not exactly an adventurous kid."

"Makes sense. Though your cousins might be leading the charge, yes? Something tells me they're a little more confident in the woods."

Katy's heart sank. She hadn't thought of that. The twins were not shy about exploring and taking risks. How could they be, given their lineage?

"Good point," she said. "Let's start with the horse trail but be on the lookout for signs they went elsewhere."

Gunnar nodded and off they went, one of at least a dozen groups of searchers, all crunching through the brush and calling the boys' names. Within minutes, however, Katy and Gunnar had isolated themselves, and the hushed, insulated feel of the woods kicked her nerves into high gear. Already the other searchers' voices faded, the leaves and brush swallowing sounds as soon as they appeared.

"You okay?" Gunnar's feet fell into rhythm with hers.

"Yep. Can't be anything else."

"Agreed. And we'll find them, Katy. You know these boys. You know how they think."

"I thought I did, but I sure didn't see this coming. I mean, I arranged this little meeting of the boys' club. You'd think it would occur to me that they might actually act like boys."

He clasped her shoulder with a warm hand. "Like you said, Shiloh's not really an 'outside the lines' type of kid. I wouldn't have expected this, either."

Katy reached up to lay her hand atop his. A tingle rolled across her skin, like a laser fusing their flesh together. She closed her eyes, enjoying for a few short seconds before pulling her hand back. More of that later, she promised herself as he put his own hand back in his pocket. For now, they had other things to focus on.

Several yards ahead, she spotted a signpost at the trail fork, its carved yellow letters visible but not readable just yet. As she squinted into the distance, trying to figure in advance which way they should go, a memory burst like a flashbulb in her brain. She's seen a sign like that not too long ago, when she and Gunnar and Shiloh had been trying to walk their way out of the woods. When they'd seen Telos.

I wish I knew where to find him.

Shiloh's voice filled her mind, a pitch-perfect replica of how he'd sounded that day. They'd been a quarter of a mile from the fjord when Telos had appeared. Of course that's where he'd go if he wanted to find the eagle.

"I've got it." She stopped and turned to Gunnar.

"You know where they are?"

Katy nodded. "Pretty sure Shiloh went in search of Telos."

His brows lowered, creasing the bridge of his nose. "Telos? The eagle?"

"Yep. We talked about him the other day. Shiloh said he wished he could figure out how he could see him again."

"But where would he go to do that?"

Certainty growing, Katy jogged toward the sign. One arrow pointed to the covered bridge, which led back toward town, and the other pointed to the fjord. "This way," she called.

Gunnar hurried to catch up. "How do you know?"

"That's where we last saw Telos, a quarter of a mile from the fjord."

He broke into a smile. "Well done, MacBain. I knew you'd figure it out."

Katy started jogging again. "Figuring it out and finding the kids are two different things. We have to hurry."

"Right behind you."

The woods echoed with their footfalls and, once again, they fell into rhythm, the pace much faster this time. Within fifteen or so minutes, they found the signpost they'd been looking for, and Katy pulled to a stop. Her heart pounded like crazy, and she knew it wasn't because of the run.

"Shiloh?" she called. "Ethan? Owen? Where are you guys?"

Gunnar paused at the sign, eyes scanning the ground like a searchlight. "I don't see any tracks leading off the path."

"Well with ground cover like this, it would be tough to see. Maybe we need to go closer to the fjord?"

"Maybe," he said. "But tell me more about your conversation with Shiloh first."

Katy took a deep breath and tried to remember the details. "I was trying to get him to relax a little, to think about the fun of being a kid, and he wasn't really having it. So, I tried to cheer him up by reminding him about our adventure in the woods, Telos included."

Gunnar sighed. "Anything else?"

"Not really. I mean, we talked about Telos helping people, that he shows up when they're in trouble, and Shiloh compared him to a superhero. That was pretty much it." She walked up and down the path as she talked, peering into the distance.

"A superhero, huh?"

"Yeah." Katy stopped and took a deep breath. "I told him that wasn't quite right, that . . ." Her brain lit up again, this time with flashes of red and yellow; emergency colors. "Oh, man."

"What?"

"Trouble. I said Telos helps people in trouble." She started into the woods, aiming herself directly toward the fjord.

"What does that mean? Where are you going?" Gunnar stomped a path through the leaves behind her.

Katy turned to face him. "Think about it. Three young boys, eager to see a superhero-like bald eagle who shows up when something goes wrong."

Gunnar's eyes lit up. "So they try to make something go wrong."

She nodded, her pulse sending a terrified beat through her body. "And then something goes wrong."

Their eyes met, and she let herself soak up his strength, his concern, his essence. They were stronger together, and if any two people could save these kids, Katy knew she and Gunnar were the two. They had to find them. Now.

Chapter Twenty-Two

"Okay, if you were nine and wanted to attract the attention of magical bald eagle, what would you do?" Gunnar stared at Katy like the answer might write itself on her forehead. She was just so damn good at figuring things out.

"Keep in mind that this particular nine-year-old really fears the unknown." She restarted her trek through the brush, sweeping her head from side to side as she walked. "Ethan! Owen! Shiloh!" she called as she walked.

"Shiloh?" Gunnar repeated. "Ethan? Owen? You guys okay?"

They paused, listened. Not so much as a crackling leaf broke the silence. "Let's just keep moving toward the fjord," Katy said. "Ethan and Owen know that area well, so they might go there."

"Makes sense." A little thrill rushed through him, a twinge of admiration for this woman who'd pretty much taken charge of his life in the past several weeks. He watched her stride ahead, voice strong and determined, and though he knew this was not the moment to indulge his attraction, something inside said that moment sure as hell better come soon. Katy MacBain was the find of a lifetime—likely many lifetimes—and the sooner he made her his, the better his life would be.

Desire acknowledged, he tucked it away and got back to business. These kids might have created a world of trouble for themselves, and the sooner they discovered that trouble, the better. Swinging his head from side to side, he scanned the area like Katy, taking in as many details of the landscape as his eyes would allow.

Minutes passed, taking them farther and farther from the trail. Just as Gunnar was about to suggest they circle back and reorient themselves, something at the corner of his eye snatched his attention. He glanced back and saw the pattern, a swath of broken bush limbs, snapped on both sides like something, or someone, had charged right through. "Over here," he called and darted toward the bushes.

"You see something?" Katy's two feet made the sound of ten as she scurried in his direction.

"I think they went this way."

Gunnar sprinted past the bushes, then slammed on the brakes. Just on the other side lay a yellow nylon rope, one end tied to the base of one of the bushes. The other end disappeared over the side of a steep slope. "Oh, no," he said, before he caught himself.

"What? What? Tell me what you see," Katy yelled from several feet back.

"It's okay," he said. "They've definitely been this way."

She skidded up behind him and peered over his shoulder. "Does that rope go over the ravine? Oh my God."

Gunnar held up a cautioning hand and inched toward the edge of the slope. "It's not a ravine. It's not that steep." Holding on to the rope, he stepped as close as he could and looked over, then let loose a huge breath, panic mixed with relief. "There they are," he said.

"You see them? They're okay?" Katy rushed up behind him, eager to see for herself.

"Whoa, easy," he said quietly. Down below, he counted three small heads, all alert and looking up at him. "You guys okay?" he called, but their mix of nods and waves didn't quite offer confirmation.

"Oh, thank goodness," Katy breathed. She leaned against him, just the tiniest bit, and he steadied his feet to let her stay that way for a second. "How are we going to get down there?"

Gunnar took his own deep breath. Time to be the fire chief, the head rescuer, the example-setter. He took a couple of steps back from the edge, inching her back as he went, then turned to face her. The relief in her gray eyes washed over him, and he flashed her a quick smile.

"Let me call this in first and get some help on the way. Then let's see if there's a way to traverse our way down."

Katy nodded and started walking the edge, surveying the terrain below. He watched her as he grabbed his radio and described their location to the searchers with as much detail as possible. By the time he finished, she'd identified a path with more dirt than brush, accented by small boulders here and there that would make excellent footholds.

"Nice work," he said, coming up behind her. "We should be down to them in no time."

She nodded and peered down at the boys. "I wish we could see them a little better. I need to know they're okay."

Gunnar spun her to face him and planted his hands on her shoulders. "They're alive and they're responsive. That's all we really need to know. Whatever else is going on down there can be addressed."

Katy's mouth bent into a tiny smile. "Yes, Chief," she said with purpose. "Shall I get that rope?"

He nodded, happy to see her shift back into pro mode. "Let's take it down with us. I think we can climb down without it, but I'd hate to need it at some point and not have it at hand."

With a small salute, Katy went to retrieve it while he planned their route. Working together, they moved down the slope in a series of partnered movements, each making sure to be steady, and steady the other, before tackling the next section. As they neared, the boys yelled and cheered, and Gunnar enjoyed watching Katy's smile widen and her eyes grow brighter each time they hooted and hollered.

Finally, nearly a half-hour later, they reached the cluster of kids.

"Katy!" they all screamed, and Gunnar watched the two raven-haired twins, Ethan indistinguishable from Owen to his eye, rush to hug their cousin. He grinned, thrilled to see them jumping and moving, then glanced over to Shiloh, who remained on the ground, eyes full of tears.

His pulse stuttered. Something wasn't right. He peered closer, noticed the odd way the boy's leg bent beneath him. "Katy?" he said carefully, trying to keep his voice even and casual.

She finished her hug and glanced up at him, eyes immediately soaking up what he didn't say. Her gaze darted to Shiloh, and she hurried over, remembering to smile at the last minute. "Shiloh! There you are. Boy, you had us worried."

"Hi, Katy," he murmured, the tears starting to spill over the rims of his eyes.

"You okay, buddy?" She squatted down by his side. "What's up with your leg? Does it hurt?"

He nodded, and his eyes widened to what seemed like twice their size. "It hurts a lot. And my insides, too. I've been trying to stay real still, but it's hard."

Gunnar moved closer, and he and Katy shared an alarmed look. "I'll radio again," he told her. "Help should be here soon." He sent a call out to the group, but no answer came back. Slightly concerned, he waved the twins over and settled them nearby, then posted himself near Katy and Shiloh.

"Can you tell me what happened?" she asked the boy.

He hung his head. "We wanted to see Telos. Ethan and Owen knew about him, too, but they had never seen him. I thought if we all hung on the rope, close to where we saw him last time, and yelled for help, he would come to us."

Katy reached out and squeezed his hand. "It's okay, Shiloh. It's a pretty logical plan, just not very practical."

Shiloh nodded, slow and sad. "I figured that out when I lost my grip on the rope. I was on the bottom, and I fell really far. Ethan and Owen climbed down so I wouldn't be alone."

She smiled. "Sounds like you found yourself some good friends."

He swatted at his tears and nodded again. "Yeah, but Telos never came. Not even when I fell."

"Well, maybe he knew you tried to trick him. Gods don't like that so much."

Gunnar nodded, then stopped himself. What was he doing? He still wasn't sure he bought this god stuff of Katy's.

Shiloh's tears intensified. "But then I really needed help. And he still didn't come."

"I'm sure he had his reasons. Remember, from up there, Telos can see everything. He sees the big picture in ways you can't." Katy leaned forward and laid her hands on Shiloh's leg. She glanced back at Gunnar and sent another message with her eyes. "I'm going to need to check you out, okay? I need to see how badly you're hurt."

"Okay," the boy said, his voice now a whisper. "I don't feel so good, Katy. Can you get my mom now? I know she misses me." He leaned back against the ridge, eyes fluttering.

Katy's body stiffened. "Anything from the team?" she asked.

Gunnar shook his head, wishing he had another answer.

She pursed her lips and studied him. "I'm going to have to do something, and I don't have time to explain it all to you."

"What's to explain?" Her tone made the hairs on his arms stand at attention.

"I'm just going to say this: Remember Tux?"

"The cat?"

"Yes."

He peered at her. Had the stress softened her brain? Why were they talking about cats?

"Do you remember the day he was hurt?"

"Yes."

"And then he wasn't hurt?"

"Yes . . ."

She pursed her lips again. "That's all you get for now. No questions and no interruptions, got it?"

He nodded slowly, though he had no idea what he'd just agreed to. He watched as Katy turned back to Shiloh, then bent down and placed her cheek against his. "I've got you, buddy," she whispered. "I can help."

Gunnar felt his mouth open, but he pressed it closed. No questions, he told himself. Just give her what she asks for. He stared as her eyes closed, then moved rapidly beneath her lids like she was dreaming. Awe enveloped him and suddenly, in a way he could not have explained if the future of the world depended on it, he knew—just knew—that all things were indeed possible.

After a moment, Katy's eyes flashed open, the gray like molten silver. "I need your help," she said.

"Anything."

She smiled at him then, her face so full of love she almost seemed to shimmer. "Come closer," she said. "Put your hands on my waist."

His mind felt like one big question mark, but he shook it off and nodded. "I can do that."

"No matter what you feel or hear, don't let go," she said.

"Never," he promised and reached for her waist.

Together, they leaned forward again, Katy's cheek against Shiloh's, and Gunnar's cheek resting on her back. A slow beat pulsed out from her body, syncing his heart with hers and blending the lines between them. He closed his eyes, and a rainbow of light appeared behind them, its colors so brilliant he had to lift his lids and disengage. His hands never moved, however, never left the firm base of her body, never broke the contact between the two of them and the earth below.

In that moment, Gunnar understood her every cell, her every belief, her every yearning. As she worked frantically to alleviate Shiloh's pain, he glimpsed the shadows of her pain floating beneath. He felt her struggles and traumas, felt how hard she'd worked to handle what Brandon Fontanne had forced upon her and how she'd made peace with the boundaries of her obligation. In that moment, he understood that she'd saved herself by allowing justice to unfold in its own way. Not only did the fight not belong to him, it had, in fact, already been valiantly won.

A sharp screech cut the air, and behind him, the twins started leaping and shouting. "Telos. It's Telos," they called over and over.

The urge to look up clawed at Gunnar, but he could not, would not, move. Not until Katy said so. He closed his eyes again, let some part of him tumble into the light this time. The energy made him both dizzy and calm. Finally, the light dimmed, leveled off into a serene white glow.

"It's okay," she whispered. "You can let go now."

"Do I have to?" he said and turned his head to softly kiss the center of her back.

"Careful, Chief," she said with a chuckle. "There's still work to be done."

He gave a little laugh and sat back, now fully conscious of the uproar unfolding behind him. The twins, caught up in a happy dance, pointed and shouted at a crowd of searchers and rescuers on the ridge far above. Gunnar raised both thumbs in the air, hoping his team could see from their perch.

"What's going on?" Shiloh asked sleepily. "Is my mom here?"

"She sure is, young man," Katy said. "We have all the help we could ask for."

The boy stared at the sky, then suddenly sat up and pointed. "It's Telos!"

Katy smiled. "Looks like he was here all along."

Gunnar got to his feet and reached down to help Katy stand, then pulled her into an embrace. "It seems we have a quite a bit to talk about, Ms. MacBain."

"It seems we have quite an audience, Mr. Wolfe."

"Then I hope they enjoy what they're about to see." Grinning, he bent down and kissed her exactly as the woman of his dreams deserved to be kissed. She might be the strongest, wildest, most stubborn and surprising creature he'd ever met, but he wondered if she'd mind very much if he fell in love with her anyway.

Chapter Twenty-Three

"Are you sure you don't mind waiting back at the house, Aunt May?"

From the back of the truck's cab, Katy watched Gunnar's aunt turn and give him a seriously perturbed look. She bit her lip, wondering if and when they'd tell him they'd already met and that his Aunt May, better known as Mayme, was very likely the reason they had any future at all.

"Who, exactly, do you think you're talking to, Gunny? Is this a show for your girl?"

Gunnar grinned. "I'm just trying to be a good host."

"A good host? Does a good host take his guest to a rescue call? Does a good host leave his guest in the truck while he traipses through the woods for hours? Does a good host let his guest wait alone at his house while he sees his girl back to her house?"

Anxiety edged up the back of Katy's throat. This was not the kind of impression she wanted to make on Gunnar's only real family, especially as an encore to her emotional meltdown on the sidewalk the other day. She knew it was a bad idea to let him drive her home. She should have just gone back to the station with the team and slept there.

But he'd been so persistent, and Aunt May hadn't seemed nearly so annoyed when they decided on the plan. In fact, she'd had a twinkle in her eye that made it seem like the whole thing was her idea. Katy decided she needed to do some sort of damage control and fast.

"I am so sorry, Aunt May. This visit must be off to a terrible start for you. Gunnar, you just drop me off and take your aunt home. She needs to put her feet up while you cook her a good meal."

Practically in unison, Gunnar and Aunt May burst into snorting laughter. "Oh, she'll do just fine, Gunny. This one's a keeper. I guess searching for her wasn't a wild-goose chase after all."

Katy's mouth fell open. Jokes didn't sneak up on her often. And what was that about searching for her? She stared at Gunnar, then caught his eyes searching for hers in the rearview mirror. Though laugh lines flanked them, she saw a nervous flicker in their depths. "Welcome to the clan," he said. "Nobody gets in without passing the Aunt May test."

Or the Mayme test, apparently. Katy sat back with a deep sigh, eventually succumbing to May's musical laughter. "Wow, I was shaking back here. You were very convincing."

"Never hurts to remind the young folks who's in

charge," May chuckled. "But, on a serious note, I want you both to know what a pleasure it was to watch you in action today. I know you said to stay in the truck, Gunny, but how could I not get out and help search for those kids? When you radioed to say you'd found them, I felt like I helped save the world. And then when that eagle appeared and literally led the whole bunch of us to you two . . . well, that was a kind of magic I didn't know existed before today."

Katy's whole body warmed. They had witnessed something special today, and that was saying a lot, since magic basically defined the whole of Spellbound Falls.

"I think you might be reading a bit too much into the eagle's role, Aunt May, but I am pretty happy about the outcome."

"Oh, you weren't there, Gunny. I heard that eagle screech and screech until he was sure we were paying attention. He just kept sweeping back and forth between the searchers, almost like he was herding us from the sky. And then, all of sudden, we saw you all at the bottom of that hill. You can say what you will, but I know that bird had a plan."

"I'm going to vote with Aunt May on this one," Katy said. "Of course, I'm the one who told you about Telos in the first place."

"This girl gets smarter and smarter all the time, Gunny." Aunt May glanced back and winked, making Katy feel like she'd not only passed the test but also gained a really powerful ally.

"Well, I know better than to argue with either of you, so I guess this discussion has come to an end," Gunnar said and pulled the truck into his new driveway. "I won't be long, Aunt May. Just want to see that this one actually goes home and rests after today's heroics."

"Gunny, I am so tired after this little adventure, all I want is a hot bath and long nap. And there's a good chance that nap will stretch right through to morning. Don't you dare hurry on my behalf." She leaned over and kissed his cheek, then opened the door and stepped out of the truck. "I'm guessing you'll want to ride up here, my dear, so why don't you come on out and get a hug before you go."

Katy jumped out and dashed around the truck, a little sorry to say good-bye to this wonderful woman, especially now that she was more than a stranger on the sidewalk. She held her arms wide and gave a hug as good as the one she got. "I'm so happy to know you, Aunt May. You are clearly, and deservedly, the most special person in Gunnar's life."

The woman pulled back and looked at her, that familiar twinkle in her eye. "Not anymore, my dear. I feel certain we get to share that title." With a quick kiss to Katy's cheek, she headed for the door. "You two go . . . decompress," she said and gave them a bawdy wink. "We'll catch up tomorrow."

"Well, that's Aunt May," Gunnar said when Katy got back in the truck.

"I don't think I could love her more," she told him, pursing her lips around the secret she and Mayme shared. It would come out soon enough, she decided, and in the meantime, he had a secret of his own to answer for. "What did she mean about searching for me?"

Gunnar's eyes widened, and he gripped the steering

wheel hard before peeking her way. "Yeah . . . about that . . . I, um . . ."

Katy smiled, his reaction giving shape to what had been a string of random comments. Any firefighters catch her fancy? He never should have looked for her in the first place. A wild-goose chase. She stopped his sputtering with a raised palm. "Just answer me this: does it have anything to do with my friend Jane?"

His mouth quirked and he hung his head. "It seems wise to neither confirm nor deny her involvement."

She barked out a laugh. "Oh, you two know each other all right."

"I was going to tell you, I swear."

Katy crossed her arms and arched her brow. "Were ye now? Just when did you plan to do that?"

He dropped his head again. "I hadn't quite figured that out yet."

She shook her head and studied him. Had a kinder, sexier, more adorable man ever existed? "I forgive you," she said. "Knowing Jane the way I do, I'm pretty sure you never had a choice."

Gunnar's face brightened, and he looked her in the eye. "If it makes it any better, it was the best damned order I've ever been given."

"Well played, Mr. Wolfe," Katy said with a chuckle. "Now, let's go decompress."

They reached the campground in record time, the two of them grinning the whole way. Gunnar had held her hand as he drove, lifting the back of it to his lips at each stoplight, which, in addition to filling her with the most amazing combination of longing and tenderness, had her on sexual pins and needles by the time they finally arrived.

"So, your cabin then?" Gunnar's eyes had never looked so blue, and Katy literally couldn't find the words to answer him.

His flirty expression crumbled. "I . . . um . . . so . . . you know, we don't have to rush anything. I'm never going to be the guy who presses the issue or gets upset. You tell me when, and—"

"Go to your cabin," Katy blurted.

His eyes widened and he almost grinned. "Really?"

"Of course, really. Do you have any idea how much delicious time you're wasting with this 'er . . . um . . . so' business?"

Without another word, he flipped the truck into reverse, turned them around, and flew down the gravel road. They skidded to a stop in front of a cabin identical to hers, though without the tinkly silver wind chime near the front door. "As requested, mademoiselle. Welcome to Chez Wolfe."

She arched her brows at him. "You speak French?"

"I think Frenglish might be the more appropriate name."

"Frenglish?"

"Oui, oui."

"You better stop talking and get me into that cabin before every bit of my interest dries up, monsieur."

With a hearty laugh, Gunnar hurried out of the cab, ran around to her side of the truck, gathered her in his arms, and carried her to the front door. Then, realizing his hands were occupied, he looked at her with such concerned ambivalence she burst into giggles. "Put me down. That door key is clearly the most critical part of this equation at the moment."

He followed her directions like a man possessed, and Katy's feet hit the ground quickly but gently. She watched with bemusement as he sifted through his keys, then struggled with the lock, and finally flung the door as wide as it would go. "The famous wooden tent, at your disposal."

She stepped inside like she'd never been there before, took a second to note that his striped comforter also looked a bit lumpy and that every surface in the cabin sported a coffee cup. Either he considered them a stylistic touch or he wasn't so great at picking up after himself, either. Most of all, the honesty pleased her—no fuss and exactly as represented. Those were difficult qualities to find, in life and in people.

Saying nothing, she turned and grabbed him, wrapping him in the same sort of embrace he'd used on her in the woods. He smiled—surprises clearly pleased him—and stared into her eyes, waiting.

"I get to lead, huh?" Katy breathed.

"Most definitely." He slid his hand along her back and pressed her closer. "This time."

Peering up at him, she slowly unbuttoned his shirt. When it hung open, his broad, chiseled chest hers to touch, she pulled back and slowly unbuttoned her own shirt, eyes never leaving his.

His breathing intensified, and she felt the eager energy in his hands as they softly kneaded her back. With a tiny smile, she stepped away from him and, eyes still fixed, carefully removed every item of clothing separating her skin from his. He gasped and licked his lips but waited, just waited.

Unable to keep from touching him, Katy reached out and peeled his shirt back. She pressed her palms against his chest, then kissed the skin between her hands. He leaned forward to kiss her, but she gently held him back. Lifting up on her toes, she kissed the base of his throat, breathing in his musky, woodsy scent. Then she kissed his chin, and, finally, his lips.

They touched lightly at first, and then, just as the lines between their bodies had blurred in the forest, atoms and molecules took over, bonding and blending into a new chemical compound. Katy gasped at the feeling, at the power of simply being next to him, and a small anxious tremor sprouted deep within. What if this consumed her? What if she completely lost control? What if she wasn't ready?

She peered up into his eyes and her soul settled. She wanted this. With every bit of her, she wanted this. And to lose control in something desired, in something shared and equal and real, meant acceptance, not consumption. She was safe here, with him. They both knew it.

Aflame with certainty, Katy undid Gunnar's belt as she backed him toward the bed. He smiled down at her, eyes blazing but still gentle. Who was this beautiful, wonderful, patient phoenix of a man? He definitely needed to be rewarded, and she trembled at the thought of the pleasure his reward would give her.

"Now," she whispered up to him.

His left brow rose, just a touch, as if to ask if she was

sure. She raised hers in response, then pushed him back
onto the bed. The blending began anew, as hungry fingers explored every curve, every hollow. They kissed
until they couldn't breathe, bodies arching to be closer
and closer. How had she ever feared this?

"I don't have words for how beautiful you are," Gunnar murmured, rising up to gaze down at her with de-
votion.

Katy smiled. "Words aren't exactly what I'm after at
the moment."

His brow questioned her again, the arch higher and
more lustful this time. His fingers danced across her
skin, gliding lower and lower. "So, tell me. What are you
after, exactly?" he said, just as those fingers found their
mark.

A husky sound—part sigh, part gasp—rolled from
her lips, and Katy felt her eyelids flutter. "Exactly that,"
she managed, the words escaping in a long, breathless
moan. "Do so much more of that."

Arching her back, she pressed herself into his rhythm,
into the music of her pleasure. As the waves built within,
promising the most delicious explosion of her life, she
opened her eyes and literally felt herself lifted into his
gaze—into an endless blue sky, ocean water, sea of del-
phinium state of bliss. She grasped his forearm and
matched his cadence with her pelvis, claiming the sensa-
tion and letting it claim her in return. Why, oh why, hadn't
they done this so much sooner?

When the intensity ebbed and, with a tender, body-
scorching kiss, he entered her, Katy knew why. Here and
now, every cell in her body was ready for this moment,
and she quivered with new hunger. In this space, the

space of their bodies, there existed nothing but nature's poetry and fluidity and purpose. Nothing was taken, and everything given, as they pressed and wound and wrapped themselves into each other.

Katy again lost herself in Gunnar's gaze as a new kind of magic claimed her body. She gasped, seeing the power of their bond, the slow, steady build of passion and connection and, yes, love, in the infinite blue of his eyes. This time, her soul sighed. There was healing to be found here, too. She couldn't mess this up; it was her destiny.

They climaxed as one, the power of pleasure rolling through them until they could move no more. Never once letting go of her, Gunnar slid to her side and pulled her close, his arm cradling her as their hearts pounded out messages to each other. Katy lay her hand atop his arm, unable to stop caressing his skin. They should probably never wear clothes again, she decided.

At some point, eons of moments later, Gunnar took hold of her arm. He ran his hand up and down several times, then lifted his head and looked at her. "It's gone," he said.

"What's gone?" she asked, mind still dreamy.

"Your scar."

The anxious tremor returned, but Katy swatted it away. Her mother had healed the skin, and Gunnar the wound beneath. Someday, she'd tell him her gift was inherited and that, in addition to having one woman in his life who could do the impossible, he'd have to deal with two. For now, though, she just wanted to enjoy feeling whole for a while.

"Yes," she said. "It's gone for good."

Epilogue

In a distant kingdom across the Bering Sea, a cell phone chimes, the text tones like tinkling piano keys. Having just settled her wee princess in her crib, the queen pulls her phone from her pocket and reads. In the space of seconds, the words take shape and her heart soars. Her dearest friend in the world is not only better and stronger, but blissful, having fallen in love exactly according to plan. The queen smiles, deciding then and there that her new family needs an immediate dose of enchantment, courtesy of the Maine mountains. Blessings abound in Spellbound Falls, and she must see them for herself.

In James Bay, off the coast of Canada, the sun shines upon a newborn island, its magical peaks and crevices teeming with ancient wisdom. Far below, scuttling like soldier ants, awestruck explorers work to discover the secrets of Atlantis, to understand this unexpected gift to humanity.

In the Bottomless Sea, a young boy, no longer fearful or isolated, laughs and calls out to his friends as they splash through the sunlit waters. Together, the three boys chatter and swim with a pair of playful dolphins, their sleek bodies leaping joyfully. Above them all, visible only to those with the most open of hearts, the air shimmers like so many fluttering angel wings.

In the heart of Spellbound Falls, beneath an enchanting canopy of string lights and maple branches, a couple strolls through the park hand in hand, her mahogany head occasionally tilting toward his broad shoulder as they smile and laugh. Around them, their community gathers—clusters of excited families and friends—all anticipating the dusk and the roaring campfire that binds and nurtures them.

Winging high above them all, a graceful eagle soars, senses attuned to those below, to their beating hearts and deepest yearnings. He watches and waits, prepared to dive as the need arises, protecting and guiding when instincts lead them astray and holding his position when the answer lies in their grasp. His eyes see what theirs do not: that magic exists in every place, person, and moment, asking nothing more than belief. Within us, and beyond us, magic waits for us all.

Dear Reader,

If the dedication in the front of this book had you questioning my opinion of firefighters, I hope reading *Call It Magic* assured you that I am fully aware it's not just about the trucks. But I also hope Gunnar and Katy were able to show you it's not about the glory, either. (Lord knows it's not about the money, as most firefighters—at least here in Maine—have to work two jobs to support their families.) And despite all the news stories highlighting the creative ways we honor our heroes, firefighters and medics more often than not continuously study and train in quiet obscurity until they are suddenly and desperately needed.

So yeah, I may have exaggerated the cockiness of my fictional responders a bit (hey, if we can't poke fun at our children, why have them), but those of you familiar with my work already know that I don't care to read, much less write, emotionally draining stories. That doesn't mean I shy away from the more serious subjects; I simply prefer to use levity to inspire hope. And like Gunnar, I, too, am fully aware that firefighting is serious business, so I hope you'll forgive my taking a few liberties with their protocols and procedures for the sake of story. I don't think I strayed too far from their collective mind-sets, though, for surely if firefighters and paramedics, our military, policemen, doctors and nurses, and everyone who works with the elderly, the feeble, and the disadvantaged, didn't step back and have a good laugh on a regular basis, they'd likely never stop crying. Not only do those dedicated men and women possess hearts befitting the warriors they are, they also have lion-sized (if slightly warped) senses of humor.

So, consider honoring your local fire and rescue squad by maybe giving them a gift card for a nearby takeout eatery, having pizza anonymously delivered, or stopping by and simply saying thank you. (But if you really want to make their day, ask if you can take a selfie with the entire team in front of one of their beautiful, badass trucks.)

And God bless all who tirelessly hit the ground running every time those alarms go off.

* * *

Okay, what you just read was originally the full extent of my letter, that is until I was nearing the end of writing *Call It Magic* and realized I had a bit of a problem.

Let me explain . . .

If you're a returning reader, you've also probably figured out by now that I'm an insatiably curious person. In fact, I may have a bit of a reputation for driving people crazy with my incessant questions. I'm not only curious about how everything in the world works, but also how people think. Such as how we connect the dots to reach the conclusions we do or why one person will judge an action as wrong and the person standing right beside them, witnessing the exact same action, will believe it to be right. Are our morals formed solely by the societies we grow up in? Or is our view of good and evil programmed into our DNA, much like our personal perspectives as to whether something is loud or quiet, tasty or terrible, and pretty or ugly?

When I first conceive a storyline, it's usually because I have a question about some aspect of human behavior that's caught my attention—usually for no particular reason that I can fathom. For example, in *Charming the Highlander*, I found myself wondering if there might ever be a circumstance where a woman is justified in not telling a man he'd fathered a child. Like what if she felt the guy was a jerk? Or a deadbeat or even dangerous? Wouldn't that be a convenient assessment if she happened to love the child too much to hand it over? (You might not believe me, but I truly didn't know if Grace Sutter was going to give up Baby even three-quarters-way into the book, even right up until I began writing that heart-wrenching scene.)

And because I apparently like looking at things from different angles, I revisited the same question in *Tempt Me If You Can*, only this time wondering what might happen if a woman—or in this case an entire town—didn't tell a man he'd fathered a child, and one day out of the blue, he receives an anonymous letter saying he should come meet his fifteen-year-old son.

I have absolutely no idea where the questions driving my stories come from. But I suspect it's my characters themselves who, wrestling with a particular dilemma, come to me—and you, dear readers—looking for answers. But here's the kicker: Your advice to them and my advice might not be the same. What you feel is right might not be what another reader feels is right or what I feel is right.

And that was the worry I had while working on *Call It Magic*.

Rape is a very sensitive subject to broach, and tragically for some, very personal. Even more tragic, it appears to be growing prevalent, especially with the advent of date-rape drugs. (Or maybe cable news and social media simply make it appear that way by finally bringing it out in the open.) And although it's more often presented as a young people's problem, anyone of any age can find themselves victimized. Not just once, either, but again in the court of social media, where everyone is free to shout their personal opinion as to whether or not the victim should have known better or even had in some way asked for it.

But I wish to draw your attention to another—and what I consider equally polarizing—question I hadn't anticipated but nonetheless found myself pondering within days of Katy and Gunnar showing up on my creative doorstep.

And that would be, is Katy MacBain a murderer?

Would you consider it murder if a person knew that someone should immediately go see a doctor but didn't tell them and that someone keeled over dead less than a month later? Even if the bastard had been raping the person at the time she discovered he had an aneurysm getting ready to burst inside his vile, perverted brain?

I imagine the answer is fairly cut and dry for some of you, in that of course Katy should have told him. For others of you, I can almost hear you applauding her decision.

So, you ask, do I believe Katy should have told him?

Honest to God—I. Still. Don't. Know.

And you know what? I don't think I want or even need to know. And you know why? Because I feel that that particular decision, having to be made in this particular situation, is nobody's business but Katy's. And I really don't want to be one of those people shouting on social media what she should or should not have done since I wasn't there and I'm not her.

This has never really happened to me before, as I always seem to be able to write my way to an answer. And because I couldn't this time, you came very close to never seeing this book.

But then I thought, wait, I know you people. We've been through quite a lot together over the last fourteen years. And you're really not reading my stories to hear my opinion of what my characters should do; you're reading them to draw your own conclusions as to what you would do in their situation. I decided to hand in *Call It Magic* despite my concern, because—big sigh—I trust you. I have faith that you are all capable of drawing your own conclusions without needing to hear mine as to whether Katy was right or wrong to withhold her information. Then again, some questions are simply unanswerable. And yet again, some answers change over time. (It wasn't all that long ago women were considered too—oh, let's go with—uninformed to vote. And too scatterbrained, emotional, unpredictable, physically weak—pick one, any one—to operate heavy equipment, pilot commercial jets, captain ships, fight fires, or wear a badge and carry a gun. Heck, we apparently used to be too dumb to be doctors and lawyers and CEOs of mega-companies, much less capable of running an entire country. Thank God we've come a long way, baby. There're still more glass ceilings to shatter, but we're slowly and surely getting there.)

Wow. Guess I'm not shy about voicing my opinion on some things. ☺

Anyhoo; I started down this long-winded path for the sole purpose of thanking you in advance (I'm writing this letter almost a year before you're reading it) for not getting upset that I don't neatly tie up every little loose end in my stories. Because, you know, sometimes it's just not possible. (And sometimes I do it on purpose, just so you can pick your own endings to some of the more minor messes my characters get themselves into. Yup, I confess, I've done that more than once. And as a heads-up, I'll probably continue doing it.)

So here is my heartfelt thank-you for taking these journeys with me anyway.

Until later, you keep reading, and I'll keep sharing the magic.

Janet

P.S. Please don't be jealous the Canadians got Atlantis. ☺ I felt they deserve a little excitement, since I hear they measure snow in meters up there.

Keep reading for an excerpt from

From Kiss to Queen

Available now!

The sharp, roaring shrill of a powerful engine shattered the slumberous quiet of the deep Maine woods. Birds scattered, chipmunks scurried for cover, and Jane Abbot instinctively ducked when a fast-moving aircraft shot overhead just above the treetops. Deciding someone was doing a bit of *illegal* scouting for next week's moose hunt, Jane frowned when she noticed the wing flaps on the floatplane were set for landing. Except that didn't make sense, since the closest lake big enough to land a plane that size on was at least twenty miles away.

Surely the pilot wasn't eyeing the pond she'd just passed.

Jane actually screamed when another plane roared overhead, this one smooth-bellied instead of rigged with floats. Her shotgun hanging forgotten at her side, she stood in the center of the old tote road and watched the sleek, twin-engine Cessna sharply bank after the first plane like a metallic hawk trying to drive its prey to ground.

What in holy heaven was going on?

The floatplane roared past again, this time low enough for Jane to see the male pilot was attempting to line up with the pond. A sudden burst of gunfire drew her attention to the second plane, where she saw a man kneeling in the open rear door holding a machine gun, his entire body jerking as spent shell casings rained down on the forest below. A small explosion pulled her attention back to the floatplane in time to see smoke coming from the nose of the aircraft as its floats brushed the tops of several towering pines. The plane was landing whether it was possible or not. No more chances for the desperate pilot to circle around and get it right. He was going down—now.

Jane finally came out of her stupor and started running at the sound of breaking branches and the sputter of a dying engine. A tree snapped with enough force to vibrate the air just seconds before the unmistakable thud of the plane hitting water echoed through the forest over the retreating drone of the deadly, victorious plane.

And then complete silence; no sounds from the pond, no birds chirping . . . nothing. Jane realized she'd stopped running and was holding her breath—listening. Waiting. Hoping.

Aw, heck. Give her a sound. Something! A whirl of water. A splash. Something to tell her the pilot of the downed plane was making his way free of the wreckage.

But still no sound, except for the sudden intake of her own breath as she awkwardly started running again. He couldn't be dead. She didn't want to witness a man's valiant attempt to save himself and lose. Jane dropped her shotgun and backpack when she reached the pond and quickly shed her jacket. Not bothering to take off her boots, she frantically splashed into the water while keeping her eyes trained on the mangled remains of the upside-down floats a hundred yards from shore. She dove into the cold Maine water fueled by a combination of adrenaline, determination, and a lifetime of braving more than one cold swim in similar waters.

She arrived at the plane, gathered her breath, and used the float strut to pull herself down under the water—the rising bubbles making the journey difficult and her vision foggy. Finding the door handle of the upside-down plane and giving several unsuccessful tugs, Jane sank lower and looked in the window to see the pilot struggling with his seat belt, his movements jerky and clumsy. She grabbed the door handle again, braced her feet on the fuselage, and pulled with all her might—only to shoot away when it suddenly opened. She quickly righted herself and reached inside and touched the pilot.

He jerked, his head snapping toward her as he grabbed her wrist and hauled her through the opening. Jane thought about panicking, but realized almost at once that his grip was loosening. She moved closer, bringing her other hand up and touching his lips. He flinched, then stilled. She freed her wrist from his grip and brought a second hand to his face, clasping his head as she touched her lips to his and sealed them. Quickly realizing her intention, the man pulled some of the air she'd been holding into his mouth.

Jane broke free and reached for his seat belt buckle at the same time he did, only to find her own strength waning. She backed out and kicked to the surface, took several deep breaths as she groped for the knife on her belt, then gathered one last supply of air and dove back down to the open door to see the man fumbling with his seat belt again. Jane touched him, he jerked, and in a repeat of before, grabbed her. Not fighting him this time, she reentered the plane and sealed her lips to his again. He relaxed slightly and pulled in more of her life-sustaining air, then went back to fumbling with his belt.

Jane simply cut through the restraint and backed out of the plane while guiding him with her. They broke the surface together beside one of the floats, and Jane found herself having to hold his head above the water as he coughed and spit and gasped, his eyes closed and his face racked with spasms of pain.

He said a word. A curse, it sounded like, in a language she didn't recognize.

"Come on," she croaked on a shiver as she started dragging him toward shore. Hearing the other plane approaching, Jane stopped swimming when it roared overhead and sharply started banking again.

"Dammit! They're back," the man ground out. "Where are we?"

Jane looked at him. He'd spoken English. "We're in the middle of the pond. Where do you think we are?"

"I can't see. Are we exposed? How far to shore?"

Jane gaped at him, realizing the skin on his face was red, as if sunburned. His eyes were running with tears and repeatedly blinking as he stared at the sky. There was a gash on his forehead, and he was keeping one hand tucked close to his side under the water.

He was blind?

"How far to shore?" he repeated, giving her arm a shake.

"Fifty yards," Jane said as she watched the plane begin another low approach.

"If they start shooting, dive under the water."

Neither had time to say anything else as the man in the plane diving toward the pond did, indeed, start shooting. She was suddenly pulled below the surface just as the water around them became a frothing web of streaking bullets. Feeling a searing sting on her upper arm, Jane silently screamed and frantically tried to surface. Surprisingly strong hands held her down until the frothing stopped and she was suddenly pushed upward.

"Where are you hit?"

"In the arm," she said, remembering he couldn't see. "I'm okay. It just grazed me."

He cocked his head, listening. "We need to get to shore," he said, shoving her in the wrong direction.

Jane shoved him in the right direction, which seemed to startle the man. She gave a small, hysterical laugh, which seemed to startle him even more.

"Don't panic on me now," he ordered harshly.

Afraid he might blindly try to slap her, Jane decided to bring him to account for his high-handedness once they were safely on shore. The plane of death flew over the lake once more, and the gunman unleashed his weapon again just as Jane and her half-drowned pilot touched shore, forcing them to run and stumble as she dragged him to a large stand of pines.

Never, ever, had she felt anything like the terror of being shot at so relentlessly. The machine gun sprayed the trees, the bullets kicking up the surrounding dirt as broken branches rained down on them. All Jane could do was crouch against the trunk of a thick pine, her knees locked to her chest and her eyes shut tight, not even able to manage a respectable scream. The pilot of the sunken plane was pressed against her, actually protecting her from flying debris and oncoming death. Jane instantly forgave him for sounding like a bossy jerk in the water. He was blind, in pain, and trying to protect her.

Well, he should! He was the one they were obviously trying to kill. She was just an innocent bystander. Heck, she was even a hero. She'd saved him, hadn't she? He deserved to take a bullet for her.

No, then she'd have to deal with a blind, *bleeding* jerk.

Jane wiggled out from between the man and the tree the moment the deafening gunfire stopped, barely escaping his blindly grasping hands. "Oh, put a sock in it!" she snapped. "I'm starting to get a little angry here. I'm cold and wet, you're bossy, and someone is actually *shooting* at me. Well, Ace, I intend to shoot back!"

With that off her chest, Jane limped over to where she'd thrown her backpack and gun. She rummaged around in the pack until she came up with a box of shotgun shells, then unloaded the bird shot from her gun and replaced it with the new ammunition.

"Come back here!" the man ordered in a guttural hiss. "Now, before they return."

She looked over and felt a moment of chagrin. If it wasn't bad enough the guy was blind, he was also in the middle of nowhere with a stranger who was semi-hysterical and very angry. His plane was wrecked and somebody was trying to kill him. And somebody he couldn't see was ignoring him.

Jane took pity. "It's okay," she assured him. "I have a gun. I can shoot back."

"What kind of gun?" he asked cautiously, apparently not knowing if he should be alarmed or thankful.

"It's a shotgun."

He snorted.

"I have slugs for it. Sabots can go through anything short of armored steel. And their range is impressive."

"What were you hunting? Elephants?" he asked dryly.

Jane took back her pity. "I was hunting partridge."

He snorted again.

"I was planning to find a gravel pit later and do some target practicing," she said defensively.

"Are you out here alone?" he asked, apparently dismissing the issue of the gun.

"Yes."

He dropped his head and muttered that single foreign word again as he rubbed his face in his hands, then sighed and looked in her direction. "How far are we from civilization?"

Jane didn't get a chance to answer. The plane was back. She ignored his second command to come to him—also ignoring the fact that he sounded rather angry himself—and stepped onto the small beach and shouldered her shotgun. She knew she'd only get off one or two surprise shots before they flew out of range, but she intended to give them something to think about before they left.

The plane swooped low over the lake again, the man with the machine gun straining out the door trying to spot his prey. Jane fired off a shot at the approaching plane, then slid the action on her gun and fired again, causing the Cessna to sharply bank away when her slug connected with metal. She quickly jacked another shell into the chamber and fired one last time at the turning plane, satisfied to see the man in the door throw himself back when the slug tore through the fuselage over his head.

She shouted in triumph at the retreating plane, then danced her way over to the wounded pilot, setting down her gun and going to her knees in front of him as she boldly stated she'd just scared those monsters silly. She never noticed he wasn't exactly celebrating with her until he reached out with unbelievable swiftness and blindly grabbed her. He hauled her toward him with surprising force, repositioned his grip on her shoulders, and shook her.

Jane squeaked in alarm and tried to break free. "You're hurting me!"

"I'm going to throttle you, you little idiot! You could have been killed!"

"Well, I wasn't. And neither were you, thanks to me," she shot back, forgetting her precarious position. "And you're welcome, you Neanderthal!"

He shook her again.

"If you don't quit manhandling me, you're going to find yourself back in the lake," Jane said, her voice a whisper of warning as she tugged on his wrists.

Although she did register the fact that she was gripping what felt like solid steel, she didn't back down from her threat, not caring if he could see her glare or not. She broke free and immediately stood up, then backed a safe distance away and simply stared at the scowling pilot.

He was a huge, wet, battered mess if she ever saw one, his face scorched and his eyes watering and blinking frantically. But even sitting on the ground in an undignified heap, the guy still looked lethal—his wet leather jacket clinging to a trim torso and his large hands clenched in either anger or pain or both.

Jane quietly stepped to the side and watched his blinking gaze follow her movement. "Just how blind are you?" she asked suspiciously.

"I can see you," he confirmed. "But you're blurry," he added, rubbing his eyes.

"Don't do that." Jane rushed back to him and gripped his head between her hands, then leaned down and studied his injuries. "You'll make it worse. Your face is red, but I can't see any real damage to your eyes. It's possible they're only badly irritated."

He leaned away from her grasp. "A fire broke out just before I hit the water."

"Well, it was a lovely landing, Ace."

He snorted again. "If you don't count the fact that my plane is upside-down in a lake."

"You walked away."

"Just barely. Ah . . . thank you," he said, trying to focus on her.

"You're welcome."

"We have to get out of here. They will be back."

Jane looked in the direction the Cessna had disappeared. "They're going to eventually run out of fuel."

"Is there a place near here where they could land?"

Jane shrugged, then remembered he couldn't see her. "The closest airport is thirty miles to the south, but some of the tote roads might be wide and straight enough in places. Do you think they'd risk landing and come after you—us—on foot?"

"I think it likely. Do you have a vehicle nearby?"

Jane nodded, then sighed, again forgetting he was blind. "It's a couple of miles away."

The man cocked his head. "Is it parked out in the open? Could the plane spot it?"

"Ah . . . yes."

"Thanks to your shooting at them, they know I'm no longer alone. Your car is not a safe destination. How far to the nearest town?"

"About twenty miles in any direction."

He stopped mid-sigh and suddenly perked up. "Do you have a cell phone?"

Jane finished sighing for him. "It's in my car. And even if I had it with me, it would take me several hours to climb a mountain to get a signal."

The man said that nasty word again. And even though she was tempted to ask what it meant and what language it was in, Jane decided the less she knew about him, the better. She was already more involved than she cared to be, and figured that once she got him to safety, the authorities could deal with him.

"What do you have for ammunition?" he asked as he slowly stood up. He staggered, then steadied himself by leaning against the giant pine and looked at her through still blinking eyes.

"I have a shotgun with maybe ten rounds of bird shot and now seven slugs. And I have a handgun with a box of twenty bullets."

"How big a handgun?" he asked, taking a step toward her.

"A .357 Magnum."

He stopped, one side of his mouth lifting slightly. "Loaded for bear, aren't you?"

Jane bristled, taking her own step toward him. "Only an idiot would come out here alone without being prepared."

He detected her movement and held his hands up in supplication. "I'm not complaining." He cocked his head again. "You seem to be able to take care of yourself just fine. Where did you learn that trick of feeding me air while I was trapped in the plane?"

"I didn't learn it anyplace. I just thought it might help."

"Well, you are most resourceful. And your lips were most welcome. You tasted of butterscotch," he added with a grin as he ran his tongue over his teeth.

Jane was glad the man was nearly blind when she felt her face heat up. "Come on. You said we've got to get out of here."

He bowed. "I am in your care, madam."

"The name's Jane Abbot."

"And my name is Mark."

"Mark what?"

"So which way, Jane?" he asked instead of answering.

Jane frowned in the direction of her vehicle. "My car is still the quickest way out of here. You need to see a doctor. Are you hurt anyplace else?"

He shrugged, then winced. "Everyplace. But your vehicle is not a safe destination."

"You think you can walk twenty miles?" she asked, thinking the hike to her car would be a stretch for him.

"If I have to. And you? Are you hurt anyplace? You said a bullet grazed you."

Jane lifted her left arm. "It's only scratched. It's not

even bleeding now." She looked at the man named *just Mark*, and then she looked at the floats out in the center of the pond. "Is there anything in your plane you might need? Medicine or anything?"

Rubbing his eyes again and looking at the pond himself, Mark seemed to think about that. Finally he sighed. "I have some things I would like to retrieve, but it's too cold to get them."

"I could get them," she offered, repressing a shiver.

Mark looked in her direction again. "It's too cold," he repeated.

"What's in the plane?" She gasped when he hesitated. "It's not full of drugs, is it? I'm not standing in the middle of a drug war, am I?"

Mark stilled, then barked out in laughter—only to quickly cradle his ribs. "I'm not a drug runner. Leave the plane. I will find a way to retrieve my belongings later."

For some reason, probably stupidity, Jane believed him. "Well, come on, then. We've got a twenty-mile hike ahead of us, because *driving* is our only viable option of getting out of—"

A long burst of distant gunfire suddenly shattered the air, immediately followed by a muted explosion forceful enough to scatter the already disgruntled birds from the nearby trees. Mark moved with surprising speed and gathered Jane into his arms, pressing her head to his chest as he looked in the direction of the blast.

"What was that?" she whispered, closing her eyes as she wondered if the plane had crashed trying to land— not that that explained the gunfire.

"I would guess your car."

She snapped her head up to look at him. "They blew up my car?"

He stepped back. "We are like sitting ducks. Do you know these woods, Jane Abbot? Can you lead us to safety without leaving a conspicuous trail?"

"Oh, yes. I've spent nearly my whole life in these woods."

He suddenly shot her a warm, genuine smile. "I have the damnedest luck. I've crashed into the arms of a guardian angel, have I not?"

"And don't I just have the darnedest luck," Jane shot back. "I was minding my own business one minute and dodging bullets the next." She picked up her jacket and backpack and shotgun. "Come on, Ace, the sooner we start walking, the sooner I can get rid of you," she muttered, grabbing his hand and heading in the opposite direction from her destroyed car.

They'd blown up her car!

"Would you happen to have any more butterscotch, Jane?"

Ready to find
your next great read?

Let us help.

Visit prh.com/nextread